Wife to the Kingmaker

A quirk of fate makes Anne Beauchamp the sole heiress to the greatest Lancastrian fortune in 15th century England; that of the Earls of Warwick. Her husband is Richard Neville, whom she regards as her inferior both in birth and importance. But she underestimates him for the gaining of the Warwick earldom fires him with a boundless ambition. The Wars of the Roses bring Richard to the forefront and Anne soon realizes that her Lancastrian fortune is being used to support the Yorkist cause. Richard's dazzling success and magnetic character earn him the nickname 'the Kingmaker', and make him the real strength behind the new Yorkist King.

Anne stands in her husband's shadow, a proud, beautiful woman who is filled with resentment. She is, however, destined to fall in love with a Neville—her husband's brother John. This is the story of that dangerous love, the discovery of which would be a powerful tool in the hands of Richard's many enemies. Above all it is the story of Anne, wife to the 'Kingmaker'.

Sandra Wilson

Wife to the Kingmaker

NEW YORK
St. Martin's Press, Inc.

For Sarah

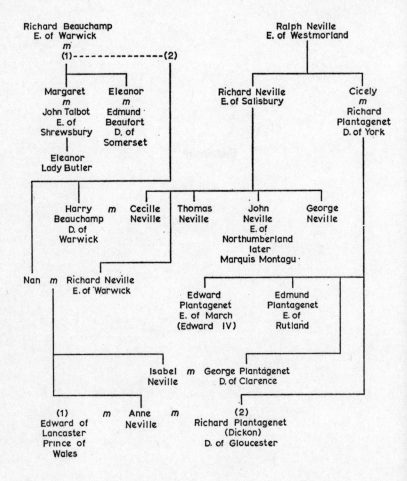

PROLOGUE

TH E Earl of Warwick was one of the most important magnates in the Lancastrian realm of young King Henry VI. His power was immense, his fortune fabulous, and he had been the custodian and tutor of the King since the death of his father, Henry V, many years before. One of Warwick's close friends was the Earl of Salisbury, and now in the early summer of the Year of Grace 1431, these two powerful noblemen met to seal two contracts . . . a double betrothal, a union twice over of the Houses of Beauchamp and Neville.

Warwick's only son, and heir, was the six-year-old Harry Beauchamp, the offspring of the Earl's second marriage. His father now penned his agreement to this child's marriage with the daughter of Salisbury. She was also only six years old and her name was Cecille.

Beauchamp straightened, waiting for the servant to heat the wax before he pressed his seal upon the document. Then he smiled and dipped the quill into the ink once more, handing it to Salisbury.

The second document was placed before them, and Salisbury bent to affix his name upon the crisp parchment. The only sound in the small room was the scratching of that quill, and the atmosphere was heavy with the acrid smell of hot wax. The names were complete, the contract sealed. Salisbury's eldest son, Richard Neville, a child of only three, was now formally betrothed to Warwick's youngest daughter.

She was five years old, a lovely child with long golden hair and green eyes. Warwick loved her above all his other children, and although he was usually a harsh, unbending man, she found from the beginning that she could always achieve her own way with her mighty father. As a result she was a spoilt, strong-willed girl with an overweaning sense of her own importance. Her name was Anne Beauchamp. Everyone called her Nan.

7

ONE

EIGHT years later, in the beautiful month of May, the grassy bank of the River Avon in the shadow of Warwick Castle echoed to the sound of singing and laughter. A colourful group of ladies sat on the spring grass, chattering gaily amongst themselves while one sang to the music of a lute. Nearby was the castle water mill and they could clearly hear the rhythmic splashing and drumming of the ancient wheel as it turned to the full flow of the waters.

The eldest daughter of the Earl of Warwick leaned forward to pluck a blade of grass. Margaret was the Countess of Shrewsbury, the wife of an ageing man, but she was happy and loved her husband. Now she stroked the blade of grass down the face of the young girl who sat next to her.

"If this weather continues, sweet Cecille, tomorrow's great occasion will be blessed by sunshine in plenty!"

Cecille blushed, lowering her gaze demurely. "The sunshine will be blessed only by those who wish to preserve their rich and magnificent clothing! I shall be happy if it is fine or if it rains!"

"Ah!" Margaret smiled knowingly. "Ah, the honey-sweet, heady taste of a first love! You are lucky Cecille, for you and my brother Harry are well-matched and have more than a passing affection for one another. Tomorrow, before the illustrious eyes of the whole of our family and the royal eyes of the King himself, you shall marry and will be safe in the knowledge that you love one another. 'Tis no small thing."

"I know, and I pray each night to the Virgin Mary in thanks for my good fortune. I am surely blessed, for I know that your sister Nan and my brother Richard have no such liking for one another." Her brown eyes moved to the solitary figure of Nan. sitting beneath a willow tree some yards away from everyone. "Tell me, why is it that your father dotes upon her so? I find him a fearsome man and can hardly believe that he is so weak where she is concerned."

Margaret pursed her lips, following Cecille's gaze. Twenty-two years separated her from Nan, a long time, indeed a generation, but she was a little closer to her youngest sister than anyone else. "Perhaps it is because Nan and your Harry are the only children of my father's second marriage. From my mother he received three daughters, myself, Eleanor and Elizabeth; every man wishes above all things to have a son and heir. When my mother died, he remarried and that second marriage was immediately blessed by the arrival of Harry. From that moment onwards I think that my father forgot any happy moments he may have had with my mother, he had his son and he was happy. When Nan arrived it did not matter that she was another girl, she came into my father's life at a time when he was happy, contented with his lot. All the feeling he had concealed for most of his life I think bubbled over then. He could not lavish his love and attention upon Harry, for one does not do that with boys . . . and so it was upon Nan that he poured that affection."

Cecille pouted. "Nan would have been better for a little less of that affection!"

"Come now! Such sourness from tomorrow's delicate, blushing bride!" Margaret poked the blade of grass down the bodice of Cecille's silk gown. Cecille exclaimed loudly and removed it. Margaret stood. "Let us join her, she looks a little lonely. She is not happy, Cecille, for all the love and spoiling she receives from my father. It can do no harm for us to be kind to her."

Reluctantly Cecille agreed, and together they walked towards the willow tree. Nan was gazing vaguely at the whispering waters which swept by close to her feet. She leaned back against the gnarled trunk of the tree, deep in thought and unaware that she was no longer alone. She was almost thirteen, and for some two months had been the wife of Cecille's brother, although the marriage could not be consummated until Richard reached the age of fourteen. She remained as yet in her father's household, and was thankful that she did not have to join her new husband who was in Yorkshire with his father and brothers. Nan's nose was disdainfully tilted as she thought of her new family, and her proud Beauchamp blood almost shuddered within her veins.

The Nevilles were a fierce brood, and were split by a quarrel over the ownership of those lands in Yorkshire where Richard now lived. The quarrel was bloody and endless, Neville fought Neville, Neville hated Neville. "Long may the feud continue and keep him there!" Nan's nose wrinkled as she murmured to herself.

Margaret's sharp ears picked up the words. "Little sister, I do not think those words lie sweetly upon your young shoulders!" She frowned, anxious because Cecille had heard.

Nan jumped, seeing for the first time that she had been joined by the others. "Those words were not meant to be overheard, my Lady of Shrewsbury! But even though Cecille be my sister-in-law I will say them again: long may the Neville feud continue and keep Sir Richard in the wastes of Yorkshire!" She had not wished to be heard, but now she defended herself by attacking.

Cecille's hand crept to her breast, and she crossed herself devoutly. "You should not speak so cruelly of my brother, for he is in great danger. Our opponents would dearly like to take the life of Salisbury's son and heir!"

Nan's lips took on a sullen pout and she refused to retract her words. Margaret grew angry at her sister's behaviour and her kindly heart hardened. "Come Cecille, we will leave My Lady Misery to her own dark thoughts and visit the nursery. No doubt you would like to see my little daughter."

Margaret had intended to hurt her sister and the effect was achieved. Nan bit her lip and stared intently at the trailing fronds of the willow tree. She loved Margaret's baby, Eleanor, and would have willingly joined them in the nursery. Deliberately Margaret took Cecille's hand and drew her away towards the other group of ladies. Soon the chattering, giggling gathering was making its way back towards the castle, leaving behind only Nan's personal maid, Alana. Alana was not much older than her young mistress, and now she sat with her lute upon her lap, plucking the strings idly and glancing frequently towards Nan's motionless figure.

A swaying tendril of the willow drooped close and Nan pulled at it, slowly ripping the tender green leaves and tossing them into the waiting waters. They floated away like tiny emerald boats. The precocious beauty of the five year old Nan had given way to a softer, deeper loveliness. Her figure was gently rounded, her small breasts pushed upwards by the tight bodice of her gown, and her creamy skin was dappled by the sunlight which glanced through the swaying branches above her head. The delicate primrose silk of her gown enhanced her golden, English fragility, looks which could capture the eye of the beholder.

A large apricot cat wandered close to her, nuzzling the deep fur trimming at the hem of her gown. She reached down and picked up the cat, stroking it, and the animal purred loudly, rubbing its head against her hand. The amber feline eyes stared up in fascination at the golden embroidery upon the net which held Nan's thick hair. The purring died away, and a furry paw reached up to pat the net. Nan smiled and pulled the paw away, shaking the cat gently. The branches moved between earth and sun and the embroidery flashed; the paw reached up again, and this time Nan pushed the cat away. Flicking its tail and looking haughty, the beast stalked away, offended.

Already Nan had forgotten, pondering anew upon the troubles of her life. She was a Beauchamp of Warwick, proud, high-born; the King of England had spent most of his early years in the same household . . . and Nan thought of herself as being somehow more elevated, more distinguished because of this. Her brother Harry was the King's closest friend, always at the royal side, and Nan was Harry's only full sister. . . . The father she knew as so gentle, kind and amiable, was in no way the same man as seen through the frightened, nervous eyes of the young King. Henry Plantagenet was weak and easily unnerved, and his custodian Warwick was unnecessarily hard upon his royal charge. Already King Henry VI was unstable, and Warwick's treatment did little or nothing to steady that undesirable trait. But all this was of little consequence to the headstrong, wilful girl who sat brooding upon the banks of the Avon.

It seemed to her that the surly face of Richard Neville stared back at her from the rippling waters. She could almost see the luxuriant chestnut hair and deep hazel eyes . . . her fingers picked up a tiny pebble and she tossed it into that imagined reflection, breaking it into wavering fragments. She disliked her youthful husband, the future Earl of Salisbury, for no reason other than that she considered herself far superior to him. Unknown to her, his reaction was inevitable; he hated her.

Trumpets sounded along the road to London and she sat up, staring along the dusty track on the other bank. At last she made out the banners and colours of her second sister's husband,

Edmund Beaufort, Duke of Somerset. Her heart fell, for Beaufort was the one other person she heartily disliked.

Somerset was proudly aware of his direct descent from John of Gaunt, of the fact that he was a prince of the realm . . . albeit through the illegitimate Beaufort line. His was a sly nature, and he chose his words with care, wrapping them in a waspish tone and regal manner which lay uneasily together. For his youthful sister-in-law, Nan, he had a lecherous desire, and already he had seen her primrose figure beneath the willow. He rode his black courser with a straight back and did not condescend to glance aside at his mouselike wife. Poor Eleanor, she was kept in a state of complete subjection by this powerful magnate who resented the power of the Beauchamps and who took his revenge against that House by punishing his poor wife.

Now the cavalcade thundered over the wooden bridge and thence into the castle itself. Nan noticed how the six lean greyhounds which capered by Somerset's horse were immediately cowed by a sharp word from him. Even the very dogs. . . .

Nan stood, brushing down her heavy skirts. She must go back to the castle, for the afternoon grew chill as the sun sank towards its rest. She watched Somerset as he dismounted. How he swaggered! She took a deep breath, thinking that if her father had been in residence, Somerset would have been more careful of his manners. Even a Beaufort must tread warily before the Earl of Warwick! She paused as she plucked at the folds of her skirts. Her father was ill, very ill, and away in France. He was unable to make the strenuous journey to England to see his son's marriage. His task was to tend to England's fast disappearing possessions in France, but he was finding his position impossible due to the meddling and changing policies of those left in England close to the young King. Chief amongst these was the Duke of Suffolk . . . a close friend and ally of Edmund Beaufort.

Nan began to walk back along the bank, smiling at Alana who struggled to her feet with her lute. Nan's skirts dragged through the succulent grass, and she picked up the hem with one hand to lighten the load. She stopped suddenly as a very tall, slender figure stepped across her path.

Somerset! The bright scarlet plumes in his peaked hat bobbed and swayed as he doffed it. He was thirty-three years old, and very handsome. His tawny hair was fashionably short, and the cut of his doublet was exaggerated and richly decorated. Now his brown eyes rested warmly on her and he took her hand, pressing it to his lips for a little longer than necessary.

She felt uncomfortable and drew her fingers from his grasp. A smile was forced to her lips. "You have just returned from France, my Lord? Did you see my father?"

"I did indeed, sweet sister. He grows weak, very weak. I spent as much time as possible with him, seeking to lighten his days."

Nan's face did not alter as she heard this, for she knew that her father despised his arrogant son-in-law, and that being closeted with him would certainly not have lightened any of Warwick's days.

Somerset misunderstood her silence. "Do not feel sad, my Lady, your father is an old man now and his life has been distinguished. Let me see a smile upon your face, I have good news for you! Your husband, his father and brothers will be here within the hour for the celebrations tomorrow. They wish to see the fair Cecille wed with the heir of Warwick!" He could not conceal his anger and resentment. He had no liking for the Nevilles and did not approve of the great match Salisbury had achieved for his daughter.

Jesu, thought Nan, did he imagine that such news would bring a smile to her lips? "My husband is coming here? I did not know." Her face was frozen.

She took her leave of him then, the turmoil within her lending her a new strength. She no longer noticed the heaviness of her gown as she swept towards the castle.

TWO

THE great hall rang with laughter and music as the marriage feast progressed. Cecille's happiness was complete, she had married her love, she sat at the side of the King of England, and she knew that her bridal finery was splendid, magnificent. She glanced shyly at Harry, turning her head then to look at the King.

Henry Plantagenet was eighteen years old, although he seemed very much younger. His brown hair was lank and greasy, his face sallow and long, and his slack mouth gave his kindly visage the expression of a simpleton. He wore a robe of purple velvet, sumptuous clothing which proclaimed him King, but already the priceless material was stained with wine and food. Henry was not of the stuff of kings, he was not interested in matters of state, choosing rather to read the Bible or compose new prayers. The sight of a low-cut gown threw him into a frenzy of embarrassment, and so the demure gentleness of Cecille drew his interest. She blushed when he spoke to her, which delighted him, and he soon found himself talking animatedly to his friend's bride.

Somerset watched Cecille's success with a sour expression. To Beaufort the King's obvious delight with Harry's new wife meant only the deeper and firmer establishment of the Beauchamps. Close by, Margaret and her husband Shrewsbury found Somerset's discomfort amusing, smiling secretively at one another. Somerset's wife sat timidly, her head bowed, her eyes downcast. She showed no feelings, nothing except a terror of her husband. Indeed, Eleanor was seldom seen now, for Beaufort kept her permanently immured in one or other of his country manors.

Nan was splendid in her new gown of oyster-coloured damask. An elegant cone-shaped headdress of scarlet velvet fitted neatly against her head, hiding the soft golden hair entirely. A silver scarf, long and delicate, trailed from the headdress, looped over Nan's wrist by a tiny golden chain. She had delighted in the day's happenings, loving every moment of the ceremony and now enjoying the tumblers who performed before the dais.

A movement of apple-green satin at her side caught her attention, and her enjoyment evaporated. Richard Neville was with her, and the remembrance spoiled her delight. He was eleven years old and his face was stormy as he sat unwillingly with his wife. His hazel eyes stared bleakly at the jugglers who now replaced the tumblers upon the smoke-hazed floor. She looked away from him, gazing opposite at the three other Neville brothers across the trestle from her.

15

There were four sons of Salisbury altogether, each a year younger than his predecessor. After Richard came Thomas, an unpleasant boy much given to practical jokes, and even now he was pulling faces at her and trying to make her laugh. She was in no mood now to bother with him, and looked away towards the next brother. His name was John, and he was small, thin and dark. He was not surly like Richard, nor was he unpleasantly boyish like Thomas . . . he was kindly and obviously impressed with Nan. Nan was drawn to him, and smiled. He blushed and returned the smile, his dark brown eyes warm. The fourth and youngest of this Neville brood was George. He was like John in appearance, but where John's face was thin, George's was like that of a ferret. His sharp eyes flickered endlessly over the gathering, and he munched his food steadily, chewing each mouthful over and over again as he studied his fellow man. A razor-sharp intelligence gleamed from those eyes.

Across the jostling, bright assembly, Nan caught the eye of her sister Margaret. Margaret had been watching Nan with her husband, and she was sad at their obvious dislike for one another. Their whole lives stretched before them, a chill proposition if they continued with their present attitude. They were young, they could not see what misery they were making for themselves. . . . She nodded her head pointedly towards Richard, obviously intimating that Nan should make some attempt at friendship. Understanding only too well, the younger girl sighed.

Nan bowed her head thoughtfully, glancing from beneath lowered lashes at Richard. Was Margaret perhaps right? Should she try to be a little more friendly with this odious boy who was to be part of her future no matter how much she resented the fact? She took a deep breath and then put her fingers to her goblet. Hesitantly she raised it towards her husband.

He started momentarily, his eyes flashing suspiciously at her. Her expression was pleading, and at last he softened and raised his own goblet. Perhaps he too wished to put their dislike behind them. The sweet mead brimmed over the lip of his cup as he turned to face her, awkwardly linking his arm around hers. Slowly they drank from one another's cup. She could feel the muscle in his arm against her own soft flesh, but as she looked into his eyes she found no gentleness, no friendship. Across the table the unpleasant Thomas continued to play the fool, and seeing what seemed to him to be silly behaviour on

16

the part of his brother, he suddenly raised his hand as if to toss something across the intervening space. The gesture was simply that, an empty threat, but from the corner of her eye Nan thought he was indeed about to throw something at her.

Instinctively she ducked, her hand jerking her cup. The liquid spilled on to the table and thence into Richard's lap, staining the clear apple green and soaking his black hose. He put his own cup down hastily and leapt to his feet, muttering an oath beneath his breath.

Nan put her shaking hands to her mouth in misery. Surely now matters would be even worse between them. How furious and how embarrassed he was . . . she closed her eyes. At that very moment she heard Thomas' delighted laughter, audible even in the noise of the hall. The tears started to her eyes as she opened them and saw the delighted mirth on his face; rage took the place of misery. In a fury of emotion she stood, pushing back the bench, then she picked up Richard's unspilled goblet and threw its contents across the board into Thomas' startled face. Before he could duck she tossed the goblet in its wake, striking him full on the cheek.

The hum and noise in the hall ended as if a thunderbolt had been cast among the guests, and all eyes turned towards her. Nan saw the sea of faces gazing at her and with a sob of mortification she ran from that awful place, her slippers pattering loudly as she fled. Her path took her past Somerset, and she heard his lazy drawl as he spoke to Shrewsbury. "Our fair sister has married into a loud-mouthed family of northern wolf-hounds I think!" Her humiliation was complete.

Outside the hall she hesitated. A group of minstrels carrying their instruments were coming along the wide passageway towards her, and seeing a doorway close by she thankfully hurried into the small room and closed the door behind her. For a long time she stood there breathing deeply to quell the sobs which shook her small body. A candlestick and an unfinished game of chess stood upon a table. The light from the candles threw a soft glow over the panelled room, lighting the ivory chessmen with an eery sharpness. She sat down wearily upon a chest and burried her face in her hands.

She did not know how long she sat there, but she started violently when the door opened suddenly to admit three persons. There stood her mighty father-in-law, Neville of Salisbury,

17

resplendent in his scarlet and gold coat. By the collars he held the figures of his two sons, and they seemed like broken puppets in his huge grasp. Salisbury was a large man with Richard's chestnut hair and hazel eyes. His complexion was ruddy and tanned by the outdoor elements, and his forceful chin was covered by a stubbly beard of a darker hue than his hair. He was thirty-nine years old and his bearing was that of a man who had known many battles and much bloodshed in his time.

Now he pushed Richard and Thomas roughly forward until they stood shamefaced before her. Nan stared and then lowered her eyes to the bristling griffin pendant which hung from Salisbury's golden collar. Jesu, this day grew worse and worse, why could he not have let the matter rest? Now Richard would hate her still further. She heard hardly a word of Salisbury's apologies on behalf of his sons, and she heard nothing at all of the humble mutterings wrung from Richard and Thomas. Thankfully she watched the door close behind them.

Hardly had they gone when the door opened again and this time Margaret stood there. "My advice went a little awry, I fear!"

"It did indeed, I pray you keep any further ideas strictly to your own self!" Nan's hurt was not yet done as she rounded on her sister. "How could Salisbury have inflicted such a scene upon me? Surely my experiences this night have been sufficient without having to endure forced apologies from my husband and his brother which neither wished to make! Oh Margaret, how could I have behaved so badly, and with the King present too. Did he say anything?"

"Who, the King? You may relax, Nan, Henry was so enchanted with the bride that he did not even notice your undignified drama. He continued his monologue quite happily, spilling his wine hither and thither. . . . I tell you something though, something which will no doubt interest you. . . ." She paused dramatically. "I followed you out, deeming you to be upset and in need of my company. Well, I almost came upon Salisbury and his two sons outside here, they were asking some minstrels which way you had taken. As you may imagine I waited in as much concealment as I could manage, not wishing to be discovered listening or in obvious pursuit of the same quarry as they. When the minstrels passed on into the hall, Salisbury took Richard by the ear, twisting it mightily, and to

18

Richard's credit he made no moan. Salisbury told him to beware of carrying his emotions so obviously upon his face where his marriage was concerned. He said that Cecille's husband had always ridden high in the King's favour, so highly that no other man had Henry's attention and trust, and now he hoped that Richard could find such a place for himself through his marriage to Harry's only true sister. That is Salisbury's dream, Nan, that Richard and Harry will have the King in their hands, barring of course the existence of the Duke of Gloucester, the King's uncle. He made some fearful threats to Richard if he did not mend his ways and similar threats to Thomas if he in any way interfered with the smooth passing of his brother's marriage. After this he pushed open this door here . . . and you know the rest." Margaret finished and watched Nan's reactions.

The pretty face at first blushed red and then waxed white with rage. "These accursed Nevilles, I will die rather than allow Richard Neville any power through *my* family! Oh, how I despise them, and how I wish I had never tried to soften his miserable little heart with a lover's toast! Never again will I make any move towards him, he will have to labour mightily in any future dealings he has with me!" She clenched her fists, banging the rough table so that the candlesticks swayed alarmingly.

Margaret reached out to steady the light, smiling. "My dearest Nan, I think he already has to labour mightily with you. He is not the soul of friendliness and charm I will grant you, but *you* my little sister can be a veritable shrew at times! You have always been spoiled, basking in the reflected glory which is Harry's. Our father loved your mother only because she produced a son, and so your arrival did not lie unpleasantly upon great Warwick's pride. He decided to spoil you, and as God is my witness he did an excellent job! You can see no further than your nose, Nan Beauchamp, and it is time you mended your ways."

Nan sniffed disdainfully, standing and picking up one of the chessmen. "The fault was not mine this night, not at all!"

At the door Margaret stopped and turned. "No, maybe not, but you gave way entirely to your emotions when you turned upon Thomas Neville in such a fashion. You caused a scene which father would have punished you severely for, and which indeed you would have thought twice about committing had he been here! Nan, you must mask your feelings a little more, such displays are certainly not ladylike and not at all worthy of a Beauchamp!"

The green eyes were hurt, but Nan was shamefaced as she nodded. "I am sorry Margaret, forgive me. I *will* try, I promise that I will."

Margaret stepped forward and kissed her sister's head. "Think on it, Nan, that is all I advise."

They walked back to the main hall together, stopping in amazement at the entrance. There were no smiling faces now, the marriage feast was strangely subdued, even the gay lilting music had faded into the shadows. Shrewsbury came towards them, his face shocked.

"What has happened?" Margaret clutched his arm.

"It is the Earl of Warwick . . . he is dead, word has just arrived from France."

Nan blinked. For so long the news had been expected and yet now it had arrived and the shock was as great as if. . . . She looked towards Harry, now the new Earl of Warwick!

There was a strange little scene there. Harry stood with his arms around the royal person of the King. Henry's hand was raised and his long fingers scratched busily at his sparse hair, while the other hand clutched a jewelled Bible. Poor Henry, his mild face was contorted by grief, the tears pouring unashamedly down his thin cheeks. The fingers stopped their scratching to brush away the tears. Tears shed for Warwick, the man who was undoubtedly responsible for the feeble-mindedness of the King, the man who had had so much to answer for. Nan's heart warmed towards Henry as he looked at her now, his trembling lips trying to smile in his kindly way. Such heart-felt sorrow, visible in his entire bearing and appearance, could not but draw compassion from Nan; she did not stop to think that this meek creature was entirely unsuited, mentally or physically, for the rigours of bearing England's crown.

The King's hands moved yet again, this time to clutch desperately at those of Harry. He grasped his friend tightly, lying his head on his shoulders and weeping noisily into Harry's wedding robes.

20

THREE

Six years later England's King at last married. His new Queen was the dark-haired, sixteen year old Margaret of Anjou; but instead of rejoicing, England was sullen and resentful. The marriage had been negotiated by the extremely unpopular and inefficient Duke of Suffolk, Somerset's friend. The price of the marriage and the uncertainty of a peace with France had been Suffolk's illegal surrender of some of England's few remaining possessions in that land. When the truth became known the English smarted at the insult, and when it further became apparent that Margaret came without a dower, England actively disliked its new Queen.

The advent of Margaret had caused unquiet in the turbulent heart of Humphrey, Duke of Gloucester who had hitherto been the King's heir and who now saw the likelihood of Henry producing a son and therefore taking the hope of the throne from his uncle. Gloucester was himself childless, and *his* heir was the Duke of York, the powerful new brother-in-law of the Earl of Salisbury. Gloucester and York had little trouble in stirring up unrest against the unpopular marriage. Suffolk's gross mishandling of the entire affair made matters easier for the insurgents.

But the weak Henry, who had previously been the willing tool of his masterful uncle, now came completely under the domination of his strong-willed bride. And so the struggle was commenced between Margaret and Gloucester, and sandwiched between these mighty foes was the unfortunate, mild Harry Beauchamp.

Nan's brother had followed a gilded career at the side of his royal friend and the King had found solace in the genuine friendship of Beauchamp. So great had been Henry's love for Harry that he had created him Duke of Warwick. Both Suffolk and Somerset were antagonistic towards Harry, and Margaret had arrived in an unfriendly land where her only friends were Suffolk and his cronies. In a space of little more than three months Margaret's tireless efforts on behalf of her new friends had succeeded in removing Harry from his court position and banishing him to his estates.

Such was her immediate power over the King. It was not Margaret's fault that her marriage had been so mismanaged by

Suffolk or that the people of England hated her from the outset. She was young, she was frightened, and her very existence depended upon Suffolk's strength and authority; she did everything possible to protect him from Gloucester's machinations. Harry Beauchamp had nothing whatsoever to do with her safety, but she cared nothing for that. Warwick, who could have been her greatest ally, became instead a sour, embittered enemy. The King's whimper of protest at losing his friend was lost in the clamour caused by Margaret's new adherents, one of the loudest of whom was Warwick's own brother-in-law, Somerset.

Nan was now nineteen and had lived for some years with with Richard at the various Neville strongholds in Yorkshire. When Harry returned to Warwick in disgrace, however, Nan and her Neville kin were paying a prolonged visit. To Nan the homecoming was welcome indeed as a respite from the interminable feuding of her husband's family.

One early June morning a slow party of riders left the castle and took the path along the bank of the Avon. The horses were led by pages who picked the way carefully through the bushes and reeds which grew so profusely at the river's edge. The ride had been intended to lighten their hearts, but a gloom encompassed them and soon they rode in silence, the only sounds the jingle of harness and the burble of the lazy river.

Nan's grey palfrey picked its hooves up cautiously, its ears flicking backwards and forwards to the sound of each wavelet upon the water, each bird call on the warm air. The wired veil of Nan's headdress floated on the breeze, a wispy white cloud, and the pearl-strewn ivory silk of her gown shone; she was bright, jewel-bright.

Beside her Cecille was as plain as a sparrow, but what she lacked in beauty she made up for in warmth and happiness. She was idyllically happy in her marriage, and that happiness had been at last made complete by the birth of her only child, a daughter named Ann who was less than one year old. Many times had Cecille conceived but only one living child had she borne, and that child was pale and listless, and the heiress to the entire Beauchamp fortune; the greatest single inheritance in the realm.

Cecille's mount stumbled and she gasped aloud as the water

seemed momentarily to reach up for her. Harry reined in, his long face anxious, and the falcon on his wrist fluttered with sudden fright. The page who led Cecille's palfrey looked fearfully up at his master, expecting a punishment for not leading the animal more carefully, but Harry's anger took another course. "Have a care, 'tis a treacherous path, as treacherous as England's Queen!"

Now the fourth member of the party spoke up, and Richard's irritation was audible. "In the name of God why do we not speak openly? Many weeks now we have been together, with events in London hovering over us like thunder clouds, and yet never once have we mentioned anything. We are brother and sister married to brother and sister, and I think it high time we acted as if we were in truth so close!" His abundant chestnut hair moved slightly in the breeze and his hazel eyes were intense and burning. He slowly dismounted, brushing the biscuit velvet of his sleeve with his hand as if to remove some imaginary blemish. They watched as he slowly pulled his mount's reins over its ears and handed them to the waiting page, then he stood patiently, waiting for Harry's answer.

Nan found herself for once in agreement with him, but even now she looked haughtily upon him. A gentleman, a future Earl, and yet he rode out with his head uncovered! She glanced quickly at her brother, noting the intricate folds of his scarlet hat with its long scarf. The differences between Beauchamp and Neville began even with such small things as hats!

Harry began to dismount and Nan looked to Richard for help. "My Lord, will you aid me?" He stepped over and his hands were firm around her waist. Briefly the wedding band burned on her finger at his touch . . . briefly . . . and then the moment was past.

The pages led the horses to a respectful distance, and soon were playing dice with one another upon the tough, wiry grass. The Avon swirled endlessly by as Richard spoke again.

"Well, my Lord of Warwick?" His voice was soft.

"What is there to say?" Harry shrugged angrily, plucking at the grass. "I have been banished by the venom of that French bitch and the friendship of a lifetime has ended in a trice! I meant her no harm, I had no ambitions to winkle her from her safe nest, it is she who sought to destroy me . . . and her success is all too evident!" Savagely he dislodged a small

23

stone with his boot and it rattled down the bank and into the water.

His wife touched his arm, the movement a tender gesture. "But surely, when her position is safer, she must relax her grip and then you will be able to return."

"You do not know the Queen, her grip will never relax. Those whom she has decided are her enemies are not likely to return to any position at court. Somerset's personal hatred of me hardens her still further; I think maybe my very life is in danger. She is well matched with Beaufort, indeed there are some whispers already concerning the Queen and my dear brother-in-law."

Nan's mouth opened in surprise. "The Queen and Somerset? But she has been married only a matter of months!"

Richard laughed flatly. "Aye, and the groom is Henry Plantagenet." There was more than just contempt for the muddle-headed Lancastrian King in his tone, there was almost an emnity.

She ignored the subtle inflexion. "Henry may be no Lancelot or Arthur, but he is good and kind, and he is King of England! She should not so abuse her position."

Richard raised an eyebrow. "I would imagine a woman such as Margaret, or any woman come to that, would find the noble King Harry VI a poor companion between the bed coverings." He looked coolly away from Nan's angry face.

Harry smiled unexpectedly. "Margaret has no knowledge of Henry's strength in *that* direction, he has never approached her except to read passages from the Bible!"

His breath hissing between his teeth, Richard looked intently at his wife's brother. "Well, I would have you know that you have my support, Harry, both as my brother-in-law and as Somerset's opponent. The Queen's party are opposed to Gloucester and therefore to my kinsman the Duke of York, and my family stands behind York."

The smile faded from Harry's face at the mention of Gloucester and York. "Well, suffice it that you are with me Richard, I do not lend my name to those who oppose the Queen. To do so is also to oppose Henry himself who agreed to and went willingly towards the marriage. My sympathies are with the King and the King alone." His tone was final.

Richard's voice held a dreamlike quality as he murmured almost inaudibly. "As are mine . . . as are mine. . . ."

Nan at last became fully aware of Richard's strange attitude, it was almost as if he did not speak of Henry at all, but some other man.

Harry stood. "Well, there is one thing the Queen can do nothing about. Henry has never in his life been without me, and now he is alone except for Margaret, and hers is not a sympathetic nature. He will send for me, I think, but I know not if I will be pleased or no. Margaret wishes me out of the way, and may take steps to ensure that I remain so." He smiled brightly, forcing away the shudder which his thoughts gave rise to. "Come on, Richard Neville, I have a mind to show you the paces of my new horse. I vow it can outpace that northern nag of yours!"

Richard accepted the ending of the conversation, and the challenge. The pages hastily put away their dice, but soon were motioned to remain seated as their presence was not required. The hoofbeats thundered loudly on the still air as the two rode away at dangerous pace along that winding pathway.

For a while the two women sat in silence, but at last Cecille spoke. "What is amiss between you and my brother? The atmosphere 'twixt the pair of you is heavy enough to carve upon."

Nan's eyelids fluttered but she did not turn to look at Cecille. Harry's falcon was perched upon a dead tree trunk nearby, its hooded head twisting this way and that as the various sounds of nature caught its blind attention. "We have no time for one another."

Cecille was horrified. "There must surely be more. . . ."

Now for the first time Nan blushed and bowed her head sharply. "After three years during which time Richard could have consummated our marriage, I remain as pure as when I was first betrothed as a child!"

Disbelief clouded Cecille's face. "You jest, I cannot believe it, not of Richard."

"Well, it is true. Oh, he is not inexperienced, indeed he has had many women, some of whom he has chosen to flaunt in front of me. I have my pride, I am a Beauchamp and strong enough to rise above the petty treatment meted out by Richard Neville."

"I will tell you something Nan, it is not you who rise above

25

his treatment, but *he* who rises above yours. You do not dislike him, even if you will not admit it to yourself. You are an accomplished actress, with your cold face and icy heart, and you are also unpleasantly given to judging others by their status rather than their merit. You consider the House of Neville to be inferior, and you resent Richard because of this. 'Tis not a pretty thought, Nan, and there are times when you are not a likeable person. *I* can tell you this as your superior, I am Duchess of Warwick . . . and also a Neville, and I can understand Richard's predicament in having such a wife as you!"

Nan's face was frozen now. "You are mistaken!" she said, her voice clipped, but within her mind was a whirlpool of uncertainly. Could all that be true of her? Was it possible that she was so unpleasant that even Cecille disliked her? And could it be true that she did indeed like Richard, somewhere deep beneath her hateful exterior. She thought now on times when her reaction to him had been unaccountable, when she had lain awake in her bed at nights, waiting, hoping. . . .

A sound of hoofbeats across the river caused them both to glance up. The pages halted in their interminable game of dice to watch the passing of a group of huntsmen. The falcon cried with excitement as the hoofbeats carried to its alert instinct, it swayed up and down, standing motionless then as the boarhounds bayed. There was no way of identifying the huntsmen. Nan shaded her eyes from the sun to watch them, seeing that their pace was slowing. Who were they? Their faces were obscured by their billowing cloaks, and their hats were pulled down well over their foreheads. Strangely well wrapped for a hot summer's day. . . .

Too late she saw the two lone figures of her brother and husband riding back along the path, too late she saw the huntsmen stop and one take a crossbow from beneath his cloak and take aim at the two who rode unheeding towards their wives, too late. . . . The arrow whistled across the rippling, shimmering waters, plucking the unwary Harry from his mount as surely as a hand plucks an apple. It was no accident, the men turned their horses swiftly and put many yards between themselves and their stricken quarry, vanishing eventually into the embrace of a small coppice.

Stunned Nan and Cecille stared, uncomprehending. Then

26

Nan was running towards the fallen figure of her brother, her slippers tearing on the sun-baked mud, her skirts pulling against the reeds and bushes.

Richard was bending over the still body, untying the laces which fastened the blood-stained collar of the doublet, but already Harry's ashen face and staring eyes proclaimed that the heart within him was still. She stood there, her hands pressed in horror to her lips, her eyes staring into Richard's shocked face. He reached out towards her as the hysteria bubbled up, and he caught her as her lips parted and the dreadful screams filled the air. . . .

Harry's own words had come true then. Margaret, Queen of England, had removed from her path the unwanted Duke of Warwick.

FOUR

LATE that same night the castle was filled with the doleful, lamenting chanting from the chapel. The sound was inescapable. Nan remained in her apartments alone, being unable to go to Cecille who had collapsed with grief and shock. Their return to the castle had been greeted with the news that a messenger bearing the King's colours had arrived. . . . Henry had indeed sent for his beloved friend.

Nan's ladies were silent as they prepared her for sleep and when they finished she dismissed them, even the faithful Alana who would have wished to remain with her sad mistress.

She knelt now at the wooden 'prie-dieu' in the corner of the bedchamber, pressing her forehead against the shelf. Oh how could such a terrible thing have befallen her family? Long she knelt there in the flickering light of a taper. The single flame attracted a multitude of moths and flying creatures and the whirring of wings was joined to the dolorous singing from the chapel. She leaned over and extinguished the flame and the whirring ceased.

There were footsteps approaching through the empty outer

27

chamber of her apartments. She listened, her head turned, recognizing the quick steps of her husband. Puzzled she stood and walked towards the doorway, stopping as she heard the door open and close again.

Salisbury's voice! "Richard, this day's work calls for a new approach to your marriage. . . ." The stealthy whisper broke off as Nan's white nightrobe gleamed eerily in the semi-light of the other room where the candles were still lit.

Her grief was forgotten as she stepped proudly before the two confused Nevilles. "You were saying, my Lord Earl?" She looked unpleasantly at her father-in-law.

He shifted from one foot to the other, his eyes flitting swiftly to his son's uneasy face.

The silence lengthened and she spoke again. "I would know what you were about to say."

"Nan, be silent!" Richard attempted to turn her from her path.

"I will not. What is all this about? I have a right to know, after all I form one half of this marriage, whether you realize it or not!"

He flushed, turning away with an embarrassed air.

Salisbury glowered at his son. "It seems that you have scant control over this shrew you term 'wife'. Such a sharp tongue deserves a thrashing now and again!" He turned his attention back to Nan, his face breaking into a smile of sweetest honey charm. She grew apprehensive. "Very well, my dearest daughter, you shall know what I was about to say, and I hope you enjoy the listening! After your father died, I was still here at War- wick when his papers and effects were returned from France. That first night after the chests were brought. I spent an interesting hour or more sifting through the many parchments which were packed away. Well, I found one paper, in actual fact a codicil to your father's last will, which I deemed it wiser to remove and destroy. 'Twas an act of the moment, but one which may now bring great wealth to you and Richard. In the normal way your late brother and all the heirs of his body would have inherited the Beauchamp fortune, and on the failure of that line *you* Nan would have come into the estate as the only full-blood heir of Harry Beauchamp. Well, something . . . or I mind *someone* . . . caused your father to ponder anew upon this aspect of his will. He penned this codicil which *included* your half-sisters in the inheritance on the failure of Harry's line. I destroyed this paper and so the will stands as it was, and you are now little Ann's only full-blood heir. You have seen the baby, she is not like to live beyond childhood . . . then all will devolve upon you, my daughter, you and Richard."

Nan was speechless for a moment. How dared this coarse Neville sift through her father's papers, how dared he meddle in her father's affairs. . . . Her green eyes flashed with pride and malice. "And you would have me concur in this Neville sleight of hand? I tell you and I tell you plain, Sirrah, I will not remain silent upon this matter. . . .

Salisbury raised his hand to stem the flow. "You would then allow Somerset to succeed with his own chicanery? Mistake me not, Mistress, it was Somerset who caused the writing of this codicil, it was dated at the very time when Somerset was in France with your ailing father, and Somerset stands to gain a healthy portion of your family's fortune should the truth be known." His eyes took on a crafty expression. "Somerset, my Lady, the ardent supporter of the new Queen, that same French woman who no doubt caused your brother's infamous murder."

She turned away from him, her grief rising anew at the mention of Harry's death. The tears sprang easily to her red-rimmed eyes.

Richard was staring at his father. "What has this to do with my approach to my marriage?"

Nan whirled to look at him, seeing the light of excitement in his eyes. He did not condemn his father's actions, he applauded them!

The Earl leaned forward. "My son, if you wish to gain the Earldom and wealth of Warwick you needs must tame this vixen wife of yours! The marriage is no marriage if not consummated!"

The silence grew so heavy that each word of the priests' chant could be heard sharply. Within the room there was a jingle of coins as Salisbury's fingers played idly with the purse at his waist. Leaving his son still staring at him, he turned upon his heel and left the apartments, closing the door softly behind him. They heard his footsteps dying away into the depths of the castle, his tuneless whistling droning, lingering tangibly long after he had gone.

Richard's eyes swung to her trembling figure. She backed

away from him, her frantic hands feeling behind her for the doorway. "Take not one step towards me!" she whispered.

He laughed coldly. "You can do nothing to stop me, Madam, you are my wife!"

Her eyes flickered to the outer door and with a lurch she ran towards it, but he stretched out and caught at her flowing robe. The white fabric tore loudly as they struggled. She was trapped now, unable to resist his strength.

"You are not going to take away my chance of the richest inheritance in England, sweet Nan!" She spat foully in his face, struggling anew in her fear. He put up his hand and wiped the spittle away. "Holy Mother, how you despise me, flaunting your birthright before me as if I were less than the dirt beneath your slippers. Well, touching *you* has been beneath *me* these years, I would not soil my body, taint myself with the taking of you. I have stood your taunts and superior bearing with a strength I did not dream I possessed. A Beauchamp of Warwick!" He sneered this last and she recognized a cruel, expert mimicry of her own voice. "Well, I am a Neville and I am about to assert my ascendancy over the noble House of Beauchamp!"

She was calm now, imbued with an icy control which was alien to the pounding of her heart. Her fingers were dead, cold, her stomach churning sickeningly, but she stared deep into his eyes. "You are beneath contempt, Richard Neville, go ahead then, take your revenge upon a mere woman. Sir Knight!"

He laughed. " 'Tis of no avail, Nan, no amount of goading, of appealing to my chivalry, is going to save you now. I have ambition, Nan, something which a Beauchamp seems to know nothing about since the passing of your thoroughly ambitious father! The consummation of this so-called marriage is not going to stand in my way now!"

Her resolve crumbled and her struggles were renewed as he bore her into the dark bedchamber. She opened her mouth to scream but his hand was swiftly over her lips. His loud whisper came to her frantic ears. "You shall be silent Madam, I thank God for that chanting that no-one shall hear you now!"

She knew nothing but the power of his body and the strength of that hand which muffled her screams. That which she had lain awake at nights for in the past came to her now, and the experience was not a thing of joy, but a nightmare of pain and humiliation.

Afterwards she lay weeping in the darkness. He was silent beside her, listening to the sobs. He did not like what he had done and did not admire himself, but given the same circumstances again he knew that he would not have swerved from his course. She was his wife in fact now, not merely in name. Conquest had in some way atoned for the countless pricks and barbs suffered at her hands in the past.

He turned his head to look at her now. She was so small, so defenceless, lying there hiding her face in the furs and coverlets of the huge bed. Hesitantly he stretched out his hand to her, but he paused then. She would not welcome his sympathy, indeed she would not believe in it.

His hand fell back to his side.

FIVE

THROUGH the mullioned window Nan watched as Richard helped the small figure of her niece Eleanor Talbot into the saddle of her small palfrey. Eleanor worshipped Richard, and her dark eyes were shining as she listened to him. She was eleven years old, a pretty child with her mother's dark hair, and Nan could faintly hear her high-pitched voice at the horses moved away from the house into the bleak January countryside.

Nan frowned a little as she saw Eleanor's black hair streaming behind her, the child would surely catch a dreadful cold by not pulling up her hood. She promised herself that she would reprimand her when next she saw the culprit. But anger could not remain overlong, for the child was now an orphan. The Earl of Shrewsbury was long since dead and Nan's sister Margaret had but recently followed her husband to the grave. Margaret's dying wish had been that Eleanor, her youngest child, should come into Nan's household, as her ward.

The view from the window was unfamiliar, an aspect over a cold, frozen township, the manor and village of Ewelme in Oxfordshire. Nan glanced around the richly-hung room with its bright tapestries and tall, elegant candlesticks. Her short, fur-lined cloak lay idly tossed upon a table, and she bit her lip as she looked towards the door. More than an hour she had been here now, coming at Cecille's request because her daughter Harry's child, lay dying.

The child was betrothed, against Cecille's will, to the eldest son of the Duke of Suffolk, whose word was law in Margaret of Anjou's England. Suffolk was bitter now at having this great heiress slip through his fingers into blessed oblivion. It was four years since Harry's death, four years since Cecille's golden, warm existence had been shattered . . . now it seemed that her only tangible memory of Harry was to be taken from her as well.

Nan's fingers tapped anxiously upon the table and she pushed the hem of her cloak first this way and then that. The damp fur left a trail of muddy moisture across the oak surface. Jesu, would no-one come and tell her what was happening? A slight movement close to the roaring fire caused her to look yet again at the silent figure of Somerset. Edmund Beaufort gazed into the twisting, spiralling flames, his hand playing with the long ears of a great dog which lay stretched near his feet. He was agitated for he now saw the Beauchamp fortune looming once more upon his horizon; maybe not all of it but at least a healthy portion. If Harry Beauchamp's daughter had survived to finally marry Suffolk's son then none of the Beauchamp sisters would inherit, but now, now. . . . Oh, how he had resented Suffolk's interference, how bitterly he had fought against the little girl's enforced betrothal to Suffolk's son. Somerset's own son could have been betrothed to the heiress . . . but Somerset must stand down before the mighty Suffolk. He started suddenly as soft footsteps approached the door, and the dog yelped as his fingers twisted its ears roughly.

The door opened and there stood the Duchess of Suffolk. Her face was white, strained, and she inclined her head gravely to Nan.

"Lady Neville, word was brought to me that you were here. Your husband? . . ."

"My husband is not here at the moment, Your Grace, but will return presently. Is there news of my brother's child? The Duchess of Warwick sent for me, that is the reason for my unexpected visit to your house." Nan's eyes moved back to the taut figure of Somerset. He stared at the flames as if he dared not look elsewhere.

32

"Lady Neville, I fear that I have sad news for you, indeed sad news for us all. My son's betrothed has . . . passed away this very hour. . . ." Her voice trailed away and she bowed her head piously.

Somerset relaxed, his slender body losing its straight, unbending stance and assuming a lazy grace as he turned at last to look at the Duchess. The silver embroidery on the hem of his short coat swung as he moved, his soft shoes making no sound upon the rushes, but the folly bells on his belt tinkled melodiously. These bells were a strange affectation of his, a fashion almost dead but living on strongly with Edmund Beaufort.

"My deep sorrow knows no bounds, my Lady, I pray you convey my solicitations to my bereaved sister, my Lady of Warwick." His whole demeanour was grotesque and Nan turned from him in disgust. He was rejoicing, rejoicing in the death of a child.

The Duchess spoke again, but her attitude was very cool as she looked at him. "I will indeed tell her of your kindness. Lady Neville, I fear that your journey has been wasted, the Duchess of Warwick is in a state of collapse and can see no-one."

Nan flushed a little at the obvious, curt dismissal from Suffolk's house. There was no mention of accommodating the weary travellers from the north, and Nan was too proud to ask anything now of the noble Duke or his lady.

"If you will be so kind as to mention my visit. . . ."

"I will do so. I bid you good day." Abruptly the lady of the house turned and departed.

Surprised at the extreme rudeness, Nan stood there. A glance through the window revealed no sign of Richard, for all she knew he would be gone for some time yet. She sighed and began to pick up her damp cloak, her nose wrinkling as the odour of wet fur came to her nostrils. Somerset leaned now against the smoky chimney breast, his eyes shining and a small curve of triumph upon his thin lips. Nan's embarrassment at the brusque dismissal of a few minutes' earlier evaporated as she watched him. Nay, Edmund Beaufort, things are not as you imagine, not at all, you do not stand to gain one coin of my father's fortune! For the first time the enormity of what had happened struck her, *she* was the only heiress, *she* would inherit all; and all because a greedy, scheming northern nobleman of the House of Neville had seen fit to dispose of a small piece of parch-

33

ment. . . . She became aware that Somerset had detected the intensity of her gaze and too late she looked away. He stared thoughtfully at her, his fingers moving lovingly over the sooty stone; his instinct told him that something was amiss.

Unexpectedly he smiled, the full force of his charm directed at her as he walked across the intervening space. "Sweet Nan, I vow that marriage suits you well, I envy your husband his bed of nights."

She flushed angrily. "My Lord, I find such remarks in extremely low taste, especially at a time such as this."

"Indeed? The expression in your eyes this moment past did not smack of grief either!" His voice was quiet, menacing, and she was suddenly very afraid of this cool Beaufort.

Her hatred for him overcame her brief fear. "I merely looked aghast at a man who could smile at the death of so small a child."

"My smile was at the infinite loss suffered by Suffolk!"

A demon alighted upon Nan's shoulders, prodding her into foolishness. She could not resist taunting him "And why should you rejoice at Suffolk's loss, his loss is not your gain!" Her green eyes were alight with her own secret knowledge.

With unexpected speed his hands gripped her wrists. "My little Neville wildcat, I *do* stand to gain. Your father did not seek to exclude the daughters of his first marriage from his will. The half-blood *will* inherit. You are not destined to be Countess of Warwick, and your oafish husband will not swagger under the title of Earl of Warwick . . . nay, Salisbury is all you will amount to!" Spittle from his lips flecked the dark green bodice of her gown and involuntarily he glanced down, his eyes lying hotly upon the soft curve of her breasts. His tongue passed quickly over his lips. Somerset was as always roused to desire for this green-eyed girl who despised him so.

"And what makes you so sure of that, my noble Somerset?" Nan's voice was cold, bearing all the infinite contempt of a woman who cares nothing for a man who desires her.

He smiled but there was no warmth to the gesture. "I saw your father write in his own hand. . . ." He stopped, seeing as if for the first time the sheer triumph upon her face. "You look, my little dove, as if you have knowledge of something which concerns me!" His fingers tightened cruelly upon her wrists, his nails biting deeply into her flesh.

34

Now the fear returned tenfold. A coldness lay upon her as he leaned closer. What a vain foolishness had overtaken her, why had she attempted to assert her triumph over him? Why could she not have left well alone. . . .

"Sweet Nan, you show no surprise at hearing this, no surprise at all! Tell me what you know, tell me I say!" Slowly he twisted her wrists.

"Unhand my wife, Somerset, or I will spit your noble carcass to the very wall!"

Richard, Holy God, Richard! Nan's relief almost overwhelmed her. Somerset released her and whirled round, the folly bells jangling now.

Richard stood in the doorway, his eyes bright as he looked disdainfully upon the hated Beaufort. Nan sank to her knees weakly, hiding her face in her hands to conceal the weeping. The blade of Richard's knife flashed evilly in the afternoon light and Somerset stepped hastily backwards, pushing against Nan's crouching figure. Terrified at his touch she sprang away, running across the room to Richard. He put out his hand and pulled her close, still threatening Somerset with the knife. "You are so brave, Sirrah, when your adversary is a woman! God preserve your miserable soul if I should find you thus again. . . . Get out of here!"

Somerset had by now regained some of his lost equilibrium. "And by what authority do *you* order *me* from here?"

Richard's hazel eyes lightened as if he were amused and he turned the blade of the knife so that it once again flashed against the sunlight. "By the authority of being the one who deems your presence no longer to be required!"

Somerset's glance fell upon the blade and he swallowed, but his apprehension was not great enough to force him into silence. "That document was witnessed by myself, I saw Beauchamp write it! I know that you have been tampering with old Warwick's will, *I know it!*"

Richard's hand absently caressed Nan's hair as she cowered against him, pressing close as if to hide within him. "Think you so, then you had best prove it had you not?" His voice was fearless, confident.

Beaufort's face closed like a mask. "The House of Neville shall have cause to regret this trickery. Do not think that it is I

35

who shall have to prove the document's existence, nay, it is *you* who shall have to prove its *non*-existence!"

But Richard did not flinch. "You think to convince the King that my wife's father penned a codicil to his will eliminating Nan from the entire inheritance? Such is an unusual step for anyone to take, my Lord, it is hardly ever that those of the half-blood inherit. Or will you tell of how you almost forced a sick old man into writing this document so that you could put your evil hands upon a portion of his wealth! I am sure that our gentle King will think kindly of you under those circumstances."

Somerset smiled. "I have powerful friends, Neville, very powerful friends!"

"One of whom you have very seriously offended this day by coming to gloat over his loss of this disputed inheritance! The Duke of Suffolk is displeased with you, most displeased!" Richard's face was bland.

Without a further word, the white-faced Somerset turned and walked towards the door, which Richard flung open, bowing graciously as Somerset stalked past.

A moment after the door closed, Richard's voice was an angry hiss in Nan's ear. "God in Heaven, but the Beauchamps have produced a tactless wench in you! A few moments more and Somerset's eager ears would no doubt have been assailed by the entire tale of my father's activities!" His hazel eyes were angry when she looked up at him.

The old hatred returned and her heart hardened. "Fear not, my sweet Lord, you came within time to halt such unwanted confessions, and your greatest wish is granted. You are now Earl of Warwick and my entire family fortune comes to you! I wish you well of it!"

He ignored her. "What arrangements are now made for us?"

"None, the Duchess of Suffolk quite definitely dismissed me from her house. We have no alternative but to retrace our steps."

"So be it, I have no desire to remain under Suffolk's accursed roof anyway!" He picked up her cloak and placed it gently around her shoulders. The gentleness irritated her; anger she could understand, force and strength, but not this cool capacity he had for virtually ignoring her. She could make no indent upon his protective shell, and the knowledge infuriated her.

They walked outside to rejoin their party, and the weary,

travel-stained horses and their riders began the homeward journey.

SIX

WITHIN a month of Ann's death, the King's uncle, Humphrey of Gloucester, was arrested. This event had a profound effect upon Richard Neville.

He was like a caged beast, striding up and down the stone-flagged floor of the private apartments at Middleham. The dark castle nestling in the wild Yorkshire countryside was one of the most important Neville strongholds. Now Nan watched her husband in fascination. His resemblance to a lion could not have been greater had he opened his mouth and roared. He thumped his fist into his palm in exasperation, stopping briefly to toss a fresh log on to the fire.

Nan's long fingers stroked the tabby cat which rubbed around her skirts. She sighed, would he never stop pacing? Since the death of Harry's daughter, nothing had been heard of Somerset who had returned to London, nursing his grievances and his spite. The arena was ominously silent, but it was not this which caused Richard's agitation.

Now he gazed thoughtfully into the hissing, dancing fire, his face illuminated by the quivering light. "My father had better kept his honour by avoiding involvement in the arrest of Gloucester!"

"Involvement?" Her voice was loud in its surprise. She bit her lip and glanced around at the faces which were now turned towards her. She glared meaningly at Alana who hastily stood and touched Eleanor's shoulder. The girl got up lightly and hurried from the room, followed by Alana and then by the other ladies of Nan's household. The door closed upon them and Nan turned back to Richard. "Involvement you say! You call it thus as if Gloucester were in the right to rebel against the King!" The cat jumped on to her lap and Richard twitched with distaste.

37

He snorted angrily. "Madam, your Beauchamp breeding shows yet again! You see nothing more than that Henry VI sits the throne and that Gloucester shows dissidence. Gloucester has little or nothing to do with what I speak of, his arrest matters nothing to me or to my father. Our concern is that Gloucester's misfortune exposes our kinsman York to danger. *That* is where my father's honour comes into dispute. He had warning enough that he was to be sent to arrest Gloucester, and during that time he could have come north and sent word to court that he was ill or some other such excuse. To have meekly taken his orders from the Queen's party and attended to Gloucester's fate smacks of idleness or out-and-out treason!"

"Treason?" What was he talking about? Salisbury had obeyed the command of the King, how could that be construed as treason? She pushed the cat away but it was persistent and soon nestled in the folds of her skirts again.

Richard turned and came close to her, putting his hands on the wooden arms of her chair. He spoke so low that he was almost inaudible above the crackling fire. "Yes treason, to the true King."

Nan crossed herself and then put her hands up to her ears. Whatever was in his mind she had no wish to hear it, no wish at all. Impatiently he pulled her wrists and she was forced to listen.

"Madam, you are steeped in the Lancastrian tradition and you can no longer imagine there to be any other cause worth fighting for."

She shook her head. "Say no more, I beg of you. If word of such talk should reach the ears of the Queen. . . ."

"It will not . . . unless you have a mind to tell her yourself!" He smiled.

Jesu, when he smiled thus . . . when he smiled so gently. . . . She shook her head. "I will not betray you."

He put his fingers under her chin and raised her face towards his own. "Nan, the rightful King of England is Richard, Duke of York. Nay, be still and I will tell you why. His claim is stronger and truer than that of your beloved Henry. The House of Lancaster traces its descent from the third son of Edward III, York from the second son. Lancaster is in power purely through the usurpation of Henry IV when he overcame Richard II. The throne is theirs through right of conquest, nothing more, and that right was founded in the murder of Richard II at Pontefract. I have no scruples in this, the wrong man has the throne . . . and it is not even as if he had something to commend him as had his sire, Henry V! Why should England have as King a man who is not only weak in the head, but also has no legal right to have the crown?"

She swallowed. "He is still the anointed King, monarch in the eyes of God."

"And so was Richard II."

"But he was murdered, surely you do not mean to. . . ."

"Put such ideas from your head, Madam, I merely wish to depose him not to deprive him of life. There is no need with such a man as Henry Plantagenet, I vow he would be happier in a monastery anyway."

Nan remembered the shy, timid boy who had grown up with her at Warwick. Perhaps there was more than a little truth in what Richard said, Henry was no majestic King, he was studious, pious and retired from the world at every opportunity.

She gripped her wandering thoughts. "Promise me, Richard, that you will not indulge in such vain hopes and ambitions."

"Why so vain? There has never been a more beneficial time than now. Henry has proved himself to be weak and indecisive, he has shown himself completely under the domination of the hated French Queen and her favourites Suffolk and Somerset. Even the ponderous Gloucester managed to stir up the land to fever pitch . . . if he can do that then think what Richard of York could do."

"I do not know York and therefore cannot comment, but I did not imagine him to be such a firebrand." Her voice was flat. She did not like such talk, it frightened her and she looked fearfully towards the shadows.

Richard frowned and his large hand suddenly swept the startled cat from her lap. "My father wanted me to rise high on your dead brother's shoulders, power at the side of a Lancastrian King. That is not my dream . . . my dream is of York as King, and since I have been old enough to reason for myself that has been my ambition. That he is now my uncle-by-marriage merely binds me closer to a vision which has always been with me. True, I too acquiesced in my father's scheming over your father's will, and I did so from thoughts of my own advancement. Now, however, the fact that I become Earl of

Warwick, with all the attendant power which the title brings, has become of paramount importance to me. Support me in this, Nan, you are my wife and I would have you with me." This last was uttered quietly, simply.

"You ask me to forsake all that which I have been brought up to believe in. My father was strong for Lancaster and he instilled in his children a like loyalty. You would have me put aside all this?"

"Yes." There were no trimmings with his words, no silver droplets of persuasion, merely the direct request. She gazed up at him. So much hatred lay between them, so many years of mistrust and unkind behaviour . . . yet when he looked at her in that way, when his eyes were kind. . . . "I . . . I have said that I will not betray you and I meant what I said."

"I asked for your support, not your silent disapproval." There was a knock at the door and he turned in anger. "What is it?" he asked testily.

Alana opened the door nervously, holding out a sealed parchment to him. "This has just arrived, my Lord, the messenger bore your father's colours." Richard's eyes glanced quickly at the seal and he took the letter hastily, breaking the seal. The red flakes splintered to the floor and Nan stared at them intently, not knowing why she did so. Richard read and then read again, his face blanching. He waved his hand impatiently in dismissal to Alana, and she curtseyed and thankfully left his presence.

He turned to Nan. "Gloucester is dead! Aye, murdered so it is believed, although none can prove the fact. Within five days of his arrest he was dead, of sorrow so they say! Sorrow!" He snorted in disbelief. "My father says that his responsibility towards Gloucester had ended on the day previous to the murder, and that his successor was a knight of the Queen's party. He puts the blame at the feet of the Queen and Somerset, the King had no hand in it."

"And York?"

His eyes flickered over her face for a moment. "Despatched to Ireland as Lieutenant! Nay, they dared not put him to death, he had done nothing openly to warrant such treatment. He is popular in the realm, such an act would be very foolish. But with York in Ireland. . . ."

"Richard, you asked me before if I would support you. Please believe me when I say that if it were merely against Margaret of Anjou then I would have no hesitation, none at all. But you ask me to turn on Henry, and that I cannot do."

He put his hand to her face and kissed her cheek. "Ah Nan, can you not see that Henry *is* Margaret . . . can you not see?"

She bowed her head. She could not strike such a blow to Henry, he was as a brother to her. Richard waited for a moment, and then he strode from the room.

SEVEN

NAN turned her head as the baby cried, glancing towards the richly carved crib. Eleanor leaned over the gurgling baby, waving a velvet ribbon before the waving arms of Nan's daughter. The child was less than a year old, a healthy girl named Isabel, and Eleanor delighted in playing with her.

Nan's attention returned to her embroidery frame and she held a brilliant blue thread against the design, pursing her lips as she decided upon her choice. The baby squealed again and her hand dropped to her lap. A girl. All these years of marriage and only one child. There had been no miscarriages, no still-births, just one single pregnancy resulting in a girl. She was twenty-six years old and in seemingly good health, why then? Why had there not been more children? She shook her head and sighed. Every man should have a son to carry on his name, and if that man was the Earl of Warwick. . . .

Her gaze was fixed now upon that profusion of blue in her lap, she no longer heard the baby's cries or the murmuring voice of her niece. Richard was at last Earl of Warwick. The King had for once chosen to withstand the pleas of his wife and Somerset in favour of the false Neville. Nan's eyes softened sadly as she thought of Henry Plantagenet, for she knew in her heart that he had stood against the Queen because of his childhood friendship with Nan and her dead brother. He had granted Richard all he wanted because of Richard's wife; poor

41

Henry, if he did but realize the true heart of her husband, the ambitious soul of the man to whom he so eagerly gave such power. She bit her lip miserably; Henry's sad eyes had smiled so warmly at her as he handed Richard the patent. . . .

Her fingers gripped the blue thread and she inhaled sharply. Such thoughts and miseries would not do. She stood and walked towards the crib, looking down fondly at her daughter, this small portion of herself. The baby recognized her and smiled, kicking excitedly, for Nan was wont to come often to the crib which great ladies did not often do. But Nan could not ignore the existence of Isabel.

"I think perhaps we should replace some of the swaddling bands, Eleanor, else the child's nurses will chide us for our lack of consideration for Isabel's health!" Her lips tightened as her niece's deft fingers replaced the white cloths and the baby complained. Jesu, it was a barbaric custom. "If God had wished us strapped thus, he would have formed us united with the bands!" But even the Countess of Warwick dared not flout custom by leaving her child free to move its limbs.

She saw Eleanor's dark eyes alight with warmth as she stroked the baby's face. "Mayhap you will soon have a babe of your own, I vow Sir Thomas Butler will not wait long before marrying you."

Eleanor pulled a face, laughing a little. "He will have to wait a suitable length of time, his father will not allow a hurried affair."

"Why should Thomas await his father's permission? He is old enough to decide for himself surely, he must at least be old enough to be your father!"

Straightening, Eleanor rocked the crib gently as the baby's eyes glazed with approaching sleep. "Did you not realize how timid Thomas Butler is? We are to live in Sir Ralph Butler's house after we are wed, and Thomas will not even consider any other course."

Nan's face showed her amazement. "Has he not heart enough to stride free of his father's yoke?"

"I think not, he has committed crime enough in choosing me as his bride. Sir Ralph disapproves because I bring no great wealth. My father had many children and I was the youngest, there was nothing left for my dower. . . ."

Nan touched her niece's arm gently. "And you, sweetheart,

what of you? Do you wish to continue with this match, I have no doubt that should you so desire the alliance could be severed. Richard has charge of you now, and the betrothal was arranged by your father when you were a baby."

"No! I would marry Thomas, he is kind, gentle, considerate, and I could do a lot worse than live my life with one such as he. That I must take his family with him does not matter overly much." The dark eyes were wide, full of some great fear. "I . . . must have . . . kindness. . . . Do you understand?"

Oh, indeed yes, I understand well. Nan's unspoken thoughts echoed her niece's words. Kindness, gentleness; how she could have wished for these very things herself. From Richard she received neither, merely coldness and a bare acknowledgement of her existence. Even now, while she fretted in the approaching heat of London's summer, Richard had been gone for many months. His fierce, overriding ambition clouded all else, and Nan's wishes counted for nought.

She walked to the window and glanced out over the towers and roofs of London. How many spires were there? Countless numbers, for there seemed a church upon every corner in England's capital. Along the street before her passed the endless stream of traffic; carts, horses, people on foot, people driving animals, street criers with their wares, women with their baskets scurrying along avoiding the deep ruts in the roadway where the wet weather had carved the path of each cart. . . . The sweet freshness of Yorkshire seemed an aeon away, or even Warwick with its beautiful river and towering walls!

And this house where she now dwelt, this magnificent establishment in the possession of the Earl of Salisbury. It was l'Herber and stood in Dowgate, not far from the waters of the Thames itself. It was a dwelling fit for a King, and the richness of its furnishings had come as a pleasant surprise to Nan's astonished eyes when first she had entered. Her father's great castle could not rival l'Herber for luxury and she liked living here . . . but nothing, nothing would make her admit so much to Richard.

Eleanor's voice broke into her daydreaming. "One of the serving-women said that she had seen the great barge of the Duchess of Suffolk entering London with the morning tide. It must be the first time she has visited the city since her husband's death." The baby was stirring and Eleanor went immediately to rock the crib.

Nan watched an old pedlar wend his way along the street, his back laden with all manner of wares, and his hat streaming with ribbons of all hues. Two pretty girls stopped and with great delight began to choose some ribbon. Suffolk. Aye, that was no longer a name to be contended with in Margaret of Anjou's party. Her favourite had at last made himself so unpopular with the realm that he had been plucked down from his lofty position, plucked down and condemned to death. Only Margaret's frenzied pleading with Henry had prevented the Duke's immediate death; the King had nodded and smiled at his beautiful young wife, and Suffolk's sentence was commuted to a mere five years' banishment. England seethed, and the hatred bubbled over; Suffolk's ship was waylaid in the Straits of Dover and he was beheaded without delay. For a while the Queen had been afraid, but the bloodlust was slaked and the land settled back to enjoy its victory. But now Suffolk had been succeeded by one more wily, more ruthless and infinitely more dangerous than his predecessor; Edmund Beaufort, Duke of Somerset, had at last come into his own. He was unchallenged, and together with the Queen, whom many believed to be his mistress, he ruled England.

Richard, Duke of York, had returned from Ireland in the hope of striking down this new threat to England's peace, but instead it had been York who was struck down. Somerset's power had been sadly under-estimated, and the mighty York had been sent scuttling back to his estates.

York's return from Ireland had caused Richard Neville's hopes to rise high; surely he was coming to claim what was rightfully his! But York had made no mention of claiming the throne, he had merely called loudly for the removal of the despised Somerset. Richard's dismay knew no bounds; the moment was right, England was with York, the people followed him, the Queen and her favourites were disliked throughout the land . . . and yet York merely asked for Somerset's disgrace! Nan's private satisfaction was sweet indeed. York's claim did not matter, did not even exist for Nan. Henry was the anointed King.

A spot of rain stained the dry stonework of the window sill and she noticed for the first time that the skies had darkened.

The church bells sounded in unison as the hour of three was reached and the air reverberated to their clamour. The rain increased its force, and now the people in the streets hurried along, eager to escape the approaching storm.

Nan pushed open the window and held her hand out into the rain. Where was Richard now? The failure of York's attempt against Somerset had resulted in York arming his men and riding against the King, still only to insist upon Somerset's removal. But for the first time York's banner of the White Rose was seen in rebellion. Richard and his father and brothers had been commanded to ride at the King's side, and for this Somerset was responsible. He did not trust the Nevilles, knowing their close kinship with the rebel Duke. No news had reached London for some time, maybe a confrontation had occurred between the two armies.

A gust of wind whipped along the narrow streets. The scents and sounds of London were stronger now and she was about to turn away when a vivid patch of colour caught her eye. The street traders pressed against the buildings to make way for the company of men who approached l'Herber on foot, their armour jingling and the rhythmic tread of their feet carrying easily to the window. Red and white! Warwick! The Bear and Ragged Staff emblem of her husband fluttered from the banners, and the Griffin of Salisbury, and the lesser colours of her brothers-in-law. The slim figure at the head of the company leapt out at her, the chestnut hair swinging as he walked in the quickening rain, his plumed helmet beneath his arm. Richard's shoulders were hunched against the elements and his head bowed; his whole appearance was somehow dejected.

Nan was puzzled, watching them as they marched into the courtyard close by. The men were dispersed to their quarters, and the Nevilles entered the house. "Eleanor, will you be my ears? Take yourself quickly to the head of the stairs, mayhap you will hear something of what they say when they come in. Hurry now, the door opens already!" Eleanor was gone like the wind, leaving the door ajar. Nan stood by it, straining her ears, but could only hear the distant muttering of male voices. A door slammed and it was silent again.

Eleanor came back, her brown eyes wide. "My Lady, I heard the Earl of Salisbury as plain as plain . . . he said that . . . that. . . ."

45

"Yes? Come on, girl!"

"Well his exact words were: 'The cause is as good as lost, York being taken means an end to everything.' And then my Lord of Warwick said, 'Aye, and York thinks we were party to the treachery.'"

Nan stared. York taken? She walked towards the stairs, thinking to make her presence known. She must find out what had happened.

The servants at the door opened it immediately she appeared and she walked in to see Richard standing by the black fireplace with his head still bowed, and a page was unstrapping the last piece of his armour. The plumed helmet lay discarded upon a chest. Salisbury was holding out his goblet and Thomas was pouring some ale out. John was sprawled wearily upon a chair, his armour entirely removed and his eyes closed. They turned in surprise to see her.

"My Lady." Richard stepped over to her and dutifully kissed her cheek. She could smell perspiration upon him.

"My Lords. Allow me to pour your ale." She took the jug from Thomas' hands and continued pouring her father-in-law's draught. His face was grey and tired. She looked at Richard. "What has happened, will you not tell me?"

He shrugged. "Aye, we will tell you, and no doubt your pleasure will be great. The two armies pitched camp eventually on opposite banks of the Thames, and York sent messages to the royal camp restating his demands that Somerset be plucked down. It was Margaret who broached the idea of sending word to York that his demands were agreed to. Henry immediately signed his name to the message, he does anything his wife requests. York was assured that he should go free and unmolested afterwards. My father and I stood by and watched it happen, and there was nothing we could do except pray that York would have sense enough to smell the trap." He rubbed his throat where the armour had chafed the soft skin. "York actually went so far as to disband his army and come across the river with only a small company of men. God's Blood and Bones, such simple trust . . . and from such a man! As he entered the tent he saw Somerset still in his place at the King's shoulder, with Margaret at the other, and as he turned to make his escape Somerset's men closed in and he was taken. Before they dragged him away he saw the faces of my father and my-

46

self, standing close to Somerset. He was not to know we had been forced to remain there. We have just this hour returned from the Tower where they took York. I do not know what Somerset intends to do with him, but I think even Beaufort will think twice before bringing York to trial on a charge of treason."

Nan listened in amazement, waiting while the page struggled out with all the armour. "And this is the man you would see on the throne? This is your fair White Rose of York? Holy Mother, even Henry seems to have more wit!"

To her surprise Richard did not show resentment at her scorn. "Aye, it passes all understanding. How could he believe in a message such as that?"

Salisbury drained his goblet, muttering that he needed rest after such a journey. He took his leave of them, followed by Thomas. They heard the heavy footsteps as they went to their private rooms.

Richard looked long at the delicate beauty of his wife. If Margaret of Anjou was noted for her loveliness, her dark unruly loveliness, then those who marvelled at the Queen had not set eyes upon the Countess of Warwick! Nan. . . .

She spoke and his thoughts were broken. "What now then? Can I hope that you have cast aside your ambitions concerning York?"

The choice of words was unfortunate. "No, you cannot! I merely wait until York's fate is decided; they must release him, he is too powerful to confine." Nan's elegant eyebrows were raised, her Beauchamp nose tilted with a superior air. In a rush of anger he threw his goblet to the stone floor and it clattered loudly, rolling away into a far corner past John's outstretched feet. "As long as your Lancastrian half-wit retains the throne England's future rolls away as surely as that! Into obscurity and anarchy, to be ruled by each successive favourite of the French whore! And all the while Henry sits mumbling prayers and hiding his mewling face from low-cut gowns! Bah, how you can remain true to him I do not know!"

"It seems to me that York has little better to offer!" She was stung, her face blushing, her whole attitude one of rebellion.

He fell ominously silent, walking across the room and slowly picking up the goblet. His fingers caressed the carved silver as he walked back, placing it upon a table. The sound echoed threateningly as he turned at last to look at his wife. His face was bereft of expression, totally and absolutely cold. Nan was afraid of him. His lips parted in a snarl, as sudden as it was horrible. "Get you gone from here, Madam, your sour visage turns my stomach. The castle of Warwick is far enough away for me to eat my meat in London without vomiting!" He strode from the room and she heard him turn in the direction of his father's apartments.

She pulled her scattered senses together, shaken utterly, and her eyes met the embarrassed gaze of John Neville. He obviously wished himself anywhere but in that room at that time.

There was a knock upon the door and Salisbury's steward entered. "My Lady, the Earl of Warwick informs me that you wish to make arrangements to leave tomorrow at dawn. . . ."

EIGHT

It was the new year before Nan returned at last to London, more than six months since she last saw Richard; now he sent his brother John to bring her back.

The Earl of Warwick's straight back was turned towards the door as his Countess entered, and he did not turn round as the door slowly closed. John looked blackly at his brother's ill manners, but said nothing.

"You sent for me, my Lord?"

"Yes Madam, I did, your presence is required at court. The Queen has expressed a desire to have you in her personal household for a while."

Nan's mouth opened and closed, then she exclaimed angrily. "Indeed! The French hussy commands that *I* attend upon her loathsome person?"

Richard tutted. "Whatever your opinion of your own worth, Madam my wife, you are still merely the Countess of Warwick while Margaret of Anjou is Queen of England! You will present yourself at Greenwich forthwith." With that the imperious Earl strode from the room.

Her mouth twisted wryly and she turned to face John. "Well, it seems that my husband has not changed at all!" She smiled and touched John's arm gently.

John smiled in return but kept his eyes averted from her face. Her hand dropped from his arm.

For three weeks Nan had been in Margaret's close circle, subjected to the Queen's spite and taunts. Richard's victory over Somerset could not be forgiven and upon Nan's shoulders fell the whole of Margaret's wrath and frustration. Outwardly Nan remained meek and submissive, but in her soul the wraith of her murdered brother waxed fat and real.

She had looked forward to seeing Henry again, but found that he remained for the most part in his private apartments with his priests. His vague manner and imbecilic smiles worried many and Nan was dismayed at his sad decline. The King's business, both great and small, was conducted almost entirely by Somerset.

One late evening Nan sat in an outer chamber of the Queen's apartments with one of Margaret's ladies, Elizabeth Grey. The royal rooms were deserted and strangely quiet, for Margaret had dismissed all her women except Lady Grey, and it was at Elizabeth's request that Nan and Eleanor remained to keep her company.

Elizabeth Grey was only sixteen years old and surely one of the most beautiful women Nan had set eyes upon, although the beauty was cold as well as perfect. She was the daughter of Richard Woodville, Earl Rivers, and his wife Jacquetta, Dowager Duchess of Bedford. She had long, straight, silver-white hair and a flawless, oval face from which gazed eyes of the brightest periwinkle blue. She was married to Sir John Grey and already had a two year old son, Thomas.

Now the two sat together, their heads bent over a gaming stool where they endeavoured to play fox and geese. Nan manœuvred her many pegs with great dexterity, while Elizabeth, with her one peg, the fox, laughed as she tried to avoid being trapped. At last the game was done and Elizabeth's fox hopelessly cornered upon the board. With a great deal of laughter they began to set up the board for another game. Nan stood, stretching, and her eye fell upon her niece in the adjoining chamber. Eleanor was standing close to the perch where the

Queen's pet monkey sat. She held out titbits to the creature, delighting in its quick movements and little chattering voice.

Nan excused herself for a moment from Lady Grey and went to her niece. "You spoil the creature even more than does the Queen herself!"

"I know, but he is such a strange little animal, I am quite fascinated. Let him eat while he may for in a week's time I shall be gone and married to Thomas Butler!" Smiling, she picked up another morsel of food and the monkey's tiny black hands reached out and seized it.

Nan was about to speak again when she heard the main door to the Queen's rooms open. She glanced up. An oval mirror hung upon the wall, a mirror which was surrounded by a golden frame covered with Margaret's daisy badge. Reflected now in that mirror she could see who entered, and she saw Lady Grey's deep obeisance.

"Ah, Lady Elizabeth, I thought perhaps that you were on duty tonight." Margaret! The Queen herself.

The lovely, dark French princess was dressed in a rich, formal gown, of peach velvet, with a high, tight waistline and huge, drooping sleeves trimmed with deep borders of ermine. Underneath she wore an undergown of white satin stitched with myriads of pearls, and the velvet overgown was caught up with a glittering diamond pin. Her black hair was pushed beneath a high, horseshoe headdress of golden satin over which was draped a trailing veil of white lace. Margaret of Anjou was every diminutive inch a person of royal blood. She was twenty-four years old and at the height of her unruly loveliness. Now the dark brown eyes gleamed warmly as she looked at another person whom Nan could not see in the mirror.

"Lady Grey, you are the most trusted of my ladies, and it would not do for my trust to be misplaced. You understand my meaning? I see that you do . . . very well, I do not wish to be disturbed for the next hour or more and I bid you turn away anyone, *anyone* who would seek my company, save that a message be brought from the King himself."

"I understand, Your Grace. Do you wish to be informed in an hour's time?"

Margaret pursed her lips, looking yet again at the unknown person at her side. She smiled slowly. Nan could bear it no longer and stepped slightly to one side and then was rewarded at seeing the face of that other person. Her eyes widened and her hand crept to the golden crucifix she wore at her throat.

Margaret was speaking again. "Yes, Lady Grey, pray knock upon the door when the hour is done." She walked towards her inner, private chambers, and the person whose arm she took was none other than Edmund Beaufort, the great and noble Duke of Somerset. The faint tinkling of folly bells came through the still air.

The door closed and Lady Grey hurried to where Nan and Eleanor stood in the shadows. Her blue eyes were worried as she put her finger to her lips. "I beg of you, my Lord, say nothing and I think it would be wiser if you now left and put from your mind anything you have witnessed this night." She glanced uneasily behind her.

"I agree that I should leave here, but as to forgetting. . . . How often does the Queen of England entertain her favourite behind closed doors?" There was an accusation in the words and Elizabeth coloured guiltily.

"It happens, Lady Warwick, but I assure you that nothing occurs which is in any way contrary to the conduct expected of a Queen!"

"Indeed, and how, pray, would you know that?"

Elizabeth's little chin was raised stubbornly. "Because, my Lady, I have listened at the door." She smiled as she saw the humour in Nan's eyes. "Aye, I listen many a time because I have no wish to be party to anything which might . . . well. . . . If I thought that they were in truth lovers then I would seek my husband's permission to leave the Queen's service. He could get me from here somehow. I tell you though, our mighty Queen leads Somerset a merry dance, he is hot for her and she denies him all but the chaste kiss and touch of the hand! Many times I have almost choked with trying not to laugh at his pleadings."

Nan stroked the monkey's head, knowing a private pleasure at the thought of Somerset's frustration. "Very well, Lady Grey, we will slip away now and none shall know of what happens here. Come Eleanor."

Elizabeth touched Eleanor's arm. "Will you perhaps be of service to me? My husband expects me within an hour and I fear his anger should he not realize I am detained. Knowing him as I do, it is a task better done in person, so will you

51

remain here while I seek him out? I will not be long and I assure you that the Queen will not leave her rooms until I call her in an hour's time. There is no risk."

Eleanor nodded her little head, following Nan and Lady Grey as they left. She closed the door behind them, turning the key softly in the lock.

Nan was almost prepared for bed when next she saw her niece, and Eleanor came to her aunt's rooms white-faced and shaken. Nan dismissed her startled women, with the exception of the faithful Alana, drawing Eleanor close to the warmth of the fire. She rubbed the cold hands. "What is it, my sweeting, surely the Queen did not find you?"

"N-no, no, she did not know I was there. Oh sweet Jesu, I am afraid." She buried her face in her hands, her shoulders trembling with a frightening violence.

"Holy Mother in Heaven, tell me what happened! Alana!" Nan gestured towards a jug of wine which stood upon a chest. Alana quickly poured some and held it to the girl's quivering lips.

Eleanor coughed at the strength of the liquid. "My aunt, I heard the Queen and the Duke of Somerset, and they . . . well, it was not as Lady Grey said. They . . . they lay together." Her eyes were huge as she put her fingers to her lips as if she had uttered a profanity.

"You mean that they made love together . . . as if they were man and wife?"

"Yes."

"Then Lady Grey was lying!" Nan's lips tightened.

"Oh no, she spoke truthfully. You see, tonight was the first time, I know because of something Somerset said. When I was left alone I could hear the murmur of their voices and I crept over to the door and pressed my ear to the wood. I heard the Queen say that it was long since time she produced an heir for England. He agreed but said that he doubted if there would be one after such a long time. This angered her and she asked if he doubted her ability in this direction. He was a little frightened of her then and hastened to placate her, saying that she remained childless only because of the King's impotency. She said that it was enough that she and the King shared a bed of nights, that what did or did not take place in that bed was

52

known only to herself and the King. She said that she wished to be with child to thwart the Duke of York who was now Henry's heir but whose hopes would be dashed in the event of her being brought to bed of a male child. He laughed then, reminding her of how they had discovered the King only a few days before, sitting on the floor, rocking himself backwards and forwards, staring vacantly at the wall. It was apparently more than an hour before anyone could bring any semblance of life into him. How could she hope, he said, to become with child by such a husband. There was a long pause and then she said that as yet only she and Somerset knew of the King's malady and that there was time before the illness became too apparent for her to conceive a child which would be accepted as the King's. I could see nothing, you understand, but I could hear Somerset's fear. He gasped and said that although he had pleaded many a time that she would allow him to make love to her, he was not prepared to get her with child. She laughed and said that he *would* do as she asked because unless he did she would throw him to the Duke of York and the Earl of Warwick. 'You have oft wanted my body, my noble Duke, well now you may have it!' I swear to you, my aunt, that those were her very words. Just then there was a slight tapping at the outer door and I unlocked it to find Lady Grey returned, but I *know* that the Queen committed adultery this night. I do not think Lady Grey realized though because she went at once to the room where the monkey's perch is and began to feed him, she did not approach the inner door. I came away at once, running straight here."

Richard's footsteps echoed along the corridor and he flung the door open. His quick eyes took in Eleanor's sorry state and he looked enquiringly at Nan. "What goes on here?"

"Nothing, my Lord, merely Eleanor's womanly tears at her forthcoming marriage." Nan nodded her head to Alana who took Eleanor's hand and led her from her aunt's rooms.

Richard watched them go and then his shrewd eyes swung back to his wife. "Well, it seems to me that Thomas Butler must be some manner of ogre to bring forth such fear and weeping!"

Nan's lips twisted into a smile, uncomfortable and unconvincing, but he was obviously in no mood to pursue the subject. He untied the laces of his doublet and began to pour himself some wine.

Undecided, Nan hovered there. Should she tell him what she had discovered? She licked her lips unhappily. He drained his cup. "I merely came to bid you good night, I shall not be joining you now as I have much to do."

"I will see you tomorrow then?"

He nodded and then stepped over to her, kissing her lips fleetingly before turning and leaving her rooms. The moment was gone and she had said nothing to him.

NINE

THE Queen was with child, Nan was sure of it. But why the secrecy? Why hide the fact? Nan was perplexed. The ladies who attended the Queen at her rising in the mornings were suddenly restricted to a select two or three, and all others prevented from close attendance.

And how Margaret fawned upon Henry in public, feeding him titbits with her own hand when they ate, and laughing often at his words. She held his hand frequently and looked softly into the gentle, trusting face of her husband. The court whispered and wondered at this sudden change in the Queen, but Henry himself appeared happy that his wife was at last seeming to love him. Henry's health had undergone a catastrophic change, however. That he had been unwell had been realized for some time, but on each occasion that the wild, staring expression had come into his eyes, he had been hustled away, emerging later fully recovered and without seeming to know that he had been ill. Whispers and rumours spread and mushroomed, but none knew for certain what was amiss, except Margaret, Somerset . . . and Nan, Countess of Warwick. The deceptions could not continue indefinitely, and one evening while the court danced and made merry at the palace of Greenwich, Henry's ailment became finally manifest in a way which even Margaret's ingenuity could not overcome.

Nan danced with the Duke of York. He was free now from his short imprisonment in the Tower, slipping through the furious fingers of Somerset who would have wished to detain such a prisoner for much longer. York was a stocky man, with blue eyes and short, curly fair hair. He was not handsome, not even aristocratic to look upon, but his manners were royal. He was a Plantagenet, and his every movement exuded a pride in his ancestry. Dancing was not his greatest accomplishment, he moved as if his thoughts travelled upon some other floor of infinitely greater importance than a mere dance. He dressed richly, favouring a dull golden velvet for his sleeveless coat. The white satin of his doublet was embroidered with his White Rose badge, and the glittering livery collar across his chest was adorned with the same pattern.

Nan was relieved when eventually the minstrels plucked the final chord and the dancers bowed low to one another. He took her hand and pressed it to his lips, smiling with some amount of embarrassment. "Forgive my dancing, sweet lady."

She was about to wave aside such apologies when her eyes widened as they caught sight of the royal dais. There was something of a stir where the King sat, and Nan's glance soon perceived that Henry was overtaken by another of his strange illnesses, and this time he had neither his wife nor the noble Somerset to hurry him away from the inquisitive gaze of his court. York followed Nan's stare, and she felt his fingers tighten over hers as he looked. He pushed his way through the now quiet crowd, his voice clear as he stood at the foot of the dais.

"Your Grace? Your Grace?" Henry's blank eyes did not even flicker at the voice. He slumped queerly in the upright chair, his mouth open slightly and saliva dribbled unchecked down his chin and on to the ermine collar of his coat. York vaulted lightly up to Henry's side, taking the limp hand and shaking the King, softly at first and then roughly. He pinched Henry's cheek, but not even this produced a reaction, although the pale skin was marked now by a fiery red spot. York snapped his fingers at some attendants and gave instructions that the King was to be removed to his private apartments. He also sent his own men to guard the King, with orders to admit no-one. The whole court knew that he was referring indirectly to the Queen and Somerset.

Henry was carried across the crowded floor, his eyes unseeing, his body unfeeling. As he passed Nan, the memories of her

55

youth at Warwick came crowding back, memories of Henry as he once had been. . . . She closed her eyes. Poor, solitary, unloved King, betrayed on all sides by those he trusted so implicity, and now betrayed by his own poor health and inherited weaknesses. The door closed behind him, and immediately a babble of talk broke out.

Richard's hand was on her shoulder, pulling her aside firmly. He led her to where York stood with his Duchess, Salisbury's sister, and all the while his fingers pinched her flesh. She knew that the strong grip was a warning to her not to speak out of place.

York's eldest son, Edward, Earl of March, stood with his father and mother. He was an immensely tall youth, already well over six feet in height, with a huge frame and broad shoulders. His bright, golden hair curled finely to his shoulders, and his flirtatious blue eyes continually scanned the gathering, seeking out the pretty women. Now he was speaking to his father: "The King is mad!"

"Hush!" Nan's fears rose immediately and she glanced warily over her shoulder.

York laughed. "Poor Nan, and who do you think is going to clap my son in irons for such a statement?" They all laughed then and Nan found herself blushing, but York's laughter was already done when he next spoke. "Nay, if Henry's illnesses persist, and one must admit that they grow daily more frequent, then England must have a Protector!"

Richard's fingers tightened on Nan's shoulder. "And there can be only one man destined for that position, Henry's heir . . . yourself!" His voice was cool.

Further talk was halted by the appearance of the Queen. Margaret strode into the room, quite obviously unaware that anything was amiss. She talked gaily to her escort, the inevitable shape of Somerset, now and again turning to include Somerset's eldest son who accompanied them. Richard's eyes narrowed coldly as he looked at the hated favourite, and his fingers stroked Nan's skin. She shivered.

The hall was now ominously silent and gradually Margaret's footsteps faltered, her dark eyes searching the room for the cause of the strange atmosphere. She halted at last as her gaze fell upon the empty dais.

Hastily York detached himself from the crowd and went on his bended knee before her. He told her what had happened.

Margaret's face went white, for without Henry both she and Somerset were powerless! They acted only through the King, hiding behind his name and authority. "And no-one saw fit to inform *me* of the King's illness?" Her voice was dangerous, her fear making her prepare once more to defend herself, as it had on her first arrival in England.

York rose to his feet, his voice loud so that the whole room could hear. "Your Grace, my men are at this moment still searching the building for you—you were not in your apartments!"

Somerset's frightened face blanched and he shifted his stance. No need to ask where the Queen had been, thought Nan acidly.

"And the King is now in his rooms? I must go to him." Margaret made to hurry away, her intention obvious, but York restrained her.

"Sweet Madam, you must not go now. The physicians attend him and they have informed me that no-one is to enter until they have completed their examinations."

The Queen's head turned this way and that, her confusion and fear written large on her face. She saw the triumph in York's eyes, saw and reacted inevitably. Her hands flew to her stomach, the swelling of which was concealed by the high-waisted style of her gown. "My husband, my dear lord . . . what of my child now. . . ." The words were carefully picked for maximum effect, the actions precise and perfect. She swayed slightly, forcing York to put out his hand to steady her. She leaned against him, burying her face in his broad chest and weeping pitifully. Nan heard Richard's ill-concealed exclamation of disgust.

The buzz of chatter spread around the room. The Queen was with child! If the child should be a son! The less easily swayed element raised its eyebrows; with child yes, but by whom?

York's smile of triumph faded, this was one aspect which he had not foreseen. As Margaret's weeping gradually subsided he spoke again. "With child?"

She wiped her tears sadly. "It is so, the babe comes some time in October. I fear that it is not long now. The secret was kept because the King wished it to be so, and I would not go against his desires. . . ." As if the mention of Henry twisted a dagger in her heart, she fell to renewed weeping.

Nan smiled. Clever, clever Margaret, her scheming had been

successful and she was with child before Henry's illness made it impossible for such a pregnancy to be believed. If he recovered he would be presented with a child whom he might possibly acknowledge; if he did not recover, then Margaret could claim the child to be Henry's and no-one could gainsay her. I pray God he recovers, thought Nan, for Henry will not acknowledge Somerset's bastard, *he will not*! Her breath hissed between her clenched teeth, her faith in Henry not yet shaken beyond redemption.

The grieving Queen was helped from the room, her small figure seeming somehow lost and helpless as she stumbled back to her rooms. Margaret was safe, safe from the hatred of England because she carried a child within her. But Somerset! The Duke was visibly trembling as he looked at the suddenly important York, and York's wrathful, vengeful eye fell upon the Beaufort. It seemed to Somerset that the whole room crowded in on him, menacing and hating.

Nan's secret knowledge came bubbling to the surface now, she could not stand by and let Margaret's scheming go untold. She grasped Richard's arm and her anxious face made him take her to a quieter corner of the room.

"Richard, the child she carries is not the King's!"

"You think I do not realize that?" He laughed unexpectedly.

She was surprised. "Is that all you are going to say?"

"What more is there? I can guess that Somerset has got her with child. It matters not, all I am concerned with is that if the child should be male then York's position becomes intolerable. He will not find it easy to take the throne then."

"If he ever attempts such a course! Even before he knew of the coming child he thought only of a Protectorship! Richard, York does not *want* the throne!" She looked intently at him.

"He does, sweetheart, he merely needs convincing."

"And the golden tongue of Richard Neville is ever whispering in his ear?"

He smiled.

On 13th October, 1453, Margaret of Anjou gave birth to a son, named Edward. The bells of London joyously pealed at the news. Richard, Duke of York, Protector of England, smiled outwardly, but beneath the smile he seethed with the injustice of his position. Now he was no longer even heir to the throne.

Margaret for the first time was popular and the people were in no mood to be deprived of their future King. A great wrong had been done to York, and he came closer to the point of open rebellion—closer, but not yet to the final step.

Somerset heard the bells from his cell in the Tower. In his private apartments Henry sat unmoving, unspeaking, unknowing.

For eighteen months the King of England remained thus.

TEN

FOR a year and a half the King had remained a prisoner of his mental sickness, and for all that time Richard Plantagenet, Duke of York, had been Protector of England. He was popular, and even Nan had to admit that he performed his duties with care and justice; there could be few complaints at his exemplary conduct. Only Somerset could perhaps be justified in complaining, for he was imprisoned in the Tower without trial for the entire duration of York's supremacy. Margaret made no move to aid her former favourite, she was safe as the mother of the future King of England, and she wisely abstained from all political tamperings. She needs must wait and see if Henry's sanity returned, and then pray that he acknowledged Prince Edward as his son.

Richard of Warwick had risen high at the side of York, becoming a member of the Privy Council. He had worked tirelessly towards his ambition, but York remained obstinately set against seizing the throne. Perhaps he hoped that Henry might recover and refuse to recognize Margaret's bastard son. . . . Warwick must be satisfied to wait and watch. As for Nan, she had seen Richard blossom, radiate confidence and draw men inexorably to his side like a candleflame draws moths. She had felt the strength in him, the coiled power which threatened to burst forth and pluck England by the ears. He was now twenty-nine years old, the greatest Earl in England, untested, untried. . . .

He was still frustrated by York's refusal to seize his opportunities when at Christmas 1454, the King suddenly recovered. His first action, to Nan's horror and final dismay, had been to openly acknowledge the child brought before him by Margaret as his own. Margaret was triumphant! She commanded the release of Somerset and that delighted, amazed lord came forth to take up his old position. The pendulum swung back and England was beneath the Queen's iron hand once more. The Duke of York and his supporters were relieved of their positions and they hurried back to the safety of their estates to await the outcome of this turn of events.

The hunt sped recklessly through the wooded hills, dashing the creamy daffodils beneath horses' hooves, bruising the uncoiling stems of bracken. Horns sounded, voices cried, and deep in a thicket Nan could hear the death scream of a wild boar as the hounds fell upon it. She reined in, her stomach sickened as always by the ending of a hunt; the chase was thrill enough, the slaughter seemed to drain all pleasure from the sport. . . .

The screams seemed endless and she could bear it no more, pulling the palfrey's head sharply and kicking her heel savagely. The horse jerked nervously, its legs scrambling up a mossy bank, and then it plunged down the opposite side and away through the fresh spring wood. The revulsion past, Nan drew the reins yet again, pulling the horse's velvety ears affectionately. What hyprocrisy, to hide her ears from the boar's death, and yet to willingly and eagerly sit down to eat the flesh when the day's work was done!

A small stream tumbled down the Yorkshire hillside, its tinkling murmur like music upon the scented air. She dismounted and watched as her palfrey dipped its muzzle into the cool waters. A sound behind her caused her to turn sharply, and she knew a keen surge of pleasure as she saw Richard astride his large chestnut charger. He raised his hand to pull aside an overhanging branch of catkins, and a shower of golden pollen cascaded over his dark brown jacket. The horse's eager nostrils scented the stream, and it walked resolutely to where Nan's palfrey still drank. Richard lifted his leg over the pommel of the saddle and jumped down lightly, leaving the horse to follow its thirst.

He leaned back against the trunk of an old holly tree, the

dark green shiny leaves in strange contrast to the soft yellowy greens which surrounded it. He pulled off his scarlet hat, unwinding the long decorative scarf which coiled about his neck. The sun burnished his chestnut hair and Nan felt an excitement deep within her at being close to him. They were still strangers to one another, and yet the past eighteen months had seen a change in Nan. Now she fretted at the rift between them, wanting more than anything to admit to him that she loved him, but being unable to find the words, the right moment. . . .

"I saw your departure from the kill." He smiled.

"I could not bear those dreadful screams, the agony that beast suffered." The horses stamped in the waters and droplets spattered on to the russet folds of her skirts.

She glanced at him, her fingers shaking. He must know, she must tell him . . . about . . . about. . . . "Richard, I believe I am with child again." No, no, that was not what should have been said first, no.

He leaned forward and grasped her hand, and his smile cut through to her very heart. "Nan. After all this time I thought that we would have no more." He drew her hand to his lips gently, but did not kiss her palm."

To his surprise her fingers coiled about his, holding him tightly. "Richard, there is more, there is much which I should tell you." She stopped as the hunt passed close by beyond the trees, the trumpets sounding loudly and the voices of their fellow huntsmen easily recognizable. "No, do not join them yet, I beg of you hear me out." Richard turned back towards her, his face puzzled. The sounds of the hunt faded into oblivion, and the natural sounds of the wood filled the air once more. She swallowed, conscious that she still gripped his fingers and yet daring not release her hold for fear that he would leave. "You once asked for my support, for my help in your dreams. I was stubborn, indeed I was my father's daughter, when I turned my face aside and refused. My faith in the House of Lancaster has at last been finally and irrevocably shattered . . . when Henry accepted Margaret's child, that was the moment when I shed my coat of Lancastrian splendour. I want no more of Henry, no more of the old loyalty. I will wholeheartedly sustain your allegiance to the Duke of York."

She realized slowly that his fingers were now returning her grip. "Why?" he whispered.

The birdsong of the woodland shrieked aloud, tumultuously, as Nan's senses reeled. Here was the moment, she must tell him now, now. . . . "Because of you." He waited, tightening his hold, she knew that he wanted to hear her say that she loved him. "Because I love you." The air sang.

His voice was husky. "Jesu, Nan, but you take a lot of winning!"

Her arms slid around his waist, tight, protecting, as if she could spirit away all problems. He put his fingers beneath her chin and raised her face to his, and then he kissed her. It was as a first kiss, the first heady embrace of youth, intoxicating and possessing. Her desire for him overwhelmed her, consigning the earth to a nothingness, a void. She would not release him.

"Would you have me take you here?" He laughed nervously. She could feel his heart beating quickly.

"Aye, my Lord, I would." The green eyes were luminous, warm. He put out his hand and unfastened the white lace of her headdress, his fingers lingering on the pale, soft skin of her throat. He tossed the heavy headdress aside, twining his hand in the warm mass of her hair as it tumbled down. For all the many, weighty folds of velvet, and the fur-lined cloth of her short cloak, she seemed as light as a feather as he picked her up and carried her to a shaded bank and laid her down on the springy moss. There he took her, fiercely, urgently, and Nan had never before known such a sweet gratification of her demanding senses. Her consciousness swayed before such ecstasy. The horses turned their heads curiously, their ears flicking forward. . . .

She lay wide-eyed beside him afterwards, her arm encompassing his head as it rested against her shoulder. It was she who heard the soft hoofbeats of a walking horse approaching through the undergrowth, Richard gave no indication that he was aware of anything. His eyes were closed. The overhanging catkins stirred some yards away from her and she saw the white head of a horse. Her startled glance encountered the equally startled face of John Neville. His face flushed as he took in the scene, and then he hastily turned his mount and was gone. In the distance she heard his voice calling to the others. "I can find no trace of them, mayhap they have returned to Middleham!" She smiled.

There was a sudden wild splashing from the stream and

instantly Richard was alert. The horses snorted and threshed about, their ears flattened against their heads. Richard relaxed as the cause of all the trouble came loping through the muddied waters and flopped wetly down on the bank at their side. One of the huge boarhounds had found them and now panted, its straggled tail wagging. Richard ruffled its head affectionately. "Sir Hound, if you had startled those horses into bolting, I should personally have had your loathsome pelt to decorate my walls!" The dog whined, pricking its ears.

Nan laughed. "Shame on you for speaking so but using such a gentle voice, see, he thinks you are commending him!"

His face grew serious as he turned back to her. "Mayhap a gentle voice would have aided us many a year ago. How much have we lost, Nan. . . ."

She leaned her cheek against his. "No thoughts must dwell on the past now, we must live for the moment and for the future!"

He kissed her and then drew back, his hazel eyes looking earnestly at her. "How lasting is your new allegiance to York? Nay, I do not mean to cast doubts upon your faith, sweetheart, it is just that I have this day received word from York and my father which makes your answer of great importance to me."

"I will have no more of Lancaster, Henry has demolished my trust."

"Very well. The letter which arrived this morning tells me that the Queen's party has summoned a Council meeting at Leicester, a meeting which excludes all Yorkists. The purpose of this spurious gathering is ostensibly to protect the King's person from his enemies. There can be no doubt that those enemies are York and his adherents, and by the same token there can be no doubt as to the fate intended for us. We will have to arm ourselves and prepare to fight for our very lives, and if self-preservation means a pitched battle against Henry, then so be it. I have given orders for all possible men to be armed and ready to march at a moment's notice; all we now await is the final word from York himself."

She plucked at her skirts. "And if you are defeated there will be a traitor's death awaiting you." She glanced at him.

" 'If' is a small word, Nan, and is the prize not worth the

63

risk?" He drew her close again, and she gave herself into his embrace.

Warwick! The name echoed magnificently across the land. For the first time Richard had shown the true brilliance upon the battlefield which was to make him a legend within his own lifetime. The Yorkists defeated Somerset's royal army at St. Albans, and Richard's sweet prize was the life of Somerset himself.

Somerset was dead, the hated enemy was no more. The King was captured and brought back to London with York's victorious army. Richard's suggestion that Henry could be disposed of easily and the story put about that he had fallen in the field were ignored. York would not put his name to such methods. Yet again York shied from putting forward his undoubted claim to the throne, even now when he was supreme and welcomed after St. Albans. Richard clenched his fists in frustration; the moment was ripe, the crown there for the taking —take it! TAKE IT!

Richard's own popularity soared. When he rode forth in London or anywhere in the land, the mere sight of his colours and badges brought cheering crowds of people to wave at him and cry his name. How the people loved a hero; they had worshipped King Henry V and now they chose Richard Neville. He was worthy of their acclaim, and he knew how to win their hearts. A smile, a hand raised in salute and acknowledgement; these things, small though they were, forced Warwick even higher in the minds of the people.

How Nan delighted in riding out with Richard, how proud she was to be the wife of this man. The legend was born. It was like riding at the side of King Arthur. And to know that he loved her, that he was hers. . . .

York's refusal to depose Henry caused Richard's anger to spill over. The battle of St. Albans had once again sent the King's sanity over the precipice, and York was once more Protector of England. When he offered his followers rewards for their support, the Earl of Warwick chose the Captaincy of Calais for himself. It was a post vacated by the late Duke of Somerset. Richard took himself away from York, away to allow his balked ambition to cool. . . . Just before the Earl of Warwick and his Countess left England, their second child was born. Another daughter, and they called her Anne.

When Margaret managed at last to bring Henry's wandering sanity back to work for her, of all the Yorkists only Warwick was beyond her reach. York allowed himself to be plucked down, allowed Henry's Queen to seize back the reins of government. The choice of Calais had been wise indeed.

ELEVEN

THE small room was hot and almost unbearable and the flames in the fire licked greedily around the dry logs. There were heavy curtains at the narrow windows obscuring the sunlight, bringing an oppressive darkness to the chamber. On a narrow bed close to the heat of the fire Nan lay still. Outside the August sun blazed over the fortress of Calais, the day brilliant and fresh, but she cared nothing for these things.

She was now thirty-two years old, beautiful still, her loveliness reborn since her discovery of happiness with Richard. Happiness? She turned her face away from the fire. How could it be true happiness when she could not give him a son? Two healthy girls, but no boy, no heir . . . and this day's loss was surely the bitterest of blows. A tear forced its determined way from beneath the lowered lid, wending its way down the sweat-marked cheek and vanishing in the dull tangle of hair across the hard pillow. Alana put a damp cloth gently to the hot forehead, soothing the weary woman who had endured one of the most poignant of all experiences; that of childbirth when the babe came dead into the world.

The heavy green eyes opened for a moment and she saw the birthing-chair still standing next to the narrow bed. She struggled to sit up and Alana tried to restrain her. "Take that thing away, take it away!" She slumped back, her strength gone with the effort. Two ladies dragged the large chair away, and it seemed to Nan that the hollow scraping sound filled the air for long, long afterwards.

In the Channel beyond the stone walls of Calais, the air echoed with another sound. Over the horizon and visible only from the topmost point of the tower, a battle raged as Richard with his small band of ships tweaked the tail of England's enemies. The Captain of Calais was by virtue of his own efforts, the master of the sea. Calais nestled between the kingdoms of two of the most powerful rulers in Europe—Burgundy and France. The Burgundians were anxious for friendship with the English and an alliance against the French. The hereditary enemy, France, was allied with Spain against the English. But both realms were beset with other problems. Where the French King was antagonistic towards England, his heir, the Dauphin Louis, was of a friendly disposition, more especially towards the Yorkists. In Burgundy, the Duke himself favoured the House of York, whereas his son Charles supported none but Lancaster. It would seem inevitable that upon the deaths of the present rulers in those lands, the policies towards England would change drastically. Nestling between the two, powerful and dangerous, was Warwick's stronghold, his personal realm.

He had often ridden with armed forces over the border into France and dealt swift blows to the pride of that adversary before slipping back into the impregnable safety of Calais. He also kept the Burgundians in a state of uncertainty by doing the same to them. England's pride in the Earl of Warwick rose higher and higher, his name on the lips of every ordinary man. Nothing Margaret of Anjou and her court party did could discredit him, he was beloved of the people and therefore untouchable.

Nan's pride in him rallied bravely as she lay there in that suffocating atmosphere. Her lips were parched and she was grateful when Alana supported her head and put a cool draught of water to her mouth. There was a knock upon the door and it opened to reveal the three black-garbed physicians who had come hurridly to Nan's lying-in when the midwives had been unable to aid her. Now their sallow faces were long and their lips pursed solemnly. Nan's hollow eyes swung to look at them.

The senior physician went on his knees before her and she looked with distaste at his tight-fitting skull cap. "My lady, we have now examined the child. . . ." She closed her eyes again. "There can be no doubt that it died because the cord pulled tight about its neck and choked the life from its body." The words were cold, unfeeling. It is my son you talk of, my son, my son. . . . "But there is more, something which it lies heavily upon me to tell you. My lady, we examined you immediately after the birth and we are all agreed that you will never again bear a child." The green eyes flashed with emerald brilliance, horror and disbelief apparent in their gaze. He glanced quickly at his fellows and then turned back to her. "Madam, there were such terrible complications, your body was so beset by the rigours of such an experience. . . ."

"You are certain?" The whisper was barely audible.

The black head bobbed up and down as he nodded. Suddenly it seemed that the sounds of the sea battle raging outside became deafening. Richard! She bit her lip in a vain effort to remain calm, but her resistance was ebbing. The golden head turned away from the sea of sympathetic faces staring down at her, and she was shaken by harsh, loud sobs. Alana hustled the physicians away, gladly closing the door on their sour faces.

She came back to Nan, taking the hot, trembling hands. "My Lady, please do not grieve so, they are not infallible. I was told that I would never have a child and yet I presented my husband with my daughter Ankarette! Take heart."

Nan clung to her and the words were just discernible between the sobs. "I cannot take heart, for now Richard will have no son, I am barren."

"Not barren, you have two daughters."

The sobs were quieter. "Aye, but he should have a son. Such a man should have a son!" The small fists were clenched again as she beat her hands on the coverlet. Beads of perspiration stood out on her forehead again. "Alana, I pray you extinguish that cursed fire, after all there is no babe to protect." Her eyes closed and it seemed to Alana that at last her mistress slept. Outside the Channel air was silent.

The evening tide brought home some of Warwick's ships, his flagship ablaze with the red and white Bear and Ragged Staff badge. The news soon spread through the town that a great victory had been won and that many enemy ships had been taken as prizes and were now being escorted to England.

Richard himself came straight to the castle to see Nan. He knew something had gone seriously wrong by the quiet atmosphere and unwilling eyes of those he met. His anxiety rose as he neared his wife's apartments and he ran up the stone steps to be met by Alana.

He stopped, catching her arm. "What is wrong?"

Quickly she told him all. He fingered nervously with his dagger, and then stepped into Nan's rooms, pushing aside the velvet drapes and looking down at the sleeping face. He bent and kissed the pale lips gently.

She opened her eyes, his name already on her lips. "You are safe, God be thanked you are safe!" Her eyes drank in every loved detail of him, from his dirty, blood-stained clothes to the hair sticky with salt.

He touched her cheek softly. "I have spoken with Alana, she has told me all."

Nan's fingers moved convulsively. "I am sorry, I am sorry. . . ."

His hand was over her moving lips, stemming the flow. "Nay, nay, say no more, I beg of you. I do not reproach you, never, never would I do that!" He buried his face in her hair.

She put her arms around him. Jesu how she loved this man, was it possible that she had once so despised him? But what of the battle she had listened to all day? "How did the day's voyaging go?"

He raised his head and the light of victory was bright in his eyes. "This day I struck a mighty blow for England. Some merchants of the Hanse plying their way south had the temerity to refuse to dip their flags to me! Such impudence! I put flames upon their decks which set them scurrying. Each one I took as my prize and at this moment they are under escort for England. I vow that this latest escapade will entrench me deeper yet in Margaret's hatred!"

Nan's brows drew together. "Richard, the merchants of the Hanse? Mayhap your deeds will be construed as little less than piracy!"

He grinned wickedly. "And what of it? They insulted me and knew the consequences of their foolishness. England now has their cargo of salt to last the winter through. Anyway, my sweeting, you know full well how the good people of England will react, they will shout my name loudly and triumphantly, singing as they take home the precious salt. Hanse! Spaniard! Frenchman! What does it matter so long as England rules the seas! The pride is restored. Every Englishman is a pirate at heart." He continued to grin at her and she knew that he was trying to drive away her own sorrow.

The evening air was cooler and she shivered. The old stone of the castle lent a peculiar chill to the summer. He gently picked her up from the bed and placed her on a blanket close to the embers of the fire. The red glow danced off his chestnut hair.

"Rest here now. I will call Alana to prepare your bed-chamber."

She caught his hand as he made to leave her. "If York rises again will you support him? Will you leave all that you have built here, the power and the dazzle which is yours and yours alone . . . leave it for a slight chance that York will succeed in overthrowing Lancaster?"

He crouched low at her side. "My love, the hopes and dreams that I set out before you all those years ago are still my aim in life. When I gained this Earldom of Warwick I gained the wealth and power of your family to aid York. Now as Captain of Calais I have earned the influence with the common people to put York on the throne. He *will* rule and it will be said by every man that Warwick put him there, that Warwick *made* him." His eyes blazed with the intensity of his feeling, then he smiled at her and was gone to look for Alana.

Nan looked at the dying fire. The baked logs winked and flashed on the dusty hearth. "My love, my love . . ." she murmured, ". . . I pray to God that your ambition does not prove your undoing."

She was asleep again when Alana came.

TWELVE

THE barge dipped and swayed on the rising tide of the Thames as the river swept past Greenwich. Nan pulled her cloak tighter around herself, her teeth chattering in the winter chill. The waters which swept beneath the bows of Warwick's barge were grey and unfriendly as she peered down into the murky depths.

Richard's attack on the salt fleet had indeed brought the wrath of the royal party down around his ears, and now he was called to account. She watched him as he stood in the prow, his cloak billowing and blustering around his body. He gripped the carved handrail as if he gripped the kingdom itself, and his sharp eyes scanned the passing shoreline. How she wished he had refused this command that he appear before the Council, how much easier it would have been to avoid Margaret's revenge by remaining in the safety of Calais.

Ahead loomed the dismal white walls of the Tower, bleak and evil to look upon. Gulls swooped and screamed above the barge, their white wings almost brushing the long banners of Warwick which flew proudly from the mast. Oars creaked as the men strained to pull the bows around to face the nineteen arches of London Bridge. The hum of the city came clearly across the smoke-filled air, the cries and shouts which were the spell of England's capital. The skies were heavy with snow as the Bridge grew out of the haze, filling the eye of the beholder with its splendour and the close, toppling houses which bulged along its sides as if they were about to fall into the swirling waters beneath. The drawbridge was raised to allow the barge to pass, and as they swept between the tall, narrow sides of the gap, she heard the cries of the people above as they leaned over to watch. "Warwick! Warwick!" Richard glanced up and waved his hand to them, a small gesture which cost him nothing but which bound them even closer to him.

The bridge was behind them at last and she smiled with relief, for she was always afraid of London Bridge at the height of the tide. The swift waters around the arches had claimed many a victim in the vicious whirlpools.

Soon now they would approach the low cluster of buildings which comprised the royal palace of Westminster where awaited Margaret of Anjou and her vultures. The torch on the bows flared in the stiff breeze, sparks floating down into the river and extinguishing with an audible hiss. The landing pier of the palace jutted out into the water, and they could see the men running to help with the mooring of the great barge. Nan suddenly hurried to where Richard was preparing to leave the craft.

She put her hand on his arm. "There is yet time to change your mind. The Queen has no intention of letting you leave London alive!"

He smiled, his hair whipping across his face. "She will not dare, sweetheart, the mob will rise against her!"

"Richard, the chance of being rid of you might be worth the vague risk of a mob."

The bows bumped against the wooden steps and ropes were thrown to the waiting hands ashore. Her breath caught in her throat. "I am coming ashore with you."

But already he had left and did not hear her words. She beckoned to the captain of the barge. "I bid you listen well, when we have entered the Palace you will turn the barge about and be at the ready to depart with all haste . . . *with all haste*!" She did not wait for the man's answer but was hurrying up the narrow gangplank.

Richard turned at the entrance to the palace and saw her. He frowned, but then extended his hand to her and they walked in together, with his small bodyguard behind. Inside their footsteps echoed on the stone flags and they soon became aware of the silent groups of men lounging on corners and along the passages; men everywhere. Her heart began to beat faster, she sensed the trap yawning before them.

Her fingers tightened on Richard's arm and he glanced quickly at her, his face was tense, his eyes watchful. On they went, deeper and deeper into Margaret's web, until they came at last to a large hall where still more men stood about. These men wore ordinary clothing, and there was no sign about them of concealed weapons, but there was that air of danger which caused the hairs on Nan's neck to prickle.

A page announced their arrival and a silent wave of alertness pierced the air at Richard's name. Soon another page approached to escort Richard to the Council Chamber. He pressed Nan's hand to his lips, his fingers warm and strong. "Bide here, and at any sign of trouble make good your escape! Do not loiter for me!" Before she could reply he was gone.

She stood alone in the centre of the hall, her green eyes watching the strange groups of men. Richard's bodyguard waited in disciplined lines along one wall. The silence was oppressive, ominous. From the distant Council Chamber she could hear the murmur of voices, and once Richard's loud laugh. A man detached himself from a small party and walked towards her. She did not know him and waited for him to speak, but instead he walked past, deliberately brushing against her and almost knocking her from her feet. He walked on, making no attempt at an apology. There was an angry stir from

71

Warwick's men at this huge insult. A burly man in the bright red and white colours caught the arm of the offender and a loud muttering ensued between the two.

Nan was confused. Unwittingly she had been used to create an argument, soon she feared that weapons must be drawn as tempers flared higher and higher. Her frightened eyes turned to the narrow corridor down which Richard had walked, but there was no sign of him. Shouts were raised, Richard's name called in defiance! A dagger flashed in the pale light and then the fight was commenced. She screamed as the dagger pierced a man's throat and the red blood streamed from the wound. Now from doors and corridors around the hall poured still more men, and they were armed. The trap was sprung in earnest.

An arm was around her shoulder, half pushing and half dragging her towards the exit. Her slippers slithered sickeningly in the pool of blood where the wounded man lay, but it was Richard who ushered her on, Richard whose arm protected her now. His men carved their bloody way through the press, and her horrified, unaccustomed eyes saw many a sight which she feared would remain with her for all time. Screams and shouts echoed around the buildings. Richard's knife slashed through a velvet drape and the hidden shape of a waiting murderer slumped lifeless to the floor. Sobs forced their way between her stiff lips now as she ran on leaden feet towards the open air and the barge.

The sounds of the turmoil within had reached the waiting ears of the captain and already the craft was poised for escape. One man stood on the pier where the restraining rope was coiled around a wooden bollard, and down the starboard side of the barge the oarsmen leaned their oars against the pier waiting to push away into the safe waters midstream. The Bear and Ragged Staff gleamed in the evening light and snowflakes were beginning to fall through the driving wind.

Richard almost pushed her down into the barge, vaulting down after her, and then the craft lurched wildly as his body-guard followed him. On to the landing stage poured the Queen's men, but already their victims were out of reach, slipping silently downstream towards the sea.

Nan clung to Richard and his fingers pushed back tendrils of her hair which lay against her face. He seemed unaffected by the closeness of his escape, rather he seemed regenerated, exhilarated by the combat. But the hairsbreadth timing was too much for his wife, her teeth chattered not with cold but with fright and she feared she would vomit her terror upon the decks.

In the estuary the barge hove to in the now dense snowstorm. A small boat was lowered over the side and two men climbed down into it, rowing ashore in the fading light. In their pockets were a bag of gold and two letters, one for the Duke of York and one for the Earl of Salisbury.

Soon news of Margaret's attempt on Warwick's life would be spread through the Yorkist camp, and thence throughout the realm. The common people should know that their beloved Earl had barely escaped the French Queen's spite. . . .

THIRTEEN

THE castle of Ludlow dreamed in the autumn woods above the winding River Teme. The trees were beginning their slow mellowing from crisp green to warm golds and reds. Spring and summer had passed since that day at Westminster, and outwardly all was peaceful and tranquil at Ludlow, the Yorkist stronghold. Within, the castle seethed with activity. All were preparing to fight for their lives against the mounting royalist re-arming. The Duke of York himself, with his sons and his Duchess, and the Earl of Salisbury and his sons John and Thomas; all were there. One prominent supporter of the Duke, however, was absent for the moment. Richard of Warwick.

Nan walked along the battlements, her fingers nervously tapping the coral rosary twined about her wrist. She wore no cloak in the September warmth, and the scarlet folds of her gown rustled along the stone like the leaves themselves which would soon fall. Down below some children played amongst the trees, their laughter ill-matched with the martial atmosphere of the courtyard. Her thoughts went winging back to Calais where Isabel and Anne remained in safety.

She glanced up at the many banners which streamed from

73

the towers, colourful and brave: the White Rose of York, the Sun in Splendour of the Earl of March, York's son, the Griffin of Salisbury. . . . Aye, the attempt on Richard's life had brought about this new confrontation, this rallying of their forces against the Queen's might. Now they gathered together at Ludlow, waiting for the arrival of the Earl of Warwick.

He had set foot on English soil with a mighty company of six hundred trained men, their scarlet and white jackets proclaiming their allegiance for all to see. Towards London they had marched, heralds riding along every road, through every street, shouting the name of Richard Neville and raising Kent to support the beloved Ragged Staff. She had left him on the outskirts of London, coming on to Ludlow alone, while Richard had ridden openly into the city. The following morning he had ridden out again, unaccosted and free. The Queen dared not strike openly at him, for her it must always be by stealth, behind closed doors. Now Richard approached Ludlow by a circuitous route, visiting his estates as if there were no danger.

Nan halted, taking a deep breath, her fingers tightening about the rosary. Why must he always act so flamboyantly? Why could he not have ridden straight to Ludlow on landing in England and forsaken such flagrant taunting as he had indulged at the capital? Why? She smiled to herself. Because he was who he was, because already he was a legend in his own lifetime and he sought always to nourish that legend, keep it alive, and strike fear into the hearts of the enemy.

Surely he must be safe now? With six hundred men wearing his badge, six hundred trained. . . . Her lips pursed thoughtfully. The men of Calais were led by two captains, John Blount and Andrew Trollope, and it was of the latter that she now thought. She did not like Trollope, a man with sly eyes and a flat, pock-marked face. True, he was one of the finest of Richard's soldiers, and his services were invaluable, but her intuition told her not to trust him.

A footstep sounded behind her and she turned to see the tall figure of her brother-in-law, John Neville. His dark brown hair was almost concealed by the flowing scarf of his peacock blue hat, and his long blue velvet coat was shabby where he wore it so often. "John, I vow you should be ashamed to walk out in such disgraceful attire! Have you no other clothing?"

The brown eyes creased into a smile. "I like it well enough, it is comfortable, which is more, I'll warrant, than can be said for your elaborate gown!"

She laughed. "I concede the point, Sir."

Trumpets sounded from the sloping woodland and she knew the sound. Her head turned towards the trees where the road wound downhill towards the valley. The beauty of autumn was lost upon her as the first of Richard's cavalcade appeared along that roadway. The banners fluttered audaciously in the breeze, the harness and armour shone as if freshly polished. Then she saw him. His courser pranced, its mane tossing, and his armour reflected the sunlight brightly. The red plumes of his helmet streamed behind him, finding an answer in the red hues of the trees beneath which he rode. His name was on her lips as she descended the steep steps. John stood aside to let her pass, and he watched her silently as she hurried across the courtyard and over the drawbridge. Leaning over the battlements he could see her as she ran down that winding road, her hands clutching her heavy, stiff skirts, her wired headdress flapping ridiculously above her head. But he did not smile.

Richard laughed as he saw her, spurring forward and bending down with one arm to sweep her from her feet. The headdress was crushed beyond redemption, and her velvet skirts soiled, but the heady intoxication of his presence overwhelmed her as she clung. She did not feel the cold metal of his armour biting into her body and she did not care that her conduct was unbecoming in a lady of such high rank. All that mattered was Richard.

And so Warwick rode into Ludlow, his army filling the court-yard with the might of the Ragged Staff. The noise was deafening as the horses stamped and snorted, the men shouted and laughed. Dust rose thickly around them, obscuring the sun for a while. York himself came to greet his ally, and with him were Edward of March and Edmund, Earl of Rutland, York's second son. It was the seventeen year old Edward who reached up and lifted Nan down from Richard's grasp, laughing at her as he did so. "I hope only that when *I* marry I will find a wife to love *me* thus!" He bent his head and kissed her cheek and Richard laughed, slapping him on the shoulder and making a coarse remark.

At the top of the steps leading down to the courtyard stood the Duchess of York with her two youngest sons, George and

Richard, whom everyone called Dickon. George was tall with fair hair and blue eyes, like Edward and Edmund, but young Dickon was slight, dark and grey-eyed. He was so utterly different that he commanded attention. He was seven years old and the political mayhem of England meant little or nothing to him.

Nan walked up the steps and joined the Duchess, turning to watch as Salisbury came at last to greet Richard. She saw John join them, smiling, his handsome face alight with pleasure at seeing his brother again. Then she looked behind the group to where stood Richard's two captains. John Blount was grinning broadly at the camaraderie of the Yorkists, but Trollope's flat face was expressionless. There should be *something* there she thought uneasily, *something* to indicate the train of his thoughts in a moment such as this. But Trollope hated the Nevilles, and hated Richard in particular, for his was a jealous nature. Now he was contemplating a way in which he could most hurt the object of his spite. Already he was engaged in whisperings with the more easily swayed members of the Calais garrison, and he felt sure that he could wean them completely away from the magnificent Warwick, given a little more time.

Two weeks later the King's army approached Ludlow, and it soon became abundantly clear from the scouts sent out by York that the enemy were a far greater force than anticipated. At night their camp fires lit the surrounding countryside with a strange light, as if some immense city burned beyond the horizon, and the sound of their trumpets seemed to echo from all around the hillside. The spirits of those within the castle were dampened at the prospect of riding to meet such overwhelming odds.

Nan lay sleepless at Richard's side on one such night, staring up at the rich hangings of the bed. Suddenly the door burst open and without ceremony the curtains of the bed were dragged aside and John Blount's white, frightened face peered in. Richard was awake then, a curse loud on his lips.

"God's Death, man, I'll have your hide for this!"

"Trollope has deserted with over half of the Calais complement. One of those who meant to go with him had second thoughts and changed his mind at the last moment and came to tell me, but it was too late to prevent the treachery."

Richard sprang from the bed, struggling to put on his hose and jacket. "How in God's Own Name did he persuade them to leave? I would have put my life on their loyalty!" He searched around for his belt.

" 'Twas a long business, begun not long after we left Calais. Apparently he kept insinuating that if they fought under your banners they would be guilty of treason against the King's Majesty." Blount found the belt and handed it to Richard.

His fingers closed slowly over the leather and Richard halted for a moment. "Aye, and the name of Henry Six still carries enough weight to strike fear into their hearts. He drew on the belt, glancing at Nan's motionless figure. "Get dressed, quickly, for we will have to leave in some haste. Trollope took with him not only half my company but also a complete knowledge of our strength and our plans!" He ran from the room followed by Blount and Nan could hear their boots ringing along the stone.

She lay there stunned, unable to gather her scattered thoughts, then she too got out of the still warm bed. There was no sign of her women and she tried to dress herself but the gown was too cumbersome and the bodice was impossible to fasten. Clutching the loose bodice she left the room, grabbing her cloak with the other hand as she passed.

In the main hall confusion reigned supreme, and the first person she saw was John. His eyes flickered over her disordered state and his slow smile brought a calmness to her. "My Lady of Warwick, never again do I wish to hear *you* speak of *my* clothing!"

Unwillingly she smiled and the fear which had been rising unchecked within her was somehow stemmed. "Help me with this accursed gown, please, for I cannot reach the laces!" She did not care about the impropriety of such a request as she coiled her long, unbrushed hair around one wrist and turned her back towards him. Deftly he linked the laces around the interminable line of hooks down her back.

"What is going to happen now?" She turned to look at him.

His eyes met her gaze for a moment. "You and Richard, my father, myself and Thomas, and also Edward of March, ride for the south coast if possible. York and Rutland ride for Wales and thence Ireland."

He looped the remaining hooks and straightened. She faced him. "What of the Duchess and the other boys?"

"They remain behind, there can be no other course. The two boys are too young to maintain any sort of speed and will only ensure the capture of whichever party they ride with. It is York's decision that his wife remain with them and that they throw themselves on Henry's mercy. The King rides with the royalist army and he will never countenance harm being done to a woman and children."

Richard's voice called them across the hall and John took her hand and led her through the jostling, panic-stricken crowd. No words were spoken as they hurried out into the courtyard and Nan turned her head once to see the silent figure of the Duchess of York, her hands resting on the shoulders of Dickon and George.

The drawbridge lowered noisily and it seemed that the sound must carry to the ears of the enemy. The hooves thudded and rattled over the wooden bridge and outside in the darkness of the woodland, the fugitives split into two groups, with York and Rutland riding westwards and the others turning for the south-west.

Her head rang with the steady drum-drumming of the horses through the silent countryside, over bridges, through deserted villages and fording streams. She lost count of the number of dogs awoken by their headlong flight, the frantic barking and growling as they swept on unheeding. Once her horse shied at a wayward fox which fled across their path and Edward of March reached out to steady the frightened animal. His teeth flashed white in the moonlight as he grinned at her.

Dawn stained the sky as at last they came to within sight of the sea. The small party reined in a small way from the village of Minehead with its towering tree-covered cliff. The weary horses hung their heads low and the sweat steamed from their foam-flecked bodies. The air was cool still.

Richard turned in the saddle. "We must acquire a boat somehow!"

Salisbury pushed his mount forward. "I think there is less likelihood of John and myself being recognized." His tired animal drew on its remaining strength to canter away towards the sleeping village, and John rode with his father. The others took refuge in a small copse of oak trees a small way from the road. There they waited as dawn lightened the sky, from the palest of primrose yellows to a grey-blue which merged with

78

the sea in the morning haze. The first gulls began to call overhead, wheeling and soaring in the heavens, their cries the cry of freedom itself.

Richard's sharp ears picked up the sounds of hoofbeats first and his sharp hiss of warning caused them to lie flat on the ground. Their tired horses were hidden by the trees and so weary still that their ears hardly moved as the new sound approached.

The hoofbeats grew louder and Nan buried her face in the tall grass, almost biting the wiry growth in her efforts to hide. An arm was flung over her, holding her down tightly.

Along the road fluttered the red, green and white banners of Somerset, the portcullis badge of Beaufort flashing brightly in the sun. Nan's heart almost stopped within her as she peeped out, it was not Edmund Beaufort, but his son, the new Duke. He so closely resembled his dead sire that Nan could almost hear the tinkling of folly bells as she stared at him. The party halted close by, their horses were fresh and obviously not ridden long. Somerset's handsome young face was perplexed as he gazed down the road to Minehead and then out to sea. They heard his voice clearly. "No-one has passed this way for some time now and there is no sign of a boat putting out to sea. I think we ride through the village and ignore the beach. They must be making for somewhere further down the coast." The drooping banners drew life from the air again as they spurred on at a gallop.

"May he keep riding and enter the sea itself at Land's End!" laughed a voice in her ear, and she turned her head sharply as a hand tweaked her bare breast down the bodice of her gown. The hand and voice belonged not to Richard but to Edward of March. He grinned at her. "An opportunity should never be missed, sweet lady!"

She haughtily drew her cloak tighter around her shoulders. Jesu, if Richard had his way, this young man would one day succeed to the throne! No doubt it would prove a magnificent day for the ladies of the realm!

Richard's loud whisper warned them of another rider approaching. A lone horseman came slowly from Minehead and they soon discerned Salisbury's burly figure. He grunted as he dismounted. "God's Blood and Bones, I nearly gave myself neatly into Somerset's clutches not long ago!" He spat wetly on the ground and the action was a demonstration of his contempt for the young Beaufort.

"Father, have you secured a boat?"

"Aye, that I have and John waits with the crew now. I fear, however, that they think themselves bound for Wales! The first crew I approached fair fainted with terror at the thought of navigating unknown waters 'twixt here and Calais. I was wiser the second time and lied from the outset." He grinned.

They untethered the horses again and pulled their aching bodies into the saddles. Every muscle screamed, every nerve twitched as they moved slowly along the exposed road towards the village. Salisbury soon led them off the road and on to the beach itself. The hoofbeats were muffled as they approached a large fishing craft bobbing on the full morning tide a short way out to sea. Pulled up on the beach was a rowing boat manned by one of the crew. They did not speak as he rowed them to the larger craft where John waited. He reached down to pull Nan aboard and his fingers were strong about her wrist.

When they were all aboard the sail was hoisted and the boat swung laboriously around into the wind. The timbers groaned against the waves, creaking as if they fought against the movement, but soon the land slipped away behind them.

Richard's experienced eye told him that the captain was about to set course for the distantly visible coast of Wales. He walked calmly to where the man stood and leaned to whisper in the man's startled ear. "Calais?" The man's gasp was loud enough for all to hear and the boat yawed as the helmsman allowed his attention to wander. The captain scowled at Richard. "We will not sail to such places, we have no knowledge of the seas 'twixt here and there!"

Richard held nonchalantly on to an overhanging rope, smiling. "But I do and would gladly command your fine craft."

The sailor's bearded jaw was set stubbornly. "And who may you be?"

The smile broadened as Richard drew on all his immense charm. "I am the Earl of Warwick." The words fell on the air with a simple directness which left the captain bereft of words. He was cowed at being in such exalted company and waved his hands in a gesture of resignation. "Command my humble boat where you will, my Lord."

Soon the bows swung again as the course was altered and Nan

80

realized that John was at her side. He glanced down at her. "It seems that the magic of Warwick has saved us yet again, Nan! Calais awaits us."

She nodded, not looking at him but staring all the while at Richard, her pride and love rising fiercely within her.

FOURTEEN

WITHIN a week of their return to Calais, Richard had earned the complete devotion of Edward, Earl of March. York's son followed the master of Calais wherever he went, watching his methods and marvelling at the magnetic qualities which bound men so close to Richard Neville. That Richard was no longer officially Captain meant nothing to the garrison; Margaret of Anjou could make what decrees she wished, they would not turn from him. The catastrophe of Ludlow was forgotten and might never have been. The raiding parties from Calais were once again riding over enemy terrain, pillaging and burning, and the ships flying the Ragged Staff banners were soon ploughing their way over the Channel.

The world might have forgotten Ludlow, but Richard had not. He chafed for the opportunity of striking back at the Lancastrians, and he vowed vengeance on the Judas soul of Andrew Trollope who basked now under Margaret's protection.

Kent, as ever, remained loyal to Richard, and daily fishing craft slipped over to Calais bringing news of developments in England. In the New Year of 1460 they brought the news that Richard Woodville, Earl Rivers, was preparing ships at Sandwich to come and strike at Warwick's stronghold. Rivers was the father of Elizabeth, Lady Grey, whom Nan remembered from the time she spent in Margaret's household. The temptation proved too great for Richard's sense of the dramatic, and at dawn one January day his ships stole into the harbour at Sandwich, surprising Rivers' troops and capturing every royalist craft which lay there. They also went into the town itself and took the red-faced Rivers and his son, Sir Anthony Woodville, from their beds and bore them swiftly back across the Channel! Kent rang joyfully with tales of this latest Warwick exploit, and the news inevitably reached the furious Margaret who was made to feel very foolish.

The night the raiders returned from Sandwich was a night imprinted on Nan's memory for all time. The town buzzed with excitement, the bells rang loudly, and the only lowering influence on the soaring Yorkist spirits was brought by the weather. The icy January night was wet and blustery, the gale howling through the narrow streets and whistling in the eaves of the houses.

The market square was filled with the townspeople, all agog to see what was going to happen, for word quickly spread throughout the garrison that the Earl of Warwick was about to bring his unfortunate prisoners ashore.

The town crier's voice was barely audible above the babble of the crowd and the continuous pattering of the rain. Nan stood on an exposed dais, her teeth chattering with cold and excitement.

She touched Richard's arm. "My Lord, these proceedings are worthy of a Greek theatre!" Her tone was crisp. Jesu, she longed for the warmth of the castle.

"Aye, and intentionally so, Sweetheart. I would have Calais and the world remember every last detail of my small victory over Lancaster! Hold now, here they come!" Nan felt someone's eyes upon her and turned to meet the amused gaze of John Neville. He appeared to find Richard's drama entertaining.

It seemed that the night was suddenly alight, for down the narrow streets came many men carrying aloft torches which flared wildly in the gale. The dancing light gleamed on the wet cobbles and the nearest torches could be heard hissing angrily as the rain touched the live flames. The men lined the square, pushing back the curious crowd, and then came the clatter of hooves as Salisbury and March manœuvred their nervous horses along the slippery surface. Behind them walked the prisoners, their hands roughly tied behind their backs, stumbling unsteadily towards the dais. The rear of this strange procession was brought up by the third Neville brother, Thomas, and Blount, the loyal captain from Ludlow. The only son of Salisbury who was not present was George, Bishop of Exeter. Where

82

Richard had chosen to further himself through politics, George had chosen the Church and was already embarked upon a meteoric rise to strength, but now he remained in England, quiet and not drawing Margaret's attention to himself.

To the delight of the waiting crowd, Salisbury and March then began to harangue the prisoners, calling them all manner of names and tossing insults into the rising wind. Their voices grew shrill as they strove to be heard above the howl of nature. Calais enjoyed it all immensely, and soon the crowd were joining in. After a while Nan no longer listened, her thoughts ever strayed to the roaring fire in her chamber at the castle, to the warm bed and to the sleeping children in the next room. . . . She stared at Rivers' bowed head and hunched shoulders, and then at Sir Anthony Woodville. He had the same silver-fair hair and piercing blue eyes of his sister, Elizabeth Grey. Nan wondered if Elizabeth had ever realized what had truly occurred behind Margaret's closed doors that night when she had gone to speak with her husband.

Her thoughts returned to her daughters. Isabel was now nine, pretty and vivacious. Anne was equally as pretty, now four years old and sharp witted. Nan could not admit it openly, but Anne was her favourite, born as she was after Nan had discovered her true love for Richard.

The soaked thatch of the building behind her now dripped relentlessly down upon her and the cold wetness of it lay across her shivering shoulders. Holy Mother, would this masquerade never end? She glowered at Richard as he stood in front of her. She had seen little of him recently, he was always busy and came to bed so late that she was asleep. Often he did not return at all and it was some weeks now since he had lain with her. Now he stood so close to her and yet did not glance at her; Nan felt a little neglected. John stepped over to her, untying his cloak and placing it about her. She smiled gratefully at him.

A large, cold drop of water fell from the overhanging thatch, striking her head and meandering icily down her face. Her patience evaporated. "Richard, be done with this else I die of the ague!" Her loud, angry hiss carried easily to his ears.

He glanced briefly at her white, cold face and then turned back to the square, holding up his hands to quieten the noise. Salisbury and March also gestured for silence, and then Richard addressed the square. "Good people of Calais, this night you have witnessed the fruits of our sweet victory over the regime of Queen Margaret!" Gone were the memories of Ludlow, gone for ever. . . . "I bid you all be of good heart for this is just the beginning, I promise you further glories!" He spoke for a little while longer, and the crowd were held in his cupped hands; they swayed to the intonation of his voice, hissed at the mention of Margaret and cheered at the mention of York. A small while later they dispersed, and their cheering, shouting voices could be heard as they hurried back to their homes.

The horses were brought and Richard assisted Nan to mount. She watched as the prisoners were escorted back to the castle, and she felt sorry for them for they wore only thin shirts and must surely be almost frozen. Her anger at Richard had not abated and her face was stormy as she rode between him and John.

Richard grinned at her. "Sweetheart, you would deny me my moment of glory?"

"Moment? 'Twas more like a lifetime! A pox on you and your over-developed sense of . . . sense of. . . ." Words failed her. She heard John's low laugh as he spurred his horse forward, leaving them to their argument.

"So sour?" Richard's tone was still teasing.

"Aye, and so *wet*!" She was in no mood to be teased.

His smile faded and he grew serious. "Nan, what I said was true, this is just the beginning. In a few days I leave for Ireland where I will meet with York once more. Then back here for my preparations for whatever plans we decide upon . . . oh, and then to Bruges."

"Bruges? Whatever for?"

"Because in that fair township lies one Francesco Coppini, until recently the Papal Legate in England, but now sulking after being snubbed by Margaret! Before he left England I sent word to my brother George, Bishop of Exeter, that he was to cultivate this dissatisfied Coppini, assure him of the friendship of York, and so on and so on. . . . If I can win him and with him the support of Rome, then think what a powerful weapon it will be in our hands. If Rome is seen to support the Yorkist cause. . . ." His voice trailed away as the idea took his imagination and whisked it soaring away.

Nan's heart fell. Here it was again, his ambition squeezing

84

her out of his life. To Ireland, to Bruges, and thence no doubt to invade England; would she never be alone with him? Her injured pride stirred and a quickening of the downpour crushed her spirits completely. Tears mingled with the rain on her wet cheeks and her lip trembled petulantly. "A pox on the Papal Legate . . . and on *you*!" She urged her mount forward quickly and left her startled husband alone in the deserted street.

FIFTEEN

"STARBOARD, starboard, you low-born wretch! *Starboard*, I say!" The young helmsman swung the wheel violently as the captain's voice roared through the early morning air.

Nan stood upon the deck watching Isabel and Anne playing with Alana's daughter Ankarette. Alana was close by, her watchful eye upon the small trio as they tossed hoops over a pin attached to the deck. They squealed in delight whenever they managed to secure a hoop; clapping their hands. Nan smiled, it was good to see them enjoying themselves, it was not often that children were allowed to be themselves for they were always expected to be like their parents in miniature.

The white cliffs of England loomed before them now, England . . . and Richard. Well, the Yorkist invasion of the land had been successful. Richard's army had landed in Kent, its numbers swelling with each passing mile, and the valiant Coppini telling all that the Earl of Warwick and his followers had the blessing of Holy Church—that those who were for York would gain absolution, those who did not . . . would not! London was left in the care of a small number of Margaret's supporters, but the city threw open its gates to Richard and Margaret's men took refuge in the Tower! George, Bishop of Exeter, had a persuasive tongue it seemed, for he not only won Coppini completely but also persuaded the hierarchy of the Church that Warwick's cause was true. The army of the Earl of Warwick joined with others, marching northwards to confront the King's forces at Northampton. This time it had been the

Lancastrians who were overcome by treachery, when the commander of their right wing, Lord Grey de Ruthyn, changed his colours and fought for the Yorkists. The battle was done in a short while, and Henry taken prisoner in his tent where he had sat for the duration of the fighting and apparently was completely unaware of what had been going on around him. He was taken back to London by Richard, but Margaret and her son escaped and fled to Scotland. The Queen's stranglehold was broken, her favourites dismissed, and it was to this new and pleasant England which Nan now sailed from Calais.

A tall, slim figure stepped out from the captain's cabin and she smiled at John. He returned the smile and hastened over to her, grinning as Alana was overtaken by yet another bout of sea-sickness. "I'll vow your lady will be pleased to reach land!"

Her eyes noticed the broken seal of a letter poking out from his purse and her smile was dimmed. She knew that the letter had brought sad news to John Neville, news of the death of his baby son, the only child of his marriage. It was hard to remember that he was married and had until recently been a father, for he never spoke of his wife, Joan, and certainly never brought her away from his estates. She knew that he was not happy in his marriage, for Joan was a plump, insipid creature with little or no charm and certainly no affection for her husband. Nan glanced sideways at him, acknowledging silently that he was more handsome than Richard—immediately she felt ashamed for such thoughts, but the truth must be admitted. John had none of Richard's hardness, none of his calculating brilliance; he was elegant, almost beautiful his face was so perfect, and yet there was nothing effeminate in his looks. None could doubt the warm sensuous nature of this Neville lord, he would twist a dagger in some woman's heart one day. Nan smiled at her thoughts.

"Will you take a glass of wine with me, Nan? I admit to a thirst which must be quenched with some of the captain's excellent ale!" He took her hand and led her down the steps into the pokey little cabin. The lantern swung rhythmically from the low ceiling and he ducked his head to avoid it.

She watched him as he poured the ale, wondering what it would be like to be married to him, and marvelling at the foolishness of Joan who could not hold him.

"Such a strange smile, Nan?" He pressed the goblet into her hand.

A flush stole over her face as she remembered her thoughts. "I was thinking of Richard," she lied.

"Of his great victory? Aye, but think on his dilemma. He has in his clutches the King he wishes to depose, but what can one do with a man such as Henry? He is so saintly, so damnably meek . . . there would be uproar if any harm came to him at Yorkist hands. And yet Richard's ambition is as nothing if Henry continues to sit the throne."

Nan drained her goblet and placed the cup upon the rough table. "What does the great Duke of York say?"

John shrugged and turned his head sharply as the men called above that the harbour was sighted. She found herself looking at the rich, dark brown hair which curled to his shoulders. He turned back again. "York still remains in Dublin. The battle of Northampton was won in his name, by his supporters, and yet York remains in Ireland! Richard insists that it is because York did not wish to bring an unpopular army of rough Irish tribesmen to England and therefore thought it better to remain away."

"And what do you think?"

"I don't know and that is the truth of it. I support Richard and always have done, but I do not know if I agree with his belief in York's greatness. York himself has been slow to come to Richard's point of view concerning the throne, but I believe that he is now come to the crossroads of decision. My opinion, for whatever its worth, is that York would be better employed making known the illegitimacy of Prince Edward's birth. If Margaret's spawn could be disinherited, then York could be returned to his former place as heir to the throne, and matters could proceed as they did before Somerset laid the Queen of England upon her back!"

Nan walked around the table to him. "John, think of the bloodshed when Henry died and York took the crown . . . and was left to face Edward of Lancaster's revenge."

"Edward of Lancaster could be done away with discreetly long before Henry passes on to the God he worships with each breath he takes! Edward is a loathsome youth anyway, by all accounts, and truly Somerset's offspring. But, at the moment at least, Richard has reformed the government—in Henry's name as yet— with our devout brother George waxing grandly as

Chancellor, and with my father and the Earl of March forming the backbone of the Council. And to this highly desirable state of affairs, he sends me to bring his beloved wife and daughters." He raised her hand to his lips.

"One thing puzzles me, John. Why are you not in some great position in the government of the land? You are Richard's second brother and have been constantly at his side. He honours everyone and yet you remain as you were before."

He took a deep breath and turned to look out of the tiny window where the white cliffs filled the view. "I chose to remain thus." There was a long pause before he looked at her again. "Nan, to you and you alone I express my doubts as to Richard's handling of affairs. I wish that he had taken a seat behind York—the battle is York's and should have been dealt with by the Duke himself. I have no faith in York, Nan, he is no King. Now young March is a different proposition, but he is not likely to come to any throne for many years yet. Nay, Richard's words may be true, York may be the rightful King, but to my mind he is little better than Henry. I am caught off balance, Nan, and I know not which way I should turn for I fear that Richard will seek to force York upon the throne." The thin face was close to her as he caught her hands again. "These things I have said for your ears alone, Nan."

She nodded, her lips parted in amazement. That John should be so undecided as to Richard's cause . . . John, of all the brothers. "But what of your father and brothers? What view do they take?"

He shrugged. "It seems that they one and all believe Richard to be right. It is *Richard* they all follow, not York! Somehow they seem to imagine that Richard will have the throne, not the dull York!" He snatched his hands into fists and struck them on the table. "There is a wonderful magic exuding from Richard's every pore which spellbinds them, and with them the land itself. Even my father lives for Richard's words. Nan, I mean no insult, no aspersion upon your husband, my brother, but I fear that he holds too much sway, too much power over men's minds. We will carry York over the threshold into taking Henry's throne, and thence it is but a short step to taking Henry's poor little life. There my conscience bids me hold back, not to put my name to such acts, and the cause of York would never recover from such a murder."

88

Suddenly Nan put her arms around him. "John, you under-estimate Richard, and seriously underestimate his integrity. He will not countenance the taking of Henry's life . . . his throne yes, but never his life. He knows better than any man how to hold the people's love in the palm of his hand, he also knows what will lose him that love. The trust placed in him is well placed, do not ever believe otherwise. He needs you with him, John, you more than anyone. As to York himself, well I too feel that he is no great man, but it is Margaret of whom we wish to be rid as well as putting York upon the throne, and in that respect York is infinitely preferable to poor Henry who is his wife's tool completely and therefore dangerous to England. No-one could accuse the Duchess of York of such an unnatural hold over her husband."

The narrow door burst open and Isabel dashed in, holding tightly to Ankarette's hand. Her golden curls were ruffled and her pretty face flushed with excitement. "You have been here an age, Mother, and already we have entered the harbour. Father's party approaches and he will be with us in a moment." In a flurry of rose-red silk the little girl was gone, calling excitedly as she saw Richard on the quayside. They heard his deep voice answering her cries.

Nan glanced at John and found his eyes upon her. He took her hand before she turned to leave and pressed it warmly to his lips. "God be with you, Nan, for as He is my witness I envy my brother his wife!" He pushed her towards the door and she left him there.

The fresh cool air came as something of a surprise after the warmth of the cabin. Already Richard had come on deck and he saw her immediately, and was striding to greet her. Then she was in his arms, pressed close to his body as his lips found hers. The magic, oh the magic! One could not doubt in anything he did, for he was Richard, he was Warwick! She shivered at being so near to him after such a long time, knowing that she wanted him.

John stepped out on to the deck and watched as Isabel and Anne ran across towards Richard, unable to bear being apart from him for a second longer. Richard released Nan, bending to swing his daughters high into the air, one on each arm. Nan laughed at the shrieks they made. John's face crossed her vision in a blur and she stared at him. The dark hair was blowing across his face and a huge emerald flashed upon his finger as he leaned against the rail.

Somehow a sliver of the joy she felt at being with Richard again was gone, a sliver of joy which fled from her outstretched fingers.

Richard's laugh dragged back her attention. "John, aid me with these troublesome little wenches! Come now, I need your help!"

SIXTEEN

ON the 10th of October, only a few days after her arrival in London, Nan had a very welcome visitor. There was a timid knock upon her door and a page announced Lady Eleanor Butler.

Nan held out her hands with an exclamation of delight and Eleanor ran across the room and flung her arms unceremoniously around her aunt's shoulders.

"My sweet aunt, how glad I am to be with you once more!"

"But for how long?" Nan's green eyes danced with pleasure.

"My husband has been accepted by the Earl of Warwick in a position close to the Earl's household, and this means that if you will have me, I can join *your* household!"

"Would ever I refuse your gentle company, Eleanor?" Nan took her arm and led her to where Isabel and Anne sat silently watching their mother's guest. "You have not seen my daughter Anne before have you?" Anne put down the ivory chessman she held in her hand and stood, curtseying low to Eleanor.

Eleanor smiled and immediately began to talk to the girls and soon they softened towards her and began to tell her of their long and complicated game of chess. Nan watched her niece. Eleanor Butler was now twenty-two, and even after all her years of marriage was still childless. Her small face was of a patrician beauty and her thick black hair was hidden beneath a tall horseshoe headdress held on by creamy white lace which pulled tightly beneath her chin. The wine-red folds of her brocade gown hung richly to the floor, emphasizing her tiny waistline and long, elegant figure. Nan could see in her niece the ghost of her long-dead half-sister, Margaret. But Margaret's loveliness was deep, born of a true and happy marriage with the Earl of Shrewsbury . . . somehow Eleanor seemed unawakened, her beauty crisp and untouched.

The door opened and in came Richard with his brother Thomas, and the small, thin George, Bishop of Exeter. George was resplendent in his bishop's vestments and she noticed that his soft almost feminine fingers continually stroked the heavy, bejewelled cross which hung from his neck. Here, she thought, was another Neville in the mould of Richard; the blaze of ambition was in his pale, narrow face, in his brightfire eyes. Together they would make a formidable adversary to any who opposed them.

But it was Thomas Neville who claimed Nan's astounded attention. It seemed that he had blossomed into a gorgeous courtier during the recent months of Richard's power in London. His splendid body was sheathed in golden embroidered velvet, the short gathered doublet drawn tightly around his narrow waist and hips by a golden belt. His legs were encased in bright blue hose and over everything he wore a sleeveless coat embellished with deep fur trimmings and embroidered with the Griffin of Salisbury. His hair, so very like Richard's, was shining and curled, and worn just that little too long. The whole effect was one of foppery, almost but not quite over-tipping the scales into the ridiculous. Nan saw the astonishment in Eleanor's eyes as she gazed upon this fashionable Thomas, and she looked away quickly lest Eleanor laughed aloud.

Richard saw Eleanor and a smile of delight spread over his face which was so often stern these days. He put his arms around her and kissed her soundly, the words of greeting coming easily to his accomplished lips. Nan's eyes dulled a little as she saw the ease with which he exercised his charm upon the newcomer; outwardly he seemed the same as ever he was, but inside . . . inside there lay a granite core. Nan believed that core was growing in size and density. Richard was no longer content that the realm should believe in his legend . . . he began to believe it himself. Richard, Earl of Warwick, was invincible!

91

Outside the cobbled courtyard of l'Herber rang suddenly with hoofbeats and she hurried to the window to see who rode so hastily through the narrow gateway. She did not see who led the horsemen, but above their heads flew John Neville's banners. She smiled, not turning her head to tell the others who came, but watching the arrival of the horsemen as she spoke. " 'Tis the remaining Neville brother!"

She turned at last to watch the door eagerly, glad of the chance to see John again. Vaguely she realized that she awaited sight of him with rather more pleasure than one would expect. But then he was there, his dark hair ruffled and damp from the misty October air outside. He was out of breath from the speed with which he had ridden and as he stepped closer to the fire for warmth, the steam immediately leapt from the heaviness of his cloak.

"Well, brother Richard, the great Duke of York is returned to Westminster from Ireland! He arrives with a great company of men, flying the banners of the White Rose and also . . . the banners of the King of England!"

Richard exclaimed and suddenly the room was silent of all except John's breathless voice. "Richard of York but half an hour ago entered the Lords Chamber at Westminster where the Council was meeting. He marched past his usual place and took the empty throne, and behind him stood his son Rutland. When eventually all had recovered from their surprise, he was asked if he wished to speak with the King. He answered that from now on he would go to see no-one, anyone who wished to speak with him should come to him!"

"You were there John, is he intent upon creating mischief or is he in earnest that he regards himself as King now?" Richard's voice was urgent.

John shrugged, his eyes briefly meeting Nan's and then moving back to Richard. "It would seem to be the latter for he continued to sit on the throne, commanding the Council to proceed. There was a merry scene in progress when I slipped away and came here. Henry is still too popular, no matter what Margaret and her wolfpack may have done. Richard, you must make haste for Westminster and put some measure of sense into York's regal but addle-pated head. He will dash all your hopes if he continues this course!"

Richard nodded, hardly bothering to take his leave of Nan

before he hurried from the room. Soon the room was empty as the four Nevilles made all speed for the venue York had chosen for his ill-timed bid for the crown of England.

Hardly had they gone when the door opened again and Edward of March sauntered in, biting crisply into a large apple. The casual manner and unconcerned smile with which he greeted her told Nan that he had not heard of his father's arrival. She gave him her hand, conscious of his great height as he towered over her. But already he was paying no attention to her for his eyes were upon Eleanor Butler. Hesitantly Eleanor dropped a curtsey to him, and when she looked upon him again her eyes were soft and warm. For the first time she gazed upon the heir of the House of York, upon the golden, eighteen year old prince.

Nan could not but be aware of the atmosphere which sprang up between her niece and Edward, but she shook his arm, telling him what had happened at Westminster. His piercing blue eyes narrowed and he swore at his father's foolishness. He turned on his heel and ran from the room, but even so he paused momentarily at the doorway to look again at the flushed face of the young Lady Butler. Then he was gone. Eleanor gazed silently at the door which swung wildly at his passing.

When all had sought the shelter of their homes for the night and lanterns fluttered in the dark streets, the Nevilles returned at last to l'Herber. It was very late when Richard entered Nan's bedchamber carrying a lighted taper. The curtains were not drawn about the bed and the moving flame awakened her.

He was weary as he put down the taper, tossing aside his long cloak and climbing fully clothed upon the bed. He lay back and closed his eyes, his hands behind his head. Nan slipped softly from the bed and began to unfasten the laces of his doublet. The muddy boots she drew gently from his feet, dropping them to the rushes on the floor. The hazel eyes fluttered and opened and he took her hand. "Sweet Nan."

"What happened?"

"There are times, Nan, when I thank God in Heaven for the existence of Edward, Earl of March! His father and brother Rutland are surely the greatest fools after Henry VI himself! I know not what York's youngest sons are like, but God's Blood Rutland is a splinter from his father's bull head."

Such dejection lay in his voice that her warm nature rushed to aid him. She sat on the pillow at his side, cradling his head in her lap, pushing the clinging chestnut hair back from his face.

He smiled up at her. "Well, I found York and Rutland at the palace which fairly bristled with their soldiers and henchmen . . . the building resembled a hedgepig! They had appropriated the King's apartments, sending Henry scuttling to hide in Margaret's empty rooms. I was ill put to be civil to York for he irritated me so with his posturings. I know not what happened to him during his sojourn in Ireland, whether it was the adulation he received there or whether it is just that he can no longer act a part which he feels to be beneath him . . . I know not. He lounged against a sideboard, sipping the King's wine from the King's goblets as if they were his already. I tried to dissuade him from his plan but he persisted that he was in the right, which I will admit to be the truth, but it is the timing, Nan, the timing! Then that young puppy Rutland swaggered across to me and had the temerity to speak down to me, *me!*" The outrage felt at his insult was evident in the emotion which choked his voice. " 'Fair cousin,' he said, 'be not angry for you know that it is our right to have the throne, it belongs to my father and he will have it, whatever anyone may say'." Richard's imitation of Rutland's affected voice was cruel and accurate. "Then I heard March's voice, the sweet tones of reason, as he rebuked his brother. 'Be rude to no man and all will be well' he said. 'Tis as well that one member of the brood has sense and perception. I took my leave of them then, taking March aside and begging him to mediate with his father and make them understand that the moment was not well chosen." Richard closed his eyes again, sighing loudly.

"What happens now?"

"There is to be a conference of lords tomorrow at Blackfriars to discuss the legality of York's claim. *Legality*, that is the crux of the matter. The time is gone when a mighty demonstration of power could take the throne and keep it upon a new head. York's moment was past long since when he could do that. If he seeks his own end in this fashion then he leaves himself wide open for repercussions and sends the ditherers inevitably to Henry's side as the injured party. At all costs that must be avoided. The nobles must now be brought *gradually* to accept the situation, Henry must be *gradually* and insidiously slandered until everyone believes what we want them to believe. *Then* will be the time to put York's rightful claim forward. . . ." The quake of ambition trambled in his body and Nan felt the power of it. She shivered. He frightened her a little, he hypnotized her like a snake does its prey, drawing it near against its every instinct and inclination.

He put up his hand and stroked her breast through the loose opening of her bedgown. "Nan . . . sweet, sweet Nan. . . ." He stretched up to meet her, his lips warm and demanding. Her apprehension fled, for on this level she was his equal, on this level he was as human as any other man. In the rising temperature of their embrace she could reconjure him as he had been before the legend began to rule the man.

She drew him close, her arms seeking to envelop him completely, and as he took her she cried out to that vanishing memory.

SEVENTEEN

FROST lay heavily upon the land, covering everything with a cloak of icy white. Christmas came and went in a strangely quiet London.

In a warm room at l'Herber an inexpert young voice sang to the accompaniment of a lute. Ankarette balanced the instrument upon her lap and her voice wobbled uneasily to the high notes. Alana sat nodding her head in encouragement, a fond smile upon her face as she looked at her only child.

Isabel and Anne sat demurely at Ankarette's feet, their faces rapt as they listened to the song of Robin Hood's exploits. A large black cat curled up in the folds of their gowns, oblivious to the tale of great deeds which rang about the room.

Another sound interrupted the song, the sound of raised voices. Nan looked towards the door, recognizing Richard's angry shout and the less audible tones of John. The door flew open and the two strode in, their faces red with anger. Richard waved his arms to emphasize a point and John snorted disparagingly. They passed through the room and out through the other door, slamming it loudly behind them and their argument could still be heard as they walked away. Ankarette's voice faltered, she struck a false note and then the song died away altogether.

Nan frowned at the door, irritated by the men's rudeness. She smiled then at Ankarette, clapping her hands and feigning great enjoyment at the singing. Ankarette beamed, encouraged, and once again picked up the lute to continue the song.

Nan stood and walked to the window, passing as she did so the silent figure of her niece. Eleanor's face bore a wistful, dreaming expression which had been there continually since she first set eyes upon Edward of March. Jesu, but the girl was smitten. Nan sighed inwardly, her apprehension for her niece growing for she knew that the handsome Edward was not worthy of the obvious love Eleanor held for him. A small dalliance, a tumble upon a bed, that was all Lady Butler would receive from March, indeed it was all she could receive for she was the wife of another man.

The window was misty, the fernlike fingers of frost creeping over the glass panes. Nan placed her warm hand against it, drawing it away and leaving the outline of her fingers and palm upon the glass. She peered out, but already the tentacles of frost were returning, obscuring the momentary view. Thoughts of Thomas Butler caused Nan's mind to travel over the events of the past months, for Thomas Butler was now away in the north with the Yorkist army, his task that of being Richard's messenger from Salisbury. Soon there would be a new confrontation between Margaret of Anjou and the Duke of York, and this time surely there must be terrible bloodshed, for Margaret's pride had been seriously and irreparably hurt. York himself had been the cause of this blow to the Queen.

The strutting Duke had eventually been calmed by Richard's efforts and persuasions and had agreed at last to become once more Prince of Wales and Protector of England, with Henry retaining the throne until death. Margaret's son, Edward, was put aside, ignored as if he had never been. The Queen could never forgive such a snub. York and Rutland swore before

Parliament to uphold this new agreement, and Yorkist London settled back with relief as the moment of danger passed.

Richard's stock rose higher as his part in York's taming was appreciated, he was more popular than ever; but York himself had a somewhat tarnished reputation now. She smiled, putting her hand to the glass again, carefully placing each finger where it had rested before; had it been known that Richard's actions had been wrought with a view to eventually placing York upon the throne and casting out Henry then no doubt the Ragged Staff would not have proved so popular a badge in the streets.

How Margaret had hated and seethed, how she had burned up her seemingly endless store of energy as she raged in the fastness of Scotland. Her fury had whipped up support for Lancaster and an army had gathered in the north country. The Lancastrian force was commanded by the Earl of Northumberland and the Duke of Somerset. Did Somerset have any idea, wondered Nan, that the Prince he now fought for was in fact his half-brother? This force now pillaged the Yorkshire estates of the Duke of York and the Earl of Salisbury, laying them waste and causing havoc amongst the tenants. This proved too much for York and he had decided to personally lead an army against the enemy. He took with him Salisbury, Rutland and Salisbury's son Thomas. Edward of March had left too, but he took himself off to the march lands of Wales to raise as many men as he could to his banners.

She turned as once again she heard Richard's raised voice. The door swung fiercely again, banging roughly against the wall and chipping the beautiful painting of horsemen which adorned the plaster. But this time it was only John who entered, his face red. She laughed suddenly, she could not help herself, for he looked so comical standing there with all manner of insults struggling for first place upon his lips.

After a moment he too began to smile, and he walked over to her. "Aye, well you may laugh, but this situation grows daily more difficult to bear! In the name of Jesu why did Richard elect that he and I should remain here and not where the fighting is? This endless time, waiting, waiting, seems senseless in the extreme. If Richard is intent upon showing his face to the worshipping masses in London, at least *I* could have gone, if not with the army then at the very smallest with March to Wales!" His face was flushed again with the frustration of his position, and his long fingers played with the dagger at his waist.

Nan could understand his feelings. She was taken with an urge to put her hand to his cheek, to stroke the anger away and bring back that smile she loved so much. As she realized what she did she took her fingers away hastily, feeling the blush steal over her face. He was silent, his dark eyes dwelling on her face, then he took her hand and kissed it. "Sweet Nan, you are kind to seek to calm my raging!" He smoothed over her action which had not passed unnoticed by Eleanor.

Nan turned to look out of the opaque window, her eyes following the twining tracery of frost. She was suddenly glad of the wired veil of her headdress which hid her burning face from view. Holy Mother, what possessed her? Her heart was pounding loudly in her breast, her pulses quickening as she recalled the delight of touching him. How could she not have recognized her feelings before? How could she not have known that she desired her husband's brother? The eagerness with which she awaited seeing him, the happiness she felt when with him . . . the dullness of life when he was not there. She knew now that what had been his anger at being left in London, had been her pleasure when she realized that he was not leaving her. She had been pleased too when he had recently been created Lord Montagu, it was as if he had at last decided to enter fully into the Yorkist cause.

She took a deep breath, rubbing her damp palms over the fullness of her skirts, turning to Ankarette and smiling unnecessarily gaily. "Come now, will you not sing for us again, I vow that Lord Montagu would delight in hearing you!"

John murmured his agreement, remaining at her side as the child picked up the lute. While the music rang out again, Nan felt his fingers against her shoulder, gently, oh so very gently. She closed her eyes, knowing that he guessed her secret. But why did she feel this for him? Why? She bowed her head for the question was easily answered. The love she had directed at Richard was now unanswered. Richard lived only for his politics, his ambition, and daily she took a smaller and smaller place in his life. Her need was great, she must be told of Richard's love, reassured of it; he had neglected this, or failed to understand it, and now . . . now. . . .

There was a commotion outside and the door opened. Richard stood there, his face very pale and shocked. He held the door open and stood aside while four of his men staggered in, carrying the slumped body of a fifth. Eleanor's voice cried out as she recognized the face of Thomas Butler. Richard's personal physicians hastened into the room, clustering around the immobile figure, but soon they shook their heads and a rug was brought to cover the blood-stained face. Nan watched, stunned. Eleanor stood helplessly beside the body, the shock of what had suddenly happened seeming not to have penetrated as yet. Her face was somehow . . . surprised. . . .

John regained his voice first. "What is all this? What has happened?"

Richard mutely held out a muddy, soiled parchment, and Nan could see the accurate, precise writing of Salisbury . . . precise that is until the last few lines which were almost unrecognizable in their sprawling tracks. John took the letter, scanning the page quickly.

Nan went to Richard, shaken by his paleness. He took a deep breath. "There was a battle at a place called Wakefield. They are all dead . . . York, Rutland, my brother Thomas . . . and my father! All dead." His words fell on a minutely silent room.

There was a jarring twang as Ankarette dropped the lute. Alana hustled the three girls out of the room and the door closed softly behind them. Richard swallowed, staring at the fire which glowed in the hearth. "My father had time to pen this letter and give it to Butler before he was captured. Butler hid and waited to see what fate befell my father before riding south. They beheaded him, John, they chopped off great Salisbury's head in a public place before a gaping crowd of peasants." His voice rose with the horror and grief within him.

Nan crossed herself, unable to comprehend fully that they were all gone, even poor Thomas with his gorgeous clothes and shining, curled hair, and York, who could not dance.

Richard was speaking again, his voice thick. "Butler was almost taken but escaped and managed to ride here even though he was grievously injured. He had a dreadful tale to tell, John, for the Lancastrians brought the bodies of York, Rutland and Thomas to the city of York and there they beheaded them! Beheaded dead bodies! They placed the heads

99

upon pikes at the gateway to the city, and put a paper crown on York's brow!"

Nan's face grew cold and damp and she felt the hot bile rise in her throat. She breathed deeply, seeking to overcome the nausea.

John's fingers were playing with his dagger again. "What now, Richard? Flight?"

Richard rounded on his brother viciously. "Flight? John I despair of you! I will not run like a hare before the hounds, nay, this hare will survive the hunt! We still have March, and the person of our blessed sovereign King Harry Six, God curse him. As Christ is my witness, this is the end of foolish pretence, there shall be no more false loyalty to Henry; I will put March upon the throne, no longer will I delay for the right moment in time. March shall have what should have been his father's."

The power of him overwhelmed the room, settling over his listeners like a soothing balm. She stared at him, mesmerized. What was it about Richard that so compelled belief, that so bound lives to him?

This was the Richard of the present, of the future. She did not know him, could not be close to him; he was apart, a giant among ordinary mortals. She looked aside at John's tense face, and the emotion of earlier reasserted itself. Sweet and Holy Jesu, how she prayed with relief that John had not ridden northwards with that ill-fated army. She hung her head and stared at the dead, huddled shape of Thomas Butler.

EIGHTEEN

IT was early February before Richard had prepared his forces sufficiently to be ready to ride out from London. The Queen's Lancastrian hordes were sweeping down through the land terrorizing the countryside and laying everything to waste in their path. The bloodlust was upon each one of them after the great victory at Wakefield, and England trembled before

Margaret's wrath. She sent a small portion of her army by sea to land off the coast of Wales and then advance towards London from the west. Edward of March had been at Shrewsbury at the time of Wakefield and soon heard from his scouts of this Lancastrian company arriving within his vengeful reach. He led his men southwards towards the enemy and the two met at Mortimer's Cross where Edward's victory had been honey-sweet, an eye for an eye, a tooth for a tooth. . . .

The night air was cool as Nan stood at the dark little postern gate and peered through into the courtyard of l'Herber. Richard was mustering his men for the march northwards in the morning, and the air was alive with bustle and noise. She stood now in the tiny walled garden of the house, alone and cold, regretting the impulse which had bade her come outside and walk. The torchlit courtyard seemed a scene from Hell itself, the men's faces lit by the flaring light, their breath standing out mistlike from their mouths. From the stables she heard the excited, nervous sounds of the horses, disturbed by the noise.

Above her head the doves in the small dovecote fluttered and cooed, disliking being kept awake at night by all this activity. Their soft voices were strangely calm, for when she looked up the birds were pacing and fluttering, their heads nodding anxiously. Looking back at the courtyard she saw that John had joined Richard, and she smiled in the darkness, drawing her cloak more tightly about her throat as the wind rose slightly.

The advent of the wind caught the night frost unawares, breaking its stranglehold on the petrified apple trees in the centre of the garden. Their branches formed a beautiful cobweb overhead as she turned away from the gate and walked along the narrow path to where the few small beehives stood, silent now, devoid of all life. From one of the apple trees came the low grudging tones of an owl, disturbed as she passed.

Behind her the postern gate opened and a man's figure was lighted by the torches from the courtyard for a moment. Even in that second she recognized John Neville. Her heartbeats raced as he looked around and on seeing her hurried along the path until he reached her. He took her hand and kissed it.

She spoke first. "Well, my Lord of Montagu, have I disturbed your search for peace by being here first?" The words were strangely formal and distant, but she could not help it.

He smiled. "No, I saw you looking through the gate and decided when the moment came to join you for a while. I fear it is *I* who disturbs *your* peace."

No, no, never that, never could you disturb my peace. But she said: "Are you prepared now for the march tomorrow?" How polite, how foolish, for these were not the words which her heart bade her say.

"As ready as ever I will be! To be joining battle at last will be like purging my soul after all these months of inactivity. Besides . . ." he paused, ". . . the murders of my father and brother need atoning, and it is left to Richard and myself to take the blood of those who did such foul deeds at York."

She licked her lips nervously, acutely conscious of his closeness. "Should you not be returning to your lady wife, she will be without your company for some time to come. . . ."

He seemed surprised at the sudden change of subject. "Nan, you know and I know that my lady wife cares not if I come or go! My presence is hardly of importance to one such as she. She has my name to protect her, and that suffices, in the meantime she eats and waxes fat and ever less desirable!" His voice was clipped, preventing further comment on his marriage.

The silence grew as she turned away from him, her nervous fingers moving along the top of one of the beehives. "John, I may have no opportunity on the morrow to bid you farewell, and so I will speak now. God be with you upon this mission, and grant you a speedy and safe return." To me, oh Holy Mother, bring him back safely to me . . . to me. The feelings of her innermost heart were treacherously close to the surface in her voice.

"Nan . . ." he touched her arm, She put up her hand to halt him, shaking her head, but he would take no notice. "Nan, would you let this moment slip with only those few words?"

Her pulses raced crazily now. Stop, stop, please say no more! She turned from the beehive, meeting his eyes at last. Her limbs turned to water as she saw the warmth in his eyes, everything that her heart truly wished to see there. . . . As if by some strange knowledge of what was happening in the garden so close by, they both heard Richard's voice roar out an order from the courtyard.

Nan's fear rose sharply and she took her skirts in her hands and began to hurry away. She heard John's footsteps on the path and then his hand was upon her, holding her back, forcing her to stop yet again. "Let me go in John, no good will come of. . . ."

"Tomorrow I ride from here to meet, God knows what I shall meet, but I do know that I shall go with a lighter heart if you say now what stands unspoken between us." He whispered the words.

All her senses cried out to him, but such a love was forbidden, forbidden. "John you are my husband's brother!" She was almost weeping.

"Aye, but that does not stop the love which I cherish for you, Nan." He turned her to face him, and now the faint light from the air above the courtyard lit his features.

Her resistance vanished, evaporated somehow, and she laid her head against his chest. He slowly enclosed her in an embrace, putting his hand beneath her chin and pulling her face towards him. He kissed her, gently at first, almost chastely, but soon that kiss became something more than a mere kiss. She was almost frightened by the strength of the desire which surged through her, and she could hear nothing but the deep pounding of her heart as the feeling mounted in intensity. She broke away, pressing her forehead against his chest and gripping the miniver trimming of his coat with both hands. "God help me, John, God help me . . . for I love you too."

He cupped her face in his hands, kissing every part, every beloved feature. "There is no-one in my heart but you, and never has been. Ever since I can remember I have wanted you for myself, Nan. I know how I felt when you and Richard were at odds with one another, I hated it because he possessed you even so, but that day when we missed you both from the hunt and when I found you both by that stream. . . . I did not know that anguish could be so keen." He kissed her again.

He loosened her cloak, putting his fingers against the warm skin of her throat, moving them down until they rested against the swelling of her breast. She jerked away, feeling the cold night air swamp her tingling flesh. "No, we must do no more, say no more . . . we sin enough already without. . . ."

"Is the sin greater for the doing than the thinking?" He restrained her again. "The deed is half-committed, nay, more than half."

But a small sense of perspective had returned to her reeling mind. "John, have you no fear of the consequences of a love such as this? What if Richard should discover it, he would surely kill you and I know not what he would do to me. What would happen if the Earl of Warwick discovered his wife's adultery with his own brother."

"Nan, for you I would risk Richard's anger." He made no mention of leaving the following morning, but suddenly visions of his mutilated body rose before her eyes, visions of his head upon a pike over the gates of York. . . . Caution was thrown to the winds before such portents of horror. It was true, what did Richard's anger matter when this might be the one and only time when she and John could speak freely of their love. A swirl of breeze rustled the crackling branches above and flakes of frost dropped wispily upon them. That same breeze moved his long hair slightly and as always the movement fascinated her, held her. She said nothing, for there was no need, she merely stepped closer and put her arms about him, holding him tightly.

"I make no pretty, tempting speeches, Nan, I want you and the taking will be no matter of feather beds and sweet words, but a bitterly cold garden and the knowledge that your husband is but a few yards away beyond that wall!"

She nodded, her eyes closed. She had passed the cliff's edge between safety and folly, between admitting or denying her love. He pushed her gently against the trunk of the old apple tree, and all sense of guilt fled like chaff before the wind. Nan gave herself to her husband's brother, and the joy of that giving passed all other considerations.

NINETEEN

DEFEAT! Richard out-manœuvred, almost killed! What had gone wrong. The Duchess of York stood motionless, watching

Nan's restless pacing. The Duchess' hands rested on the shoulders of her two youngest sons, and George was whimpering a little as he fidgeted with his gloves. Dickon's face was solemn, but he did not cry.

"My Lady, what do you intend to do? The choice is yours, either you remain here and await capture by Margaret or you will flee to the Low Countries with me. My ship will sail on the next high tide."

Nan stopped her pacing. She could not leave, she must wait and hope that Richard was safe . . . and John. . . . "No, Your Grace, I thank you for your kind offer but I will not leave London. I would ask a favour of you, though, and that is that you take with you my daughters and my maid, Mistress Alana."

The Duchess nodded, and immediately Nan signalled to Alana who stood near the door, wringing her hands with fear. "Alana go and prepare my daughters for the journey, pack what you will, and then go with all speed to the Duchess of York's ship where it is moored at Barnard's Castle. Take Ankarette with you, of course, that goes without saying. Hurry now for there is not much time."

There was a movement of black in the shadows and Eleanor's slender figure came forward. Her lovely face was pale with the shock of her recent widowhood, and now she went on her knees before her aunt. "I beg that you allow me to remain with you."

Nan's cold fingers touched the perfect face. "Of course, Eleanor, if that is your wish, but please realize that you take a risk for this is a Yorkist household. Now, I bid you go to assist Alana for she has much to do in a short time."

The Duchess walked slowly to the door, turning to look back at Nan. "You are foolish, my Lady, and I doubt greatly that Richard of Warwick would praise your action in remaining here. You know when high tide is due, and you have until then to change your mind. If you do not . . . then may God have you in His Holy Keeping."

She was gone suddenly, leaving Nan alone in the huge draughty room. The hounds stretched on the rushes, groaning in their slumber, oblivious to the disaster which had struck. St. Albans, the town which had once been the scene of Richard's triumph, had this time seen his downfall. It seemed that the scouts he sent to discover the enemy's whereabouts had been captured and Richard had had no intimation of how close Margaret's army really was. The Lancastrians were upon the startled Yorkists before they could gather their formations, and the battle was quickly done. Darkness alone had seemingly saved the army of Warwick, for they managed to disperse when night fell, Richard and John escaping to freedom. Now they sought their only hope, the victorious army of the Earl of March, fresh from the triumph of Mortimer's Cross.

Nan moved closer to the fire. Was it perhaps wiser to leave with York's widow? The wind sucked through the building, the flames flared briefly and then retracted, black smoke belched from the logs. The wind brought with it a momentary sound from the city outside, the panic and shouting as the terrible news spread through London. London, a city strong for the Yorkist cause, a city which had taken great Warwick to its heart. . . . A battle lost for the want of a few, solitary riders, two or three scouts who rode into the enemy's eager clutches.

The door swung quietly upon its hinges and she turned to see the black and white presence of George Neville, Chancellor of England. She dropped a deep curtsey before him, and he touched her head, murmuring words which she could not hear. He moved to the fire, holding out his bejewelled hands and sliding his pale eyes to her face.

"So, the scales tip yet again . . . Lancaster ascendant, York descendant." His voice was expressionless.

She frowned. "Is that all you have to say?"

"It was but an observation of fact. My brother Richard lives, and with luck will by now have met with young March, but their combined force is very much inferior to the many hordes under Margaret's banners. There is hope however, no matter how slender, hope for Richard that is . . . but as for John, I fear. . . ." His voice trailed away into a horrible silence.

She felt chill fingers creep over her. "What of John? Is he not with Richard?"

George pushed one of the boarhounds with his foot. "No, Richard escaped alone. If it had not been for John's resistance to the surprise attack, then no-one would have escaped with their life. John gave Richard his chance, he fought bravely for as long as he could, but he is now Margaret's prisoner!" The pale eyes were upon her now.

Did he know? Could he tell? Those eyes were so penetrating. . . . Nan strove to conquer the emotion which fought to be seen. John! She crossed herself, knowing that her fingers trembled violently, but she concealed them quickly in the folds of her gown. Perspiration stabbed between her shoulder blades, causing the embroidered damask to stick to her icy skin.

"You had best take a seat, my sister, I fear this news has shaken you a little. I had forgotten how fond you are of John." She glanced uneasily at him as he led her to a chair, but it seemed that the words held no hidden innuendo, it was merely the guilt-laden conscience within her which quivered at every phrase.

"What will become of him now?" The bloody gateway of York loomed large before her.

"His life is safe enough for the moment, and strangely enough it is because of the Duke of Somerset that John Neville breathes yet. Somerset's brother has fallen into Richard's hands. and Somerset fears reprisals if John is executed. Margaret, however, yaps and howls for a Neville life . . . how long Somerset can hold her is a matter for God's judgement."

Nan dragged her clammy fingers over the damask, her senses swimming sickeningly. George leaned over her, taking one of the hands which shook visibly now. "Nan, you had best go with your daughters to the Low Countries. Margaret's army is drunk with its victory, and the victory is the sweeter because Richard took with him into battle the person of King Henry. Margaret has regained her husband's authority and is truly supreme once more. The terror and destruction already caused by her soldiers has never before been experienced in this land . . . she would be better advised to control them more for the memory will live strongly for many a year. When she reaches London I cannot doubt that the gates will be opened to her for the citizens will fear what will happen if they make a stand. What do you imagine will befall you or any other Yorkist sympathizer still here when that day comes?"

"I will stay, I should be here when Richard comes."

"*If* he comes then he must surely be too late to save you, Nan! Make no mistake, I do not intend to remain here in a trap like a rabbit."

Nan stood. "Then you had best be gone from this place!" She bent and picked up the hem of his robe, pressing it to her lips, then she turned and walked from the room.

107

TWENTY

DAYS later London still trembled and quaked as Margaret slowly advanced on the city, waiting for her anger to fall upon those who had betrayed her cause.

Nan was awoken by Eleanor whispering with someone at the doorway. She turned her head upon the hard pillow, seeing that the day had dawned cold and grey and that a fine drizzle floated through the skies. Again she heard Eleanor's voice and now she sat up. "Whatever is it, Eleanor, has the Queen arrived before the gates?" Her fear rose sharply.

"No, not as yet." Eleanor closed the door upon whoever had been there, and now came to her aunt. Nan swung her legs out of the bed, drawing on her robe, and then she went immediately to the 'prie-dieu' to pray.

Eleanor watched and as soon as Nan had finished, she spoke. "There is some news. It seems that the London magistrates have this very morning received a group of Lancastrian knights sent by the Queen. They have agreed to open the city gates to the approaching army and are at this moment preparing a train of carts laden with food and money to send to her as a token of their goodwill!"

Nan paused before her mirror, her hand lying upon her silver hairbrush. She looked at her reflection, seeing the anger flash in the green eyes, the fierce, fierce anger which leapt across the face. Margaret to receive help from London, and that help to go forth unchallenged? Never! "Which way does this accursed train pass?"

"Close by the Palace of Westminster, and then out through the western gate."

Nan's fingernails dragged over the bristles of the brush and she looked thoughtfully at the Beauchamp face which peered back at her from the mirror. Aye, it was long since she had thought of her Beauchamp blood, but now it coursed proud and unyielding through her small body. She was Richard's Countess, his representative in the city now that George had fled. Her fate was already sealed if Margaret took possession, so what could it matter if she attempted to raise Richard's banners now? A plan formed in her mind and she turned to Eleanor. "Send a page to bring the chief steward here . . . at once."

108

Eleanor hurried away, and immediately Nan searched through her vast store of gowns for one in particular . . . at last her fingers touched the bright red and white velvet embroidered with the Ragged Staff. The steward was bowing to her, his face puzzled.

She turned. "How many of my Lord's banners are still here?"

He stroked his chin. "Perhaps close on ten."

"And jackets? How many men could be dressed in the Earl of Warwick's colours?"

"Twenty or twenty-five, but some of the jackets are in need of repair."

"That does not matter! I know that there are at least that number of men here at the moment and that it is possible to acquire quickly enough horses for them. Within the hour I wish every able-bodied man to be dressed in Warwick red and waiting on horseback in the courtyard. Break out every banner you can find. Have my palfrey prepared, in the finest trappings available, and bring also the mount of my Lady Butler. Await my arrival in one hour, that is all!" She turned away and the man bowed again.

"One moment!" She called him back from the doorway. "I believe that you are an accomplished musician, and that your prowess upon the trumpet is well known?" He nodded. "Then you too shall await in the courtyard, upon horseback and dressed in the Earl's colours. This morning we are about to make a noisy, colourful journey across London, it is time this city was reminded that the Earl of Warwick is not dead!"

A slow smile spread across the man's wizened face. He had been for many years the steward of old Salisbury, and now went willingly to serve Salisbury's son. Any act which blazed the name of Neville across the realm met with his approval. He hurried away.

The bells announced the hour of eight o'clock when Nan walked into the courtyard. The space was filled with horsemen, bright and defiant in Richard's livery, their helmets sparkling with fresh polishing, and the Ragged Staff large across their breasts. The horses were caparisoned in red and white, and above them all flew the proud banners. She smiled, going towards her palfrey and mounting it. Eleanor followed her.

The steward pushed his horse forward, the trumpet held in his right hand. "Which direction do we take, my Lady?"

"The Palace of Westminster." A stir spread through the courtyard, for everyone knew of the supplies which were passing that way to go to the Queen. The steward led the cavalcade out into the street, his trumpet sounding noisily at every corner, warning all that a procession approached and that the way should be made clear.

All the busy streets were halted in confusion at her approach, carts and horses pressing against the walls of the houses to allow her to pass. Word spread from mouth to mouth, urchins hurried in the wake of the Countess of Warwick's company. Soon a great crowd was following them, along the street towards Westminster.

Around a corner they came upon John Neville's town house. The doors were barred and the windows boarded, it seemed that Lady Montagu had not awaited news of her husband's fate before leaving the city! Nan almost scowled at the empty façade as she passed, but her anger faded to memories of John and the night before his departure. Her face flushed and she became hot even in the cold winter air.

Soon she recognized the approaches to the Palace, and in a moment they were at the entrance to the square before the Palace gates. Down a nearby street poured the baggage train, halted now because the road was blocked further on. All around the square pressed the Londoners, gathered in strength, silent as they watched the train. At the gates of the Palace stood a group of horsemen in the red and black livery of Margaret's son, and from their helmets flared great ostrich plumes. Nan recognized some of them, but one in particular. Andrew Trollope sat upon his fine white horse, his flat face proud and sneering as his eyes fell upon Nan's party. He was risen high in Margaret's service and was now Sir Andrew, and had commanded a large portion of the Lancastrian army at St. Albans. He then was the leader of the deputation received by the magistrates!

Nan's cavalcade entered the square, halting conspicuously before the Palace in a blaze of Warwick red. The Lancastrians looked a little nervously at one another, no longer so supremely sure of themselves . . . they were but a small number in this Yorkist city. The square was silent, the only sound being the hoofbeats of Nan's palfrey as she alone urged her mount forward.

The slow clip-clop sounded like cannon fire as the hooves struck the cobbles and the animal's breath stood out in a frozen cloud as it shook its head. The people watched her. Nan was very conscious that now, at this moment, she represented Warwick to them, she must emulate Richard's sense of the dramatic, bring his magic into the hearts of these people. Her heart thumped. She passed before Trollope and totally ignored his existence. Warwick! The word seemed to rustle in the air. The banners flapped noisily in the breeze from the nearby river.

Seagulls cried overhead, sharply, their voices taking up the word. Warwick. Nan had almost negotiated the square when, as one, the crowd surged forward. No word had been spoken aloud, no command given, but as a single entity they fell upon the baggage train. The Lancastrians were openly afraid now and they urged their horses through the press in an attempt to push their way to freedom. The crowd turned upon them and one was pulled from his frightened mount and disappeared beneath the swaying blanket of Londoners. Trollope, to Nan's dismay, made good his escape.

But Margaret's train was sacked. The Londoners stripped it bare in a very short time, pocketing the provisions which had been destined for the Queen's army. Nan's company turned to go back to l'Herber, and the crowds parted before her, cheering loudly, their spirits soaring at this defiance of Margaret's strength. Nan smiled and nodded her head graciously, but her teeth chattered in her head and her stomach churned with delayed reaction. In the courtyard she had to be helped from her mount and was almost carried into the house. Inside she drank deeply of strong mead, closing her eyes with relief. How easily matters could have moved in the opposite direction!

Incredibly, incomprehensibly, the scales tipped away from Lancaster. Margaret delayed, she hesitated because she knew the unpopularity incurred by her ruthless army. She dispersed a large number of her men, knowing she would be more welcomed for doing such a thing, but already her moment was past. The Earl of Warwick and his battered army had at last met up with Edwards of March, and the combined Yorkist force was marching on London. Margaret waited in confusion, and the victory slipped through her fingers.

On Friday, 27th February, Richard and March rode into the deliriously happy city to a tumultuous welcome. Without the loosing of even one arrow, the Yorkists had taken London from the grasp of the Queen.

TWENTY-ONE

OVER a month later, in the beautiful month of April, a brilliant cavalcade rode northwards through the streets of York, beneath a gateway bereft of its gruesome decoration. The horses sounded loudly on the ancient cobbles, echoing from the overhanging gables of the black and white houses. York Minster towered over them, immense and new, then they passed beneath another gateway and out into the open countryside again. Ahead loomed the dark green fastness of the Forest of Galtres, cool and inviting.

Nan's face reflected the beauty of the spring day, she was radiant. Her white palfrey gleamed as it trod lightly along the dusty road, and her dull green skirts rippled against the animal's flanks. The long white veil streamed in the breeze, billowing and swaying to the movement. Nan was thirty-five years old, but such was her happiness on this occasion that the years fell easily away and she was in the first rush of youth once more. Her palfrey stumbled slightly on the uneven ground and she adjusted its path without really thinking, for her mind was on greater things. John was safe, he was safe and awaited them at Middleham, and with him were Richard and the new King of England, King Edward IV!

She thought of Edward as he had been on the last occasion she had seen him. He had been leading an army out of London to confront the remnants of Margaret's Lancastrian forces. Together with Richard's forces, the entire Yorkist army numbered less than the enemy, but they had crushed Lancaster at the town of Towton in Yorkshire, and at last the unworthy life of Sir Andrew Trollope had been forfeit to Neville swords. Margaret, her husband and son had once more escaped capture, but now the Lancastrian cause was hopelessly tarnished.

Richard's promise had been kept, he had avenged the deaths of his father and brother, and had placed the blood of the dead Duke of York upon the throne. There had been no doubt about the support Edward Plantagenet had received from the citizens of London or those nobles who were not at Margaret's side; they had one and all poclaimed Edward's right to the crown. He had sealed his claim with this massive victory at Towton.

A splash of vivid vermilion caused Nan to look unwillingly at the woman who rode immediately behind her. Joan, Lady Montagu! How Nan loathed the foolish, empty smile which continuously graced the equally foolish, empty face of her lover's wife. Joan was small and rather plump, and always wore colours and styles which emphasized her roundness. Her tiny hands were clustered with many rings to each finger, and those fingers were always to be seen dipping into dishes of comfits and other sweet confections. Even now the podgy hands were searching in her purse, and a comfit was brought forth and popped into the open, circular mouth. Nan shuddered, to think that this woman would tonight share John's bed. . . .

The vermilion was suddenly closer as Joan brought her mount alongside. "I say again, my Lady, that litters are a far more civilized mode of transport for ladies of rank!" Joan gasped as her mount lurched alarmingly up a slight incline.

Nan's teeth gleamed white as she forced a smile. "But think how long it would then take us to travel to Middleham from London! We would be less than half way, I vow!"

Joan giggled then. "Aye, but in *my* condition I should have been happier to travel at a more leisurely pace!"

"In your condition?" Nan reined in, staring in growing horror, her eyes flickering over Joan's thick waistline.

"You have guessed it, sweet Nan, I am with child. I did not realize it myself for many months, and it was only last week that my physician informed me that far from being unwell of some dreadful malady, I was merely enceinte!" Again that awful giggle.

Jealousy seized Nan roughly, tearing the smile from her face.

A knot twisted in her stomach as she looked at Joan. John's child!

"Mother, will it be long now before we reach Middleham?" Isabel was beside her, her small face upturned, tired.

"Nay, sweeting, it will not be long now." Nan smiled down at her daughter, glancing at little Anne who also came closer on her small palfrey.

A small figure cantered past them on a brown horse, a small figure which shouted in an ungentlemanly manner. "Come on Dickon, I'll wager you cannot catch me!" George, the brother of the new King and newly created Duke of Clarence! He was an insufferable boy, given much to slyly creeping behind people and eavesdropping upon them. His pride in his elder brother's new importance took a form of condescending unpleasantness; the sneering shade of the dead Rutland looked out from George's pale blue eyes. Nan looked behind to see if York's youngest son had taken up the challenge. Dickon was now Duke of Gloucester, and he rode stiffly up to Nan, his thin little face pouting angrily. His very dark hair was fine and wispy and the eyes he now raised to her face were a steady grey.

He smiled at her raised eyebrows, manœuvring his mount in between Isabel and Anne. He was so different, thought Nan, he was not one of York's golden tall brood, he was a changeling. Now he scowled at his brother who vanished gradually into the depths of Galtres. "He knows that his animal will easily beat my poor nag, I will not give him the satisfaction of beating me!"

"Dickon, he will not like it if you refuse to join him."

He grinned broadly, his thin face lighting up impishly. "Then let him not like it, I am his brother, not his creature. Tell me . . ." he leaned closer, trying to conceal his words from the curious ears of Nan's daughters, ". . . is the Earl of Warwick very strict? He seems very fierce to me."

Nan pondered on this question. Richard was now of great importance to these two boys for they were to come into his household to learn knightly conduct, Richard was to be to them as Nan's father had once been to King Henry. Such was the honour now paid to Warwick by the new King, that his only brothers were to be given into Neville hands. Richard had a new name in the realm now, his importance and might were recognized by all, and he was called the Kingmaker. It was a name which Richard delighted in, a name which suited the legend, which nourished and sustained it. Dickon was still awaiting her answer.

"Well, Dickon, I think perhaps that he is strict, but he is not unkind or harsh and is always fair. Does that answer you? You must understand that the Earl of Warwick as seen by his wife is an entirely different man from the Warwick as seen by the boys in his household!"

This answer seemed to satisfy him for he smiled and did not appear to wish for any further words. He glanced ahead as George returned, his face stormy and obviously prepared to squabble with his younger brother. Nan sighed inwardly, reining in slightly to allow Dickon's horse to go into the lead, and then she left them to quarrel alone.

She looked around for Eleanor, smiling as she saw the black-robed figure on its bay mount. Eleanor was soon alongside and Nan leaned towards her. "I can well imagine Richard's reaction to the great Clarence!"

Eleanor smiled. "Aye, I think perhaps young George will soon be a different beast."

"God be praised." They laughed together. Nan put her hand to her purse, hearing above the jingling of harness the distinct crackle of parchment. It was Richard's letter bidding her come north to him, the letter which had told her that at last he had released John from his Lancastrian prison, safe and well. A sentence from the letter came suddenly into mind. "Bring Lady Butler north with you, mayhap the change of environment will aid her recovery from unhappiness." It was strange that Richard should think of Eleanor's wellbeing, somehow out of character. . . .

The ground was now carpeted with bluebells, their thick perfume vying with the scent of the spring trees. The forest awoke to the warm sunshine and its beauty stretched on all sides, but very quickly they rode uphill and out of the trees. Before them stretched the moors, wild and magnificent, and so very open after the enclosed woods they now left behind.

Eleanor was still thinking of Clarence. "He is not at all likeable is he? But think of the honour the King pays Richard by placing both his brothers in his care." Her voice took on a different note as she mentioned Edward.

"Hmm, that's as may be, but I could have wished Clarence

115

on some other aspiring nobleman—preferably many miles away from Richard's estates. He makes poor Anne very unhappy with his unkind teasing and rough treatment, she is very small and not at all strong."

"The Lady Anne can look after herself, my aunt, do not fear on that account. On the last occasion he tormented her, so Alana informs me, the Lady Anne kicked him soundly upon the shins—royal prince or not! I understand that the Duke of Gloucester enjoyed the incident immensely and had his ears soundly boxed by the infuriated George! The household at Middleham will not be dull, I think!"

The scented air swept over the sloping ground and Nan saw some deer ahead. The breeze carried the dangerous odour of approaching humans, and in a trice the deer were bounding away down the hillside and into the security of the forest.

Eleanor was thoughtful. "It will be good to see the King again will it not?" Her eyes were large and full of eager anticipation.

"You would seem to be looking forward to the occasion."

"Well, his company is gay and he is certainly the most handsome of men!" Eleanor blushed, biting her lip.

"He is comely enough, that I grant you, but Eleanor heed my warning when I say that Edward of England is not steadfast, do not place your hopes high." Nan could not put into words the exact meaning she intended without offending Eleanor's pride.

There was no time for further talk for sudden shouts filled the air. Clarence was waving his arms excitedly and pointing ahead, and already Dickon was gone at breakneck speed towards an approaching party of horsemen.

Eleanor's sharp eyes recognized those who came. "It is the King himself, riding to greet us . . . and Richard." She paused, straining to see more. "Yes, and Lord Montagu. Joan, your husband is coming!"

Joan nodded, searching around in her purse for another comfit. Nan glared at the podgy face. Even now the woman did not care that John was so near! A thousand poxes on her for her indifference!

But Nan's excitement was hard to conceal or dampen as she lifted herself slightly in the saddle to peer ahead. Her own party was halted now, the horses stamping and snorting, and the drumming of the approaching hooves filled the moorland.

Edward reached them first, his immense figure dwarfing the two Nevilles. He came to greet Nan, giving her the honour of his first words as she was the wife of his most important supporter, but his blue eyes searched for the slender figure of Eleanor as he took Nan's hand. He was a giant upon his large courser, and his strong body was encased in pale blue velvet and ermine. There could surely be no man in the world to rival this golden King for sheer beauty of face and figure. He turned his attention completely upon Eleanor and Nan saw her niece's doelike eyes gaze adoringly upon him.

But Nan cared nothing for Edward's dalliance at that moment for at last the two other riders were with them and her hungry eyes at last saw John. He was thinner and his eyes were a little sunken, it seemed that his Lancastrian captors had not treated him with any respect save only that upon his life depended the neck of Somerset's brother.

Then Richard was there, his presence swamping all else. He dismounted and took the bridle of Nan's mount. She reached down to him and was in his arms, but the embrace was short-lived before Isabel and Anne were pulling at his arm and his attention was drawn to his daughters.

Nan turned her head to search for John. He was there, his eyes upon her. He did not look away as their glance met. There was suddenly nothing on the moors, no sound, no movement, an infinity broken only by the love in his eyes.

TWENTY-TWO

THE House of Neville was taking occasion to entertain the King of England, and the magnificence of the banquet spread out in the great hall of Middleham was almost beyond belief. The trestle tables bowed beneath their load of rich foods, fifty or more courses each set out upon a silver or gold platter and garnished colourfully. Richard had seen that this feast was one which would be remembered for a long while.

On a raised platform at the head of the huge table were the most important members of the gathering. The King himself, resplendent in purple velvet and cloth-of-gold, his coat thickly pleated over his broad chest. When he drained his golden goblet, a page stepped forward immediately to replenish it; Edward could not help but be impressed by the pains taken to serve him. Now he leaned back in his chair, his handsome face creased into an infectious smile as he watched the antics of the dancing bear which performed before Warwick's guests.

The great beast stood upon its hind legs, held by no more than a light silver chain, and the handler was a young girl. The King's eyes were warm as he looked at her, for she was clad in little more than a draping of fine cloth and the curves of her figure were easily seen as she led the bear. Around her ankles were small silver bells which rattled merrily to each movement as she whirled around to face the bear, putting her face dangerously close to the animal's slavering jaws. The hall held its breath in fear, but already the girl was smiling as she curtseyed at the end of her performance. Applause broke out, and all eyes swung towards Edward as he stood, holding out his hand to the girl. She approached him slowly, leading the bear, and the King held out a large ruby ring to her, pressing it between her breasts. Raucous laughter broke out at this, and the girl smiled invitingly at Edward.

When she had left the hall and the jugglers took her place, Edward sat down again. Behind Edward sat his close friend and confidant, William, Lord Hastings, and now he touched the King's shoulder. Hastings pointed after the girl who had almost left the hall, and he whispered close to Edward's ear. Smiling, Edward nodded his head, and immediately Hastings left the hall.

Nan watched this with amusement, for it was obvious that Hastings was about to find the girl to warm his master's bed that night. Already it was quite obvious that Edward of England was more concerned with the pursuit of women than he was with the more onerous tasks of being King. He willingly allowed Richard to hold the reins.

On Edward's right sat Richard, carefully attired in a dark blue coat which did not outshine the King's purple and gold.

He sat back silently, putting his goblet to his lips and drinking deeply, and his sharp eyes flickered over the sea of faces before him. His glance fell upon the King's brothers and he smiled at them, the charm of great Warwick reaching across the room to touch the two impressionable youths. George of Clarence stared open mouthed at the baron whose name was a byword in Europe, but Dickon smiled shyly in return. Beside Dickon sat Nan's daughter Anne, and Nan could not help but notice how often she and the King's youngest brother were engaged in whispering and secretive giggles. They were two of a kind, both shy and somewhat over-shadowed by their siblings. With Clarence sat Isabel, but her lovely little face was haughty as George almost upset his plate into her lap. He glowered at her as if the fault lay with Isabel and not with himself. A little later however, Nan saw that they too were talking amicably together, but not with the same easy camaraderie of the younger children.

The servants began to clear away the trestle tables and the clatter of the precious plates filled the smoky air. The minstrels who had been playing throughout the banquet were now joined by four more, and the music became louder as they struck up a dance. Richard stood and came towards Nan, his chestnut hair gleaming in the haze. The King stepped down from the dais and approached Eleanor, who sat alone and still garbed in black. His voice was plainly heard as he held out his hand to her. "Lady Butler, as we two are the only unattached members of this gathering of husbands and wives, it is only fitting that we should lead the first measure."

Eleanor smiled up at him as she took the proferred hand. Black, thought Nan, seemed even to enhance Eleanor's loveliness. She watched them dance but her heart was heavy as she saw the love on her niece's face.

Richard's voice was in her ear. "Nan, this dance shall be our first in a long passage of time!" He pressed her hand to his lips and then led her to where others already joined the King and Eleanor. The sleeves of Richard's velvet coat were so long that the scalloped tips brushed the floor as he danced, the rich, swaying fabric dragging through the food and mess which soiled the clean rushes.

Nan's eyes moved back to Eleanor. "My Lord, it was a kind thought of yours that my niece should come north with me."

He grinned. "Many years have you been my wife, Nan, but

119

you obviously know little of me. No such thought crossed *my* mind at all, 'twas the King's notion that she would benefit from leaving London." He saw Nan's troubled eyes and drew her aside from the dance. "Sweet Nan, do not worry yourself about Lady Butler, she is a widow and thus free to do as she wishes. Edward will not force her against her will, such is not his way."

"Richard, she is a babe compared with him! Widow she may be but worldly she is not. He cannot know the effect he is having upon her—a small dalliance to him is a great matter of the heart to her."

"Then more fool the lady! Nay, sweetheart, I cannot believe that Eleanor, who has been a wife, is so lacking in experience as to mistake the King's advances for something more than a brief desire. Smile now, she will be safe from him soon anyway for within the week he returns south."

"And you?"

"I remain here. I have chosen the north as my platform, my nutshell you might say. Here I shall rule."

Her attention was fully upon him now. "Richard, the King grants titles and prizes in many directions after this last victory, even to that lecherous Hastings . . . but what of you, the man who aided him most, who made him what he now is?"

He drew her close. "What would a Dukedom benefit me? I am Warwick, premier Earl of England, master of great tracts of land across the English countryside. My name is known by all, were I to become Duke of This or Marquis of That then I would have to begin again, instilling *that* name into the minds of the people. Nay, I am content to remain as I am, as also I am content to remain here when the court returns south."

She looked up at him, noting the stern set of his jaw. Why was it that he wished to stay here? There could be only one reason and that was that Edward would be wildly acclaimed and adored when he returned to his capital, a victorious, youthful, handsome King, a brilliant general, proved beyond doubt. Richard would be shadowed by Edward's glory, and that was a comparison which he had no wish to see drawn. She smiled a little, as his wife of many years she knew him perhaps a little better than he imagined!

Her nerves tightened suddenly as she saw John and his wife approaching through the crowd. A thought took her and she

120

touched Richard's arm. "What of your brother so recently returned to you, does he return south or remain here?"

"No! John stays with me, I have great need of him."

Her heart surged with relief and she smiled brightly at Joan, curtseying quickly and then holding out her hand to John. "My Lord of Montagu, how it pleasures me to see your face once more, I feared at one time. . . ."

His fingers were firm about hers as he drew her hand to his lips. "Nay, Madam, by the grace of God . . . and the noble Somerset . . . I am safe and well!"

Joan was chattering animatedly to Richard, her words pouring forth relentlessly. Once Richard rolled his eyes heavenwards and even John smiled with amusement. In an effort to stem the flow of inanities, Richard led his sister-in-law out to dance, and for the first time Nan was left alone with John.

She knew that her love was written in her eyes as she looked at him. "I have prayed to God in Heaven for your safety, and my prayers have been answered."

They moved away to a less crowded corner of the hall, and as he smiled and inclined his head to an acquaintance they passed, he whispered quietly to her. "I had wondered if . . . you would regret our last encounter."

A blackness surged before her eyes momentarily. Regret? Oh sweet Jesu, how could he believe that? "Never . . . ever." She smiled at Hastings who hurried back into the hall through a doorway close by and he gathered himself into a low bow before scurrying on in search of Edward.

She turned to watch him, seeing that Edward still partnered Eleanor. Richard had deserted Joan and stood now with Edward's priest, Robert Stillington, the Dean of St. Martin's in London. Stillington was often in the King's company, although after Hastings he seemed a somewhat unlikely choice of companion.

John's hand still held hers, concealed in the voluminous skirts of her satin gown, and his finger caressed the moistness of her palm. She bowed her head, flushing. He tightened his grip suddenly. "Let us walk together a while—away from here."

She started. "Is it wise?"

"Wise for a man to walk with his sister-in-law? I know of no law which forbids the practice!" He was laughing a little, but she could detect the tremor in his voice.

Slowly they walked towards the doorway, passing the guards in their scarlet jackets who held flaring torches above their heads to light the entrance. Nan's satin skirts seemed unnaturally weighted as she moved, almost appearing to hold her back. On they walked, talking lightly, smiling and nodding to those they met. No-one paid great attention to Lord Montagu and the Countess of Warwick as they walked on down a now quiet, darkened passage in the outer extremes of Middleham Castle.

They halted at last by an embrasure which opened into one of the tiny slit windows. Listening, they heard no sound of any-one approaching, no sound at all except for the fluttering of the torches which were at long intervals down the passage. John drew her into the small space, and the blackness of its shadow engulfed them as the stone walls obscured the torchlight. His arms slipped about her and he pulled her close, kissing her lips as if for the first time. She melted against him, her mouth cling-ing to the sweetness of him. Their excitement mounted, desire rushing foolishly towards. . . .

A sound broke the heady silence. She pulled away, frightened, and she knew that John had heard the footsteps as well. Two people were approaching!

"Sweet Eleanor, how refreshing is your shy nature, how refreshing and desirable!" The King! Nan's heart almost ceased its frantic beating as she recognized Edward's smooth voice.

John's hands held her firmly, pulling her against him, his fingers stroking her throat.

There came the unmistakable sounds of a slight struggle, then Eleanor's breathless whisper. "Your Grace, I beg of you, do not. . . ."

"Do not what? Kiss you? Ah, Eleanor, your delectable lips beg me with each passing moment for a kiss."

Eleanor gasped. "You . . . frighten me."

"Frighten? God's Blood woman, you have known a husband, how can I frighten you? You are no virgin fresh into the world!" His tones were slightly less bantering now.

"I will not lie with you, Your Grace, save you force me!" Eleanor was unexpectedly firm.

"By the Rood, the day that I have to force a woman will be the day I take to my bed to die! Force you I will not, but have you I most certainly will!"

"I will not disgrace the name of my aunt in whose household I now am!"

Nan's face waxed hot with shame at such words. Disgrace her name? If only her niece could know the truth! John's arms tightened around her and she hid her face in the dove grey brocade of his doublet.

"The Countess of Warwick? And what, pray, does that noble lady have to do with this? You are a widow, Eleanor, and as such free to do as you wish!"

These were the wrong words to have picked. "Very well, Your Grace, then I shall now exercise my rights!" Eleanor's slippers tapped quickly on the stone flags, the sound diminishing until there was silence again. Lady Butler's attitude was most unexpected.

But Edward, was he still there? After a moment they heard his low laugh. "Very well, my little prudish Eleanor, you leave me no choice but deceit. All is fair in the pursuit of the fair lady." Another pause, and then an irreverent laugh. "I shall have you, without force, oh sweetly without force . . . in a marriagebed!" He walked away but in the distance they heard him repeat the last word, laughing still. "Marriagebed!"

Nan heaved a huge sigh, her legs weak with the fear she had felt. If Edward had discovered her in such circumstances! John moved slightly and the torchlight fell upon his face. He smiled gently. "Well, our spell is broken for the moment I fear!" He kissed her.

She nodded. "We should return while the way is clear!" Her eyes sought his again, and he put his lips against the warm flesh of her shoulder. She shivered anew at his touch.

He stepped out into the deserted passageway, pushing back a strand of her hair which had strayed from beneath her headdress. Together they walked back along the stone flags, gradually mixing with more and more people as they approached the hall. Again they nodded and smiled as they sauntered along, disguising their love completely. "What do you think the King intends?" she whispered, leaning closer for a moment.

He shrugged. "His meaning was plain enough, he intends to deceive Eleanor into thinking she is married to him. Some secret ceremony with a false priest, no doubt, it has been done before."

"I must warn her."

"And admit to her that you were also in that deserted part

of the castle with a lover? Such an admission would be foolish. My advice is that you stay well outside any of Edward's concerns, well outside. Beside which . . ." he halted and pressed her hand to his lips, ". . . neither you nor I are in any position to offer advice of that nature."

She blushed, but nodded her agreement. There was nothing she could do, even Eleanor would wonder at Nan's knowledge of her conversation with the King. Such wonderings could lead to others, and an awkward conclusion might be reached.

A bright flash of crimson and vermilion spread across the doorway, shuddering and twinkling in the torchlight, and there stood John's wife. She popped a comfit into her mouth before hurrying forward to where they stood. Nan listened to Joan's trivial talking for a moment before excusing herself and walking back into the hall.

For the remainder of that evening she found herself watching Edward, and when she and Richard finally took their leave, Edward was still there, his arm thrown about the thin, hunched shoulder of Robert Stillington. The royal lips were whispering conspiratorily in the priest's ears.

TWENTY-THREE

THE moors were bright in the late summer sunshine, the heather purple and misty to the distant hills. The pages walked slowly, leading the ladies' palfreys through the stubbly grass, past the tangled yellow splashes of gorse which sprawled along the vaguely discernible path.

Nan's errant thoughts wandered aimlessly in the drowsing warmth and she looked around her at the open beauty of this northern moorland. How she had grown to love Middleham and the other northern castles belonging to Richard, but most especially she loved Middleham itself. Now the stately lines of Warwick Castle seemed a lifetime away in the dim reaches of yesterday.

Throughout the summer she had seen little of her husband or

of John, for they were mostly away along the northern boundaries of England quelling any troubles which arose. The Lancastrians were quiet for the most part, with Margaret of Anjou being in France seeking to raise support with her royal cousins there. London basked happily under the new Yorkist regime, idolizing the bright young King who replaced the unhealthy gloom of the unfortunate Henry. Nan bit her lip as she thought of Henry, for she had no lingering sense of loyalty, no small iota of that fierce support she once had held for the friend of her youth. To her Henry was now an unwanted burden, a false prince who had almost destroyed the peace of England.

The other palfrey behind her snorted as a lapwing started from the grass beneath its hooves. The page steadied the beast, his voice sounding out of place in the quiet of the afternoon. Alana smiled as her mistress looked around at her, trying to appear happy and pleased at the ride, when in truth her every bone ached and every nerve cried out at the bouncing, swaying movement.

Nan saw the tired face. "Poor Alana, I fear that riding is no longer a favourite pastime with you." Her voice was gentle.

"Madam, my every joint creaks at each step!" Alana could no longer conceal her misery.

"Well, soon Middleham will be in sight. I am sorry to inflict these rides upon you, rest easy for I will choose another companion to ride with me next time."

Alana's brow was troubled at these words for she did not know whether to be pleased or not. What if her mistress should find a more youthful, more congenial companion and turn away from her old servant completely? But then she smiled to herself, for she knew that Nan would never desert her.

They continued in amicable silence for a while, and then Alana coughed discreetly. "My Lady, I have a request which I would dearly wish to put to you."

The timid tone surprised Nan and she told the page to halt, turning to look enquiringly at the older woman. "Speak then."

"It concerns my daughter, Ankarette. You will know how close she is to the Lady Isabel . . . well, I was hoping that you might consider the possibility of placing her in your daughter's household when it is formed."

"Of course she will join Isabel, no doubt my daughter would have requested so herself shortly."

They moved on, the hillside slipping away before them to reveal the clustered village of Middleham with the fortress rising solidly behind.

"Mayhap my niece would like to accompany me upon these rides in future. . . ." Nan's voice was a murmur, she spoke really without thinking too deeply on the point, but she turned quickly on hearing the sharp intake of breath from Alana. The woman's face had blanched dramatically. "Whatever is it, do you see a spectre?"

"No . . . oh no, my Lady!"

"Well?"

Alana looked miserably uncomfortable again. "I do not think Lady Butler is well enough to ride."

The hoofbeats clattered loudly upon the wooden drawbridge and they heard the jingling of mail as the soldiers saluted the Countess of Warwick as she returned. The pages stopped in the inner courtyard and more came to assist the ladies to dismount. Nan said nothing as they walked into the castle, but once inside and out of hearing of anyone, she put her hand on Alana's shoulder. "What is wrong with Lady Butler?"

"Oh, Madam, I know not for certain, merely that she is unwell. You must have noticed that she has not been seen much in company these past weeks." Alana avoided the steady green gaze.

Nan's fingers pulled thoughtfully at the fastenings of her light riding cloak. It was true, Eleanor had been conspicuous by her absences. She handed the cloak into Alana's outstretched hands. "I shall be with my niece should anyone enquire after me." She turned quickly and walked away, her amber skirts rustling loudly.

Eleanor was standing by the window of her bedchamber, her hair blowing free in the slight breeze which crept in through the narrow slit. She did not hear her aunt enter. Nan watched for a moment as her niece stretched her arms lazily above her head, a smile touching the young lips as she gazed towards the southern horizon.

"Good day Eleanor, I trust that I do not find you still unwell."

The girl gasped and hastily drew her loose wrap about her body. "My aunt, I did not hear you enter."

"So I noticed." Nan smiled and she sat down on the bed, the curtains of which were drawn back to reveal the ruffled sheets where Eleanor had recently been lying. She looked up at her

126

niece, seeing with surprise the agitation which her presence had somehow wrought in the girl.

Eleanor left her place by the window and moved to the table, her nervous hands moving over the carved binding of a Bible which lay there. Nan saw the dark shadows beneath the large eyes, the pale face, and somehow generally unwell appearance of her niece. "Eleanor, it grieves me that you did not think it necessary to tell me you were unwell. What is wrong?"

The girl smiled shakily, her noice brighter than necessary. "There is nothing wrong, merely a little tiredness which will soon pass." She bit her lip.

Close to the Bible lay a dish of apples, some of the first of the harvest, and Nan stretched forward and picked up a small red fruit. She bit into it, but it was not juicy being rather dry and tasting of parchment. She grimaced and put the apple down upon the table, chewing unwillingly upon the piece she had bitten. Eleanor watched in horror, her face waxing white, and to Nan's shock her niece suddenly retched violently.

"Jesu, Eleanor, I had not thought an apple would so affect you!" Nan hurried to bring a damp cloth to press to the hot forehead.

The nausea passed after a moment, but beads of perspiration glittered along the dark hairline. Nan stared thoughtfully, her heart going cold within her. "You are with child." It was a statement of fact, not an accusation.

Eleanor began to weep, springing to her own defence rapidly. "And if I am?" She glared defiantly at her aunt.

Nan put her hand on the girl's arm. "Do not speak thus to me, I will not admonish you for I think I know who has got you in this condition. Our high and noble monarch, is it not?"

Eleanor gasped, biting her lip again. "You will say nothing, promise me you will say nothing."

Nan spread her hands helplessly. "Shortly there will be no chance of concealing your condition, already your waist is gone."

"I shall be leaving soon anyway."

"Why? Where can you go?" Nan was anxious.

"The King wishes me to bear the child at his manor of Wigmore, I am to go there as soon as he sends word."

"At least he acknowledges his offspring! Wigmore? That is

127

near the Welsh border is it not? Lands he holds as Earl of March?"

"Yes."

"And what then, Eleanor? What will happen to the child?"

"It will receive the honours due to its birth . . . I am the King's wife!"

Nan closed her eyes briefly, all the memories of Edward's laughing mention of the marriagebed returning. "Wife? When did he 'marry' you?"

"Two days before he left Middleham and returned to London."

Nan suddenly swept the dish of apples from the table and the fruit rolled in all directions. "You fool, Eleanor, do you really imagine that Edward married you? You may be of noble birth but you are most certainly not destined to be England's Queen; Think girl, if he truly married you why is there such a need for silence? He is King and unmarried, you are a widow . . . there can be no real reason for such subterfuge if indeed the marriage was truthful!"

Eleanor's head snapped back as if she had been slapped. "You will tell me next that Robert Stillington is no true priest!"

"Stilling. . . ." The word escaped slowly between Nan's lips. "Stillington performed this marriage?" She paced up and down, kicking aside the apples. Her head was spinning, if the Dean of St. Martin-le-Grand had officiated then how could there be doubt? She glanced again at Eleanor. Could it be possible that Edward had thought again, that he had decided to treat Eleanor honourably and make her his Queen? "Was there anyone else to witness the marriage?" Eleanor shook her head. "What reason does the King give for the secrecy then?"

"He said that he does not truly think the moment ripe for his marriage to be made known, he wishes to be firm upon his throne and he wishes to win the Earl of Warwick's favour in this matter!" Eleanor looked sideways at her aunt.

Richard! Nan thought then of her husband, who now spoke of some great foreign match for his King. Richard, who sought to lend his name to the negotiations for the hand of some princess of Europe. "Aye, that *is* a problem indeed, for I doubt if Richard will find the matter congenial."

Eleanor flung away angrily. "Why should the Earl of Warwick's permission be given for the King of England to wed?

128

Edward is King in his own right, not merely on the sufferance of Richard of Warwick!"

Nan's own anger rose to the challenge. "He would not be King had he not been made so by Richard of Warwick . . . the Kingmaker!"

"That is a debatable point, my aunt, for Edward is stronger, more ambitious than is realized by your husband!"

"Even so, do you really think that Edward would have won if Richard's forces were in opposition to him? Nay, I think not, for it is because Warwick rallied to the Yorkist flag that your lover now sits the throne. He wears the crown, my Lady, and leaves Richard to govern the land as *he* sees fit. Your lord Edward prefers to while away his time in less ardous pursuits, already his amours are talked widely of. . . ." She broke off as she uttered these last words, seeing the hurt upon her niece's face. She walked quickly over and took the trembling hands. "Eleanor, if Edward has made you his wife, and that is the truth before God, then I wish you well and give you my blessings. Richard will be affronted for a while, but I doubt if the wound will be permanent, even to Richard's enormous pride. You are close to him, not through blood but through me, and you have been in his household for many years of your life. He will perhaps see the advantages of such a match. If he doesn't . . ." she shrugged, ". . . well, there is little he can do about it anyway."

Eleanor gripped Nan's hands tightly, her face anxious. "Promise me that you will remain silent about your discovery. Do not tell the Earl, I beg you! I vowed to Edward that I would hold my tongue until the moment was right, if he should discover that I have chattered to you of all people. . . ."

Nan warmed to the girl's pleas. "Dearest Eleanor, of course your secret is safe with me, I would have no wish anyway to impart such information to Richard! It would be better if Edward told him himself. You may rest assured that I will act as if I know nothing . . . see, I swear upon his Bible!" She picked up the carved volume and pressed it to her lips.

Eleanor relaxed then. "You will never know how relieved I am to be able to tell you of all this, for I am more than a little frightened at being so alone. What can we say to the Earl when I have to leave for Wigmore?"

Thoughtfully Nan stared at the Bible. "When Edward was

here, you went to him with some problem over your estates from your late husband did you not?"

"Aye, that is so, when Thomas died he left me two manors, but my father-in-law, Sir Ralph Butler, sought to relieve me of my inheritance. Edward granted that the manors were mine and that Sir Ralph had no right to them during my lifetime."

"There is your answer then, Richard will be given the impression that you leave for your own lands. He will not question such a course, indeed I doubt if he will give it more than a passing attention."

"You would not mind deceiving your lord thus on my account?"

Nan almost laughed aloud. Deceive! Holy Mother, had the girl but known the immensity of Nan's deception where Richard was concerned. Her life was become one single fabrication, a continuous tissue of deceit. . . . She swallowed, feeling for the first time a prick of guilt.

TWENTY-FOUR

ISABEL and the young Duke of Clarence danced exquisitely together, and the room was silent but for the music of the minstrels. Dancing was George's one saving grace and for his age he danced with great accomplishment. The two children twisted and turned, their faces almost frowning with the effort of concentration upon the steps, especially Isabel who sought to match George. As the music came to an end the applause broke out, and George bowed, breaking the spell with his unpleasant smile.

A page stood before Nan, a sealed parchment in his hand. She took it and waved him away, her fingers eagerly breaking the seal which she recognized as Eleanor's. How she missed the gentle company of her niece, gone these months now to the secret manor of Wigmore. Around her bowed head the Christmas revellings continued, the dancing and merriment loud and happy.

130

With a smile she read that at last Eleanor had been brought to bed of a son! His name was to be Edward, after his sire. A son. Nan raised her head, gazing at the smoke which wound up from the fire; England already had an heir but nothing was known of his existence. She crushed the letter and tossed it into the fire, watching it blacken and then flare into flames.

Nearby she saw the slender figure of John as he leaned against the wall laughing at the antics of the Lord of Misrule who rode wildly about the room on his ribboned mule, commanding people to do the most ridiculous things. No-one dared to flout his commands, and there were shrieks of loud laughter.

How empty Christmas seemed without Richard. Nan looked over the throng to where his emblem of the Ragged Staff gleamed from a beam, visible even through the smoky haze. Warwick's castle . . . but no Warwick. Queen Margaret had invaded from the north and Richard had easily driven her back, but now rumour was rife of various Lancastrian invasions which were imminent, and so Richard was away with the King in London and the southern counties, raising troops and reinforcing the defences of the realm. Middleham was without its Lord. John remained to control the now quiet north, for even such apparent peace could not be left without the firm hand of the House of Neville to steady it.

Lady Montagu squealed loudly as the Lord of Misrule pointed his jingling staff in her direction, commanding her to choose a partner and then dance with her back towards him. The minstrels struck up a fresh tune, a wickedly fast dance, and Joan found her voluminous skirts a great hindrance as she giggled and danced, turning to look at her partner every so often. Nan's face was cold as she looked at the ridiculous woman, for Joan was a mother now, having born John a sound and healthy son. The corpulent figure of John's wife was scarcely less round than when she had been big with child.

The small, slight shape of Dickon moved across the floor, hesitating at first and then going to speak with John. Nan's heart yearned; how she longed to go to him, to kiss him on the mouth there in front of the entire gathering! How she longed to shout aloud her great love for John, Lord Montagu. Now was the time of festivity and happiness, and Richard was many miles away. . . .

A tumbler crouched before Nan, suddenly leaping back-

131

wards in a complicated somersault. Nan gasped with delight and clapped her hands in appreciation. His place was taken by a juggler with long yellow ribbons streaming from his arms, and the ribbons fluttered as he tossed scarlet and blue balls into the air, five, six, seven and more. Nan watched, but her concentration was no more as again and again, unbidden, came the yearning for John Neville.

Joan was giggling helplessly now. She had consumed a great deal of wine and was already far the worse for wear and undoubtedly, once asleep, would not awake before the noon of the following day. Nan glanced anew at John. He was alone again for Gloucester had left him now. He looked down at the goblet he held, swinging the contents slowly round and round. The moss green of his coat glowed bronze in the firelight.

Nan stood. Would ever there be another chance such as this, with Joan so befuddled she would not know the month of the year before long, and with Richard so many miles away. . . . She walked towards him. He saw her and turned his head, smiling. The noise of the room was eclipsed.

He took her hand, pressing it to his lips. She smiled, bowing her head in salute to his greeting, but he alone could hear her whisper. "Come to me tonight." Her eyes were bright as she raised her head.

His fingers tightened momentarily in surprise. "Your women. . . ."

"Can be dismissed." She smiled.

Later she lay in the huge, empty bed. The night lamp glowed softly in its bowl of oil, the light gentle and reassuring. She was alone in her apartments, having dismissed her women until the morning. The curtains were pulled back, and the golden embroidery shone and winked in the dimness, moved by a vague draught from the window. Outside the Christmas night was sharp, ice-filled, and she could hear the voices of the guards as they stamped their feet and rubbed their hands to keep warm.

Would he come? She bit her lip. No, it would be the utmost foolishness to do such a thing. The drapes across the doorway were pushed quietly aside as someone entered. She sat up, straining her eyes to see, and then he stepped into the light of the night lamp.

"You came." She stretched out her hand to him and he

clasped her fingers. He sat on the edge of the bed, feasting his eyes upon her. Her hair was her only cover as it streamed down over her shoulders. Her skin shone in the warm light.

"Jesu, you are beautiful," he whispered, pushing her hair back with his fingers. Then he leaned forward and cupped her face in his hands and kissed her lips gently. His hand traced the outline of her breast. "My brother does not deserve you, Nan, for he neglects you so. Were you mine I would not neglect you. . . ." He buried his face in her breasts and she held him close, tight and cherished. As she gave herself to his embrace she heard him say: "No cold London garden this. . . ."

The full moon shone brightly through the narrow window, falling obliquely across the bed, and Nan sat up to look at John as he slept at her side. How she loved this man, she put her hand against his warm hair, unable to resist the urge to touch him. Why had it been decreed that she should marry his brother? She knelt up and drew the curtains around the bed, enclosing them in an inky darkness. Lying back with her head against his shoulder, her drowsy eyes closed, and a weary, intoxicating sleep overtook her.

Suddenly there was a candle in the room, a candle which fluttered wildly as someone carried it to the bed. Nan gasped in horror as the curtain was stealthily pulled back and the candlelight shone brightly across her face. It was Alana who leaned in to see her, and Nan heard the shuddering gasp as her maid looked upon the face of John Neville.

Hurriedly Nan pulled her night robe about her body and climbed out of the bed, gesturing to the startled Alana to follow her. Once out of the bedchamber Nan faced the shaking woman. "Alana Burden, you have witnessed nothing this night, nothing! Do you understand?"

"But my Lady, should you be discovered the Earl will surely kill you! To take a lover is foolish enough, but to take. . . ." She gestured vaguely at the bedchamber where John slept on.

"Do I have your promise of silence?"

Alana smiled. "Of course, my Lady, I would never before God betray you. You were not to know that it has always been my practice to come back to see that you are sleeping soundly. You would have been wiser to include me in your secret, for then I could remain out here and turn away anyone who might come."

Nan walked to the drapes which hung across the doorway and pulled them gently aside to look at the bed. "I love him," she said simply.

The other woman nodded. "I suppose that it was inevitable that your heart would turn elsewhere. Your husband can charm everyone, man, woman and child alike, he is like some great magician, but with his own wife. . . ." She shrugged.

Nan swallowed, she did not like being reminded of Richard. "Alana, will you keep watch here for the remainder of this night?"

With a nod, Alana held back the curtains to allow Nan to pass through. Nan discarded her robe when she reached the bed, and climbed naked between the warm sheets. John moved slightly in his sleep, his arms reaching out to her and drawing her close. She curled up against him, her arms stealing across his chest. Soon she slept.

TWENTY-FIVE

NAN looked down at the letter and then back to the mud-stained messenger who had brought it. Eleanor's writing leapt out at her. It was three years now since Edward's accession, three years of the Earl of Warwick's political brilliance. She frowned and returned her glance to the letter:

"My dearest aunt, by the time this letter reaches your hand I shall have entered a convent. This news will come as a great shock to you, but I have no other course to take. My Lord the King has forsaken me, he wishes to ignore the past as if it never were, and to take another woman as his wife. He visited me but a few days ago and stayed only as long as was absolutely necessary as he had to return to London for an important meeting with the Council and with the Earl of Warwick in particular. The woman he has chosen is Lady Elizabeth Grey, that same lady we both met while in the service of Queen Margaret. She is a widow now, and from the descriptions I heard from his loving lips her beauty has not diminished with the passing years. She did as I and refused to bed with him, saying that she was not good enough to be his Queen but was certainly too good to become his mistress. Only once before has he met with such a refusal and on that occasion he married in order to obtain his desires; now he has taken the same step again but wishes to acclaim Elizabeth as his wife. She has no knowledge of Edward's previous contract with me, and he tells me that if I seek to make the fact known then he will of course deny everything. Stillington has been threatened should he be foolish enough to speak out. Even had I wished to harm my dearest Lord, I would have had no choice but to step out of public life, but I would never wish to seek revenge upon him whom I love so dearly. I know only that I am his rightful wife and that my son is trueborn. One thing I beg of you, my aunt, and that is that you honour the vow of silence you once made to me. Not one word of my secret must pass your lips. I would that the King and the Lady Elizabeth have a happy and fruitful marriage and that his plans are not foiled by me in any way whatsoever. For my sake and the sake of my child and the great love I bear you, keep your own counsel in this. I shall not name the convent I now go to, my whereabout shall not be known and neither shall I tell of my son's whereabouts. His life would be in danger were the truth known. Think on this and grant me my request, no matter how serious the matter may seem to you. Eleanor."

Elizabeth Grey! The daughter of Richard Woodville, Earl Rivers, who had been treated so ill by Richard at Calais. She looked for a last time at the letter. There was no trace of spite or reproach, no hint of the immense hurt and unhappiness which her niece must have felt . . . only the great love she bore this fickle King. Nan ripped up the letter into tiny pieces, knowing as she did so that she was tearing the body of Edward Plantagenet limb from limb. She walked to the window and tossed the fragments out into the wind and they were carried away like snow, scattering widely.

The mellow autumn sunshine soaked into the stone of Middleham, and high above the lapwings wheeled and dived in the blue skies. The moors blazed with purple beauty as the heather bloomed proudly upon the rolling slopes. She watched as a gay group on horseback approached the castle, recognizing the chief members as being her two daughters and young Gloucester. A little to one side rode the solitary figure of Clarence and even from this distance Nan could see the sullen expression on his face. He was fifteen years old now, almost a man, and his allegiance was firmly given to the Earl of Warwick. He moved endlessly in Richard's immense shadow, cleaving ever closer to Warwick and ever more estranged from the King. At least a part of the reason for this lay in Isabel, now thirteen, for Clarence was in love with his fair cousin, even though scarce a day passed without an argument between them. The group passed beneath the shadow of the walls and were lost from view.

Nan's heart was heavy as she turned back to the room, seeing that the messenger still stood there. "You may go to the kitchen and have some food to refresh you before you leave. Have you any knowledge of where Lady Butler now is?" He shook his head and she could tell that he was not concealing anything. She waved her hand and he hurried away.

She sat alone in her room, thinking of her beloved Eleanor, when suddenly the door opened and John was there. In spite of her sadness she smiled at him for she was still under his spell. She had not seen a great deal of him, even with Richard being away, for he was occupied with crushing the various Lancastrian uprisings which sprang up along the border. Twice he had led a small force against a large Lancastrian army and had succeeded in defeating the enemy. He had captured many of Margaret's noblemen including the great Somerset. But John had no reason to spare Beaufort's life, no brother to fear for; Somerset was executed. The King had shown his appreciation for the invaluable service of this second Neville, and now John was Earl of Northumberland, the title being taken away from the mighty House of Percy who supported Lancaster. The former owner of the title now languished in the Tower, hate-filled and awaiting the moment for revenge upon John.

His eyes moved swiftly about the room, but she was absolutely alone. He came close, crouching before her and taking her hands, pressing both palms to his lips. Her sadness almost fled as her fingers tightened about his, twining against the bright hard rings he wore. Then his lips were upon hers, warm and honey-sweet. She shivered, her eyes closing with pleasure, but then she opened them in surprise as she sensed that he was drawing back slowly. "What is it?"

"I came to tell you that Richard will be here within the hour, he has sent a herald ahead to inform us."

Her head spun with the cold news after such a heady embrace. She would not release him, gazing deep into his dark brown eyes. "Kiss me again, for it may be some time before. . . ." He bent his head near, his hand moving over the bodice of her gown and slipping behind the stiff brocade to caress her breast. She almost wept with delight, but now they could both hear the hurrying footsteps of Isabel and Anne as they came to tell their mother that Richard was coming.

John was standing behind her chair when the door opened and they came in.

The hall was ominously silent, the only sounds being the noises of people eating and the servants as they brought in fresh dishes. The minstrels were silent and there were no jugglers, tumblers, or jesters to entertain the gathering.

Nan fingered her meat, her appetite almost non-existent. She looked at Richard's dark, brooding face as he drained his goblet. Hardly a word had he spoken since his return hours earlier, and he had not even smiled a greeting to his wife. Word had soon spread, however, and it was known that Richard had returned because of the King's unfortunate marriage.

Down the table sat the King's brothers. They too seemed bereft of appetite as they glanced continually at the lowering storm which had seemingly seized Richard. Even Joan, John's wife, was quiet, the normally senseless, endless chatter having left her this night. Alone of the gathering John seemed unaffected, indeed Nan had a strange suspicion that he found the situation somehow amusing. His brown eyes met her gaze, and then she was sure that he was close to smiling openly.

Richard stood and if possible the silence became deafening. Even the hounds looked up from their dozing to stare at him. His long velvet coat of kingfisher blue glowed in the smoke filled light, and his golden collar flashed as he turned to his brother.

"My Lord, I have supped my fill, I bid you accompany me now to my chambers that we may talk."

John nodded and walked with him, and as they passed through

the doorway, the noise and chatter burst out in the hall, only to die away abruptly as Nan got to her feet. By her movement she reminded them that even if Warwick were absent, then his wife certainly was not. A sea of faces turned towards her, and then a bench scraped upon the stone floor. She turned her head and saw Dickon making his way towards her. He offered her his hand and she smiled gratefully at him. The King's youngest brother had presence; small he was, thin and somehow insignificant one would think, but now and again he was magnificently regal. Even the golden King himself could be diminished by this dark boy.

The silver pendant which hung from her waist chinked against the floor as she walked, her fine white veil floating behind her as she left the hall on his arm. Once again the babble broke out.

"I thank you," she murmured, curtseying slightly to her escort.

He smiled and his grey eyes were alight with warmth. "My Lady, if at any time I may be of service. . . ." His voice trailed away, then he took a deep breath and grasped her hand quickly. "Madam, please forgive my words now, but say them I must. I love and revere both yourself and the Earl of Warwick, but I am first and foremost the King's brother." Having said this he sighed with relief as if the words had been lying with leaden weight upon his conscience.

She smiled. "Of course you are, I would not expect otherwise."

His eyes swung to survey her face. "Maybe *you* would not, but as to the Earl. . . ." As if fearful of having spoken out of place he suddenly turned on his heel and hurried back into the noisy hall.

She watched him, a little sad that Richard's political ambitions and schemings should put Gloucester in such a difficult position as regards loyalty. From a nearby room she could hear a voice raised in anger and she knew that Richard and John were close by. She pushed open the door and inside she saw Richard angrily pacing up and down before the fireplace where a page struggled to kindle the fire as the autumn evening chill encroached. His fingers shook as he held the candle to the freshly laid fire, for to be close to Warwick's fury was a fearful thing for one so small. Richard stopped as she walked in, and then he frowned. "You would be better to remain away, Nan, my anger brings no pleasant atmosphere for a lady!"

138

"I have endured your anger before without scar!"

Unexpectedly he smiled. "True enough. Pray come and sit here, then, and listen to my woes." He led her to a chair where John leaned with one leg upon the arm. Her arm brushed against his thigh as she sat, but he did not move away.

"You have heard by now what has happened?" Richard was pacing again. There came the crackle of flames from the fire and the page stood, his face red with the effort of kindling the reluctant sparks. Bowing low he then scurried away, thankfully closing the door upon his master.

"I have heard that the King has married Lady Elizabeth Grey."

He poured himself a fresh draught of mead. "A Woodville! What manner of Queen is that for England! Perhaps I should begin a little earlier than the actual marriage. As you know the Dauphin Louis is now King in France, and Louis is a vastly different proposition to his predecessor who always hated England. Louis is greatly for an alliance with the English, a putting aside of past differences, and I must confess to a like desire. Meanwhile, in Burgundy our old ally the Duke grows old, and his son, the Count of Charolais, waits eagerly for the power to come to him. He is a supporter of the House of Lancaster, even going so far as to meet in a friendly manner with Margaret of Anjou herself! Louis can see that the situation in Burgundy will soon become critical, and he constantly courts my friendship, seeing in me a way of gaining the desired alliance with the English. Some time ago he intimated a wish for a marriage to be arranged between King Edward and a French princess. I put the proposition to the King and he gave no sign of disliking the idea of such a contract. Deeming this to be some manner of agreement to the proposal, I pursued the matter and time and time again brought the contract before Edward for his final agreement. Again and again he put me off, murmuring small excuses which should have told me that he wished the proposed French marriage in Hades! I continued my negotiations with France, only to discover that Edward is making friendly gestures towards Charolais in Burgundy! And this while I am dealing openly with the French! The situation became intolerable and so a meeting of the Council was arranged to clarify matters—who were we intending to ally ourselves with, France or Burgundy? The entire Council attended this meeting, for all were intent upon gaining Edward's

139

yea or nay in the matter of a marriage, be it with France or not. The whole land cries out that the King take a wife and give England an heir. Before long the matter is mentioned and Edward stands, leaning casually against the back of his chair and smiling—nay beaming—at the Council." Richard swung his arm in a gesture of incredulity at Edward's behaviour on so important a matter. "Then he states that he will have none but his own choice for a bride, and that his choice is Lady Elizabeth Grey! Well, as you may imagine, we thought him to be joking, but then something in his face warned me and I gained the measure of his mood. I was careful then not to reveal the anger I felt at his treatment of me in allowing me to continue the French negotiations when he had no intention or inclination for such a match. He treated me as if I were some lapmonkey! But where I remained suddenly silent, the others spoke up. The King could not marry this lady, they said, she was not of royal birth, she was a widow and already had two sons, she was much older than the King, and so on and so on. The smile faded from Edward's lips at the hindrances they heaped upon his choice, and then his tone was short and gruff. The matter was closed, he said, as he had already married the lady! England already had a Queen!"

Nan felt a surge of sympathy for Richard as she listened, for truly Edward had excelled himself in his bad behaviour. He had trifled with matters which were of vital importance, and he had made Warwick look a fool before Europe.

Now John spoke, leaning forward to place his goblet upon a table. "My brother, somewhere along this ragged trail you have forgotten that it is Edward who is crowned King and not the mighty Warwick!"

The ensuing silence tingled and Nan held her breath as she watched Richard's face. He stared at his brother who now appeared in a traitorous light. "What say you?"

John stood. "I said, Richard, that somewhere along this ragged trail your overweening arrogance has pushed aside the fact that it is not you who wear the crown! Nay listen, you are Warwick, you made Edward what he now is, but you must accept that at some point the moment *must* come when he strikes free of you. It seems to me that this is the moment he has chosen. For the past three years or more you have reigned over England and Edward has allowed the situation to continue. I do not say that I agree with what he has now done, his timing or his choice of bride, but *you* must see that he is no longer your catspaw, he is King!"

Richard almost snarled as he turned upon his brother. "Serpent! Are you my brother or are you not? It seems that Edward's gift of an Earldom has unhinged your mind! Has he only to dangle a gift before your nose for you to bray like a donkey and follow his lead?"

John walked slowly to the door. "The gift you speak of so disparagingly was a gift well earned . . . not an Earldom come upon by devious means! But as to your other words, yes, I am your brother and as such I feel I must say these things to you as no other rushes to perform the task!"

His hand was upon the door as Richard spoke again, this time in a quiet, controlled voice. "Which are you first then, John . . . the King's man or my brother?"

There was no answer as John hesitated, then the door closed quietly upon him. Richard turned to Nan. He was severely shaken and suddenly he ran his agitated fingers through his hair. "I no longer know who to trust, it seems that those I love the most are those I should mistrust the most."

She was beside him then, her fingers on his arm. "My sweet Lord, John is true to you, you must believe that."

His hand touched hers briefly. "An' if I believe you about my brother, what then of the King whom I loved and cherished? Does he think that I am some minor lordling whom he may rap over the knuckles whenever he pleases? I am not foolish enough to imagine that our new Queen has been chosen simply and solely because of her beauty. Edward may be of a sensuous nature, but he is not sensuous to the point of idiocy over a single woman! Nay, she was chosen because of her family, she has hordes of unmarried brothers and sisters, a voracious grasping brood which already gathers around the throne waiting for the honours to be given out. I have not trained Edward all these years without getting to know his thoughts a little. He now seeks to temper the power of the House of Neville by introducing the House of Woodville. The Nevilles are the most powerful family in the land."

"But why do that? Your family are the King's allies."

He smiled. "Sweet Nan, things are so clearly black and white to you are they not, you do not see the greyer hues in between.

141

What if there should be a rift between the King and the Nevilles? No other House can match us for power and strength. So Edward has to introduce another faction, and the Woodvilles are many and will owe their power simply and solely to the King's marriage with one of their number. They will remain true to him whatever happens, otherwise they will lose all. There is no-one so keen and adept at holding on to his wealth than one who has but newly come to such a state!" He glanced down at her and she knew from his expression that he was thinking of his own inheritance of the Beauchamp fortune and the power it brought to him.

"Nan, hearing John speak now makes me think perhaps that in my quest for power I have neglected those whom I should woo. I have sadly neglected you, my love, can you forgive me?"

He caught her unawares and she stared guiltily at him. He raised his eyebrows. "Jesu, it must be long since I last spoke gently to you, you are so taken aback! Perhaps I can tell you something which will make you happy. Plans are going ahead for Isabel's marriage to George of Clarence!"

"The King has agreed?"

"No, the King has not agreed, the King does not know . . . it is somewhat difficult to approach his most noble majesty now on such a subject. We have sent word to the Pope for dispensation as they are first cousins, but there will be no stumbling block there."

Nan's heart slowed. "I pray God then that Edward agrees to the match, for otherwise he will be antagonized still further by such negotiations going on without his knowledge!"

Richard was irritated again. "God's Blood woman, there can be few greater heiresses in England than the daughters of Richard Neville! Should Edward disagree then perhaps it is Warwick who will be antagonized!"

She stiffened and her chin rose defiantly at his resumption of his old tones. He scowled at her, angry at her for her words and angry at himself for forgetting so soon that he had wished to be gentle with her.

Neither would unbend and so they walked haughtily back to the hall together, in silence.

TWENTY-SIX

THE court was at Windsor, and the day now finishing in a blazing spring sunset had been full of festivities. The occasion had been the christening of the King's daughter, Princess Elizabeth of York. A daughter, not the yearned for son, but at least Edward's Queen had proved herself capable of bearing him a healthy child.

After the full day, the evening was quieter, and now Nan sat in the Queen's apartments watching as Elizabeth and her ladies learned the latest dances. Elizabeth's beauty had indeed not diminished with the passing years, although that certain coldness remained with her. Now she was garbed in the magnificent gowns and jewels of the Queen of England, and it was hard to imagine her as the young lady-in-waiting to Margaret of Anjou of all those years before. But gone now was the smiling friendliness of that Lady Grey, and in its place was a cool superiority, an ice-cold manner which had already dealt many a snub at the Countess of Warwick. Nan was not alone in being snubbed, however, for this Woodville Queen had made it her policy to treat all those of the old nobility, whether previously of higher rank to herself or not, with the same disdain and rudeness. Such was her fierce pride in her new power that she made many of them kneel while in her presence, and had even been known to cause her own mother to kneel for two hours because of some minor argument which had passed between them. This then was the woman whom Edward had chosen over the kind and gentle Eleanor Butler.

Nan bowed her head as she thought of Eleanor. She had heard nothing further from her niece, and the silence worried her. There was a commotion now from the entrance to Elizabeth's apartments, and Edward and his gentlemen entered. Nan looked at the young King who was resplendent in indigo satin and black hose, and her face revealed the resentment she felt on Eleanor's behalf. Oh faithless, heartless King, you have a wife and a fine son who bears your name, but you cast both aside for the sake of this calculating Woodville who already is hated throughout the land.

Edward greeted his wife who nodded coolly at her royal spouse. Nan was amazed at Elizabeth's manner, she carried herself as if she were of royal blood born and Edward were of a lower class! It was almost eighteen months since she had become his wife but already it was rumoured that he sought his pleasures elsewhere. Nan raised her eyebrow as the King danced with his Queen; Elizabeth did not seem to be of a warm enough temperament to hold one such as Edward Plantagenet who was essentially a sensuous man.

Nan glanced around the room which was now crowded with members of the court. Her sharp eyes picked out the many Woodvilles who stood amongst the nobles. The Queen's family was already begun upon its path to power by marrying into various great families, and this very day a whisper had been brought to Richard of one particular Woodville betrothal which very much affected the Nevilles. Since Richard himself had no son, then the heir to the House of Neville was John's son, George. Both Richard and John had been negotiating for the hand of the daughter of the Duke of Exeter for George, but now it had become known that Elizabeth had bribed Exeter to consider her brother Thomas Woodville for the girl instead. Elizabeth's meddling in such matters dealt a mighty blow at Richard's pride, and was yet another penny to heap upon the pile of discord.

Nan was proud of Richard, proud of the way in which he had seemingly risen above the swirling tide of Edward's plottings. He had this day stood as godfather to the new princess, and none could tell from his smiling face the angry heart which lay beneath. There was a smoothness about him, a lack of expression which was almost uncanny, and which the Beauchamp blood of his wife could well understand as it brought to her echoes of her dead father. She looked at him as he stood with John across the room from where she sat. Richard was thirty-eight now, but apart from a slight greying of the chestnut hair, he had not changed over the years. His body was still slender, there was no ugly thickening to mar his appearance. John was if anything thinner than he had been. His dark brown hair was still clear and rich in colour, but his fine face was unexpectedly lined.

Now John bowed his head, smiling, as the Duke of Clarence joined the two Nevilles. Nan glanced quickly at Edward and saw that the King's smile had faded into a glower. Edward did not like the close bond between Warwick and Clarence, nor did he like the love Clarence held for Isabel.

144

A small figure approached [her] and was bowing elegantly before her. Nan smiled at Dickon of Gloucester. He took a seat beside her, his grey eyes friendly. "My lady, I would tell you how glad I am that my Lord of Warwick and my brother the King have apparently put aside their disagreements today."

Nan raised her eyebrows and looked anew at Edward who scowled still at Clarence. "Indeed! I agree that it would be better if there were no discord."

The dark head nodded slowly, the long, nervous fingers plucking at the heavy gold embroidery of his sleeve. "It is to be hoped that the Queen forgets the slight which was thrust at her on the occasion of her coronation."

Nan shifted uncomfortably. Elizabeth had indeed been slighted, for Richard had conspicuously absented himself from her coronation, leaving John to represent the Nevilles. Elizabeth would find it virtually impossible to *forgive* such an insult, let alone forget it. " 'Twas no intentional insult, Your Grace, my Lord had most pressing business in Calais. But if the insult was meant, then you may be assured that the Queen's Grace has more than recouped by her treatment of myself!" Nan was in no mood to allow Elizabeth's ill manners to pass without comment.

Unexpectedly he smiled. "Your anger is well placed, and I will admit to you that I have no admiration for either my new sister-in-law or her vulgar family!" There was supreme distaste upon Dickon's delicate face as he spoke, and Nan was astounded that he choose to speak so openly of his feelings against the new Queen.

"It could be that you speak unwisely, Dickon, for I am of Warwick's faction and therefore no friend to the Queen."

His teeth gleamed white as he smiled wickedly. "There would be little point in telling a Woodville would there? I told you once before that although I love Warwick I am first and foremost the King's brother. This still holds true, but as God is my Witness, I find it hard to absorb these Woodvilles into that loyalty."

"You will remain loyal to him, Dickon, for that is your nature. Your brother is a handsome, brilliant prince, blessed by a fruitful marriage, and a realm which loves him. He is secure now in the knowledge that the person of King Henry is safely under lock and key in the Tower since his recent capture . . .

145

he needs only to lay hands upon Margaret of Anjou and her son to have complete satisfaction in his security. There can be few clouds upon his horizon."

"Save perhaps those surrounding Warwick. Nay, sweet lady, let us not pretend that the smiling face which your husband presents to the world is the true Richard Neville. He has been abominably treated, even I will admit that, but now is the time to put aside all differences . . . now, before the rift between the two widens irreparably. Tell me, why is it that Warwick will not take the hint which is so very obviously given by Edward that he has no wish to ally England with France? Time and time again I have heard my brother attempt to pass over any such talk, and time and time again I have heard Warwick insist upon dragging up the subject. Were I on the end of my brother's answers, I would long since have dropped all mention of France!"

Nan sighed, looking closely at the young Duke. "I will tell you then, Dickon, why it is that my husband will not let go. It is because he really and truly believes that England's future lies with a French alliance. He will not desist while he believes Edward will eventually come around to the same belief. That is Warwick, that is how he is."

The long fingers were still plucking at the embroidery, but now they stopped. "Then Warwick had best admit that his ambition is cast aside, for soon my brother intends to make a Burgundian alliance!"

Nan's hand flew to her throat. This above all things would alienate Richard. The Woodvilles he could rise above, the petty insults would roll off his strong back, but the forfeit of his French dream, the dream which grew and grew in his vision. . . . "When?"

"Soon, and the alliance will be finalized by the marriage of my sister to the Count of Charolais who has recently become a widower."

"Jesu, Jesu . . . when Richard discovers this!" Nan's green eyes flashed with rage and she turned on Dickon who flinched before her. "Why then does your brave brother not say openly that he wishes nothing to do with France. He hum's and ha's, smiling and prevaricating, and allows my husband to continue with the French talks. Has the King of England no notion of how he estranges Richard from his side?"

146

Dickon put his hand over hers. "My Lady, I think that Edward does not realize how deeply Warwick feels all these barbs and taunts. Edward intends them because he wishes Warwick to realize that the years of his supremacy are at an end, but he does *not* intend to force Warwick into a corner. What Edward may not realize, however, *I* do, and I have no wish to see an open confrontation between them. And so I come to you, my Lady, to ask you to broach the delicate subject of the Burgundian marriage with your lord."

"Never! I have no influence with Richard, and certainly have no wish to meddle in his politics. I am his wife, no more, no less. I will tell you something, Dickon, your royal brother's motives are not all so clear. He is also moved by not a little jealously over the way in which Clarence clings so close to the Nevilles. I have seen Edward's face when he looks at Clarence, and I know this to be true. He does not like it that George has chosen a Neville for his future bride."

She stood and he stood too, taking her hand. "Then he will be doubly displeased when he eventually realizes that his other brother has chosen a Neville as well!"

Nan turned sharply at this. "Anne?"

He nodded. "I have more than a cousinly fondness for your second daughter and would eventually make her my bride."

"Well, I cannot imagine that Warwick will object to such a contract, but as to Edward. . . ."

He smiled. "I will achieve my aim, my Lady, on that you may be sure. I have spoken to Anne herself and I know that she loves me as I love her. If I have to turn England upon its tail I will have her to wife. But there is time enough, the perfect moment must be picked. Edward can be manipulated if one picks one's time. I have much patience, it is one of my few virtues. My Lady. . . ." He still held her hand, restraining her. "I would have you tell Warwick that he has a friend in me, but not a friend who will take up arms against the King."

The evening was suddenly cold and Nan's voice a mere whisper. "You think this quarrel will ever come to such a pass?"

He sucked in air between his teeth, his face thoughtful. "I know not, I know not, but I pray that all will be smoothed over soon." His grey eyes were grave as he looked at her.

TWENTY-SEVEN

THE hoofbeats were dull and regular along the rough track as the party sped towards the north. The ladies urged their mounts to greater efforts but they had great difficulty in maintaining pace with the large coursers of the men.

Nan was weary, hot and uncomfortable, and she saw no real reason for this breakneck speed, save Richard's anger and frustration which forced him along in competition with the wind itself. Her own anger rose and suddenly she reined in, calling out to him.

His head turned sharply and he raised his hand and the party stopped. The dust swirled chaotically around them, obscuring vision for a moment. Richard's face loomed out of the cloud, his brows drawn together in a frown, as indeed they seemed always to be now. "Well, Madam?"

"My Lord, I fear you must continue the journey without the encumbrance of ladies to hold back your speed. If we continue at this rate we will break our necks. I pray you leave but a small escort for us and we will follow at a more leisurely pace!" Her green eyes were hard and she raised her head obstinately. Nearby she heard Joan's murmur of agreement.

He continued to scowl for a moment, but he recognized the stubborn expression on her face. His eyes swept over her, taking in her dusty cloak, the colour of which was now totally lost beneath a coating of England's earth. Her white veil was now grey and even her eyebrows were coated with the choking dust. Then he nodded, the hardness of his face softening and a glimmering of his great charm visible in his hazel eyes. "Forgive me, Nan, my anger ever did urge me to punishing extremes. We will rest a while here and then proceed, as you say, at a more leisurely pace!" He slipped lightly from his huge bay horse, moving around to hold up his hands to her.

She leaned down to him and he lifted her down to the dusty road. He gave the orders to rest to the others in the party, and soon there were sighs of relief as they all dismounted. Joan's voice was loud in its complaints, and Nan signalled to Alana that she should attend upon the Countess of Northumberland.

Nan turned back to Richard but he was gone. Her eyes searched the surrounding woodland and at last she saw him. The trees crept down the hillside through a thick carpet of bracken, and a small distance away she saw Richard leaning against the trunk of one of these trees, gazing down at the sparkling water of a brook. She followed him, pushing through the cool-smelling bracken with its strange scent which reminded her vaguely of her childhood.

He did not turn his head to look at her as she approached, and so she made no attempt to join him. Instead she sat down by the bank of the stream, listening with pleasure to the melodic tinkle of the water as it splashed over pebbles. She took a deep, long breath; she was weary, weary of the continual struggle for power and the continual plottings and counter-plottings which enveloped the affairs of Edward IV.

It was now more than two years since the birth of the Princess Elizabeth, and the Queen had but recently been brought to bed of yet another daughter, not the prayed-for son. The rift caused by Edward's marriage had widened, deepened, but the rift caused by Edward's behaviour regarding Warwick's French hopes was almost a complete severing. Relations between Richard and his King were strained because of Edward's opposition to the marriage of George and Isabel . . . opposition which had culminated in him calling both his brothers to task and forbidding them to entertain any ideas of marrying Warwick's daughters.

Edward had been a little worried by Richard's reaction to this, and had sought to placate the mighty Earl by agreeing to allow Warwick to visit France as the representative of the King of England. This alliance with France was still Richard's fervent desire, a desire which mounted with each exchange of letters between himself and Louis of France. Richard had a great admiration for the French King. He had gone across the Channel with Edward's smiles and handclasps to speed him on his way, but the sails of his ships had barely vanished over the horizon when a Burgundian embassy arrived in London. They came at Edward's invitation, a fact which he had taken great pains to conceal from Warwick. Richard's brother John had accepted the situation calmly, doing all that Edward asked of him, but the other Neville brother, George still Chancellor of England, had taken to his bed for the duration of the embassy's visit. George was afraid to have any contact with the Burgundians in case he should in any way cross his brother Warwick's policies and path. Edward's reaction had been simple and swift; he had taken the chancellorship from George Neville, saying that he had no place for a man he could not trust absolutely to do his bidding. Edward's choice as successor to George had proved somewhat illuminating to Nan; the new Chancellor was Robert Stillington, now Bishop of Bath and Wells. Ah, the faithful, ever-present Stillington! Then the old Duke of Burgundy had died, leaving Charolais, the pro-Lancastrian heir, to step into the seat of power. The Burgundian embassy had hurried away.

Richard had returned from France, bringing with him a French embassy. How Warwick rang with the tales of his magnificent reception in France, telling Edward how truly meant were Louis' gestures of friendship. Edward had reverted to his former sullen attitude regarding Richard's negotiations; he had snubbed the puzzled French embassy and left Richard to look after them while he returned to the Queen at Windsor. Once again Richard had been made to look more than foolish, and on top of this he soon discovered about his brother's deposal from the Chancellorship.

These then were the reasons why Richard, Earl of Warwick, was now riding northwards for his estates. His anger had frothed over, his enormous pride had forced him to retire from Edward's vicinity and lick his wounds in the relative privacy of Middleham.

A water rat plopped into the water, vanishing instantly from view, and Nan smiled. She pulled a nearby foxglove close, plucking one of the pink bells. She pushed her finger into its velvety depths, stroking the smooth surface. She leaned back, gazing at the soft green fronds of bracken which waved like lace above her head. From this little haven it seemed that such matters of state were a lifetime, nay a world away.

Soon another party would ride for Warwick's estates, and chief among them would be the Duke of Clarence who still adhered to Richard in spite of the King's efforts at breaking the relationship, and John, Earl of Northumberland. Richard was displeased with his brother for receiving the Burgundians, and it was inevitable that there would be a fiery encounter between the two Nevilles when at last the two were alone.

Nan's heart warmed as she thought of John. Her love for him had not lessened, and she respected his viewpoint regarding Richard and Edward. He still maintained that Richard should have been content to let Edward rule as he obviously intended to do. Alone of Salisbury's surviving sons, John of Northumberland was in no way hardened against his ungrateful monarch.

The sunlight was suddenly blotted out as Richard stood over her. The brilliant scarlet of his coat glowed in the July air as he stood there, his hands on his hips, looking down. "Do you seek to sleep, Madam?"

She sat up, and he took her hand and pulled her to her feet. She made to turn to go back to the horses, but he held her hand still. "Nan, forgive me that I do not think often of you, it is not that I have no affection for you." His fingers brushed the dust from her eyebrows, and his lips were warm and soft as he kissed her.

Guilt screamed within her, a terrible surge of self-disgust which submerged her. She gripped his arm, tears starting from her eyes. How could she have so betrayed him, how could she. . . .

His arms were around her and he laid his face against her forehead. He misunderstood the tears. "Nan, pardon my unforgivable neglect. My beloved Nan."

She dissolved into helpless weeping.

TWENTY-EIGHT

THE wind howled ferociously around the stone walls, encasing Middleham in a vortex of spinning air. For more than a day now the great gale had blown and already there had been much damage caused by the force of the storm.

Trees bent before the weight of nature's wrath, their leaves whirling like green snow, ripped and tattered, and the endless rain lashed the moorlands. Above the skies were leaden, dull and low; gone was the brightness of summer in this August hurricane.

In the solar Nan sat with her ladies, and their spirits were dampened by the weather, even the music they played was sad and slow. Nan was not thinking of the storm, her thoughts were of John. He had come to Middleham at last with the Duke of Clarence, and Nan had been in the courtyard with Richard to greet the new arrivals.

How calm had been her heart, how very, very calm. She had looked upon her husband's brother at last without passion as he rode into the confines of the castle. There had been nothing, absolutely nothing left of her former love and desire as he dismounted and came to speak to his host and hostess. His lips had been warm against her hand as he kissed it, but her stomach had not tightened, her pulse not quickened. Was this how it was then, that a chance remark by Richard could change her entire outlook, could bring the truth to face her? Forgive me, he had said, forgive me my neglect. They were small words, he had said them before, but this time . . . this time. . . . She sighed. What a fool she had been, what a vain, selfish fool. She had given herself to Richard's brother only because her pride had been hurt when the Warwick ambition had supplanted her. She had not loved John, she had loved the image of Richard she saw in him.

She stood, an anxious worry churning in her stomach as she thought of the danger she had courted, the risk she had flirted with in order to indulge her passion for John of Northumberland. She looked out of the window at the bowed trees along the brow of a distant hill. Thick, murky clouds scudded across the horizon, and the damp air was cold.

A small door was open slightly and Nan could see a solitary figure seated in the adjoining room. She walked to the door, pushing it open more. Her daughter Anne was alone, her head bowed, her face hidden by the curtain of golden hair which hung down past her waist. Since Clarence's arrival Anne's quiet unhappiness had been obvious, but now the weather seem to have nourished the low frame of mind of Warwick's younger daughter. Nan closed the door behind her and went to Anne, putting her hand on the warm shoulder.

Anne started, her head turning with surprise, and Nan saw the tears which lay wetly on the soft cheeks. "Anne, why do you weep?" Nan sat with her, putting her arms around the trembling shoulders.

The girl shook her head, swallowing to hold back the tears, but her mother's kindness only drew more and soon she wept loudly. Nan held her close, laying her cheek against the shining hair. "Is it Dickon of Gloucester who causes your sorrow?" Anne nodded, hiding her face away from her mother.

It was inevitable, thought Nan, that Gloucester's actions in staying with Edward in London should be misconstrued by Anne. If Clarence could come to Isabel, why then could not Gloucester come to Anne? "Listen my sweeting, do not judge Dickon by the same rule as Clarence. He is no less constant or loving because he chooses to support the King. He once told me that he meant to have you as his wife, no matter what, and that he would choose his moment carefully before putting his choice before King Edward. Believe me, and have faith in your love. Dickon of Gloucester is canny, as they say the Scots are!" She smiled, squeezing Anne's shoulders.

Her reward was a bright smile from the red-rimmed eyes and shaking lips. Anne dried her tears, sniffing noisily, but her spirits were lifted visibly. Nan was relieved, for Anne's misery had lain heavily upon her mother.

There was a discreet cough from the doorway. Alana stood there, and immediately Nan stood and went to her.

"My Lady, the Earl of Northumberland has sent a message that he wishes to see you. If you will follow me. . . ."

Nan's lips parted in dismay. Since John had come to Middleham she had not seen him except when in company with others, and now, quite obviously, he had an opportunity for them to be alone together. Not to go now would only postpone a meeting which must take place eventually.

Alana led her through the maze of passages which formed the main building of the castle, up and up until at last they came out into the early evening air upon the battlements. The storm swallowed the pale sunlight and the summer eve was like twilight. Already torches were lit, the flames burned irregularly in the strong wind, sometimes almost extinguished, sometimes shining brightly in a momentary calm. Leaves flew through the stream of air, as if autumn were arrived already, but the leaves were green and fresh. . . . Shattered twigs drifted along the stone walk, rustling and cracking loudly as their slippers trod upon them. Where the sun should have been there was an oyster-coloured stain in the heavens, and once again raindrops splattered upon the damp earth.

Nan shivered as the moist atmosphere struck her. She

noticed that there were no sentries pacing their steady way along this stretch of the walls, and was surprised. Alana halted suddenly, her finger to her lips. They were by a small doorway, reached by descending some steep steps. Alana nodded todwards the door. "He awaits you in there."

With a reluctance which was evident even to the unknowing gaze of Alana, Nan descended to the door, knocking gently upon the ancient, black wood. The door swung open violently in the sucking gale and a pile of broken twigs scurried frantically around in the space at the foot of the steps.

A single candle burned in the tiny room, and by its spiralling light Nan could see John waiting for her. He was alone. She shut the door behind her and faced him.

The closing of the door shut out the shriek of the storm, and the silence which plunged over the room was loud. The wax of the candle dripped on to the table and the sound could be heard. John was still, he made no move towards her. The moments trailed by, and she saw his fingers begin to play with the dagger at his waist. He was uneasy. At last he spoke. "It is finished is it not?" The dark brown eyes were piercing as they stared at her.

She lowered her eyes, unable to meet him. She nodded. Once again the stillness of the room pressed in on her.

"Why?"

Her hand moved helplessly. "I . . . realized. . . ."

". . . That it was Richard all the time?"

"I suppose so. I am sorry, John, sorry if I hurt you now." Jesu, how could she be so dispassionate with this man who had known her body, had shared her soul for so many years! The reversal of her emotions struck anew, surprised her anew.

"Nan. . . ."

"There is nothing, John, nothing. Please."

"After all we have known, is this to be how it ends? I cannot believe that I see standing before me the woman I have loved and cherished to my heart for most of my life. Nan, tell me that you tease me, I beg of you that you tell me that!" He leaned forward on the table, and the candleflame hissed in the sea of molten wax.

" 'Tis no teasing."

He closed his eyes as if she had struck his face, but she felt no urge to rush and comfort him, caress the thin, lined face she had once dreamed of with each moment. Nothing; a void. A mouse scuttled across the floor, disappearing into the inky shadows in the corner. She heard it squeak.

John was staring at her now, and she could see the huge hurt she had inflicted on him. "Mayhap it is just as well, then, Nan, for tomorrow I leave to patrol the Scottish border, but afterwards I do not return here. I am bound for London, for the King. You may think me a treacherous brother, leaving Richard when his need for me is greatest, but I can no longer ride two mounts. My conscience, my whole heart, bids me be loyal to the King. There is soon to be great strife in the kingdom and I do not stand at Richard's side." He paused. "I am about to wrong Richard bitterly by allying myself with Edward, it is more honourable not to wrong him by my love for you as well."

"He will feel your defection keenly, John. It will be as a dagger thrust in the back."

"The moment will pass soon enough, Richard is like a cork upon water, he will always rise above adversity. Besides, he has two great Georges to support him, Clarence and Neville, they will more than make up for my loss."

She shook her head. "It is you he leans on, John, only you. Will you take up arms against him?" She could not believe that John would indeed fight against Richard.

He breathed deeply. "I know only that I cannot take up arms against Edward, as to the other. . . . I pray God the dilemma will not present itself."

"It must, John, you know it must! Richard and the King veer ever further from one another, and there is not room in England for two such men."

"Nan, Richard is in secret correspondence with Louis in France, still determining on the French alliance, even while the King prepares his sister to become Burgundy's bride! Through Louis, Richard is suspected of being in contact with none other than Margaret of Anjou herself! Nay, nay, I will finish now that I have begun!" He held up his hand to silence her. "I am not blind, and neither is Edward. Richard makes it plain that he intends to be powerful in England, if not under Edward, then under another. . . . What Warwick has made, Warwick will unmake! Clarence hopes and dreams that the Kingmaker

155

will turn his genius to put him on the throne, and so Clarence cleaves ever closer to Richard."

She laughed, the sound forced jerkily from her lips. "Clarence as King! You jest, Richard would never seek to place George Plantagenet on the throne!"

He did not smile. "I said only that that was Clarence's hope! It is my belief that Richard has another in mind. Why do you think your daughter Anne remains without a betrothed? Isabel is destined for Clarence, there can be no doubt, but Anne remains uncontracted. Richard holds out no hopes for Gloucester's suit, I doubt if he would accept Gloucester now anyway! Nan, think now. Richard is in contact with Margaret of Anjou. If he can restore Lancaster to the throne, who would be the greatest and most eligible man in England then?"

She turned away, her skirts rushing over the dusty floor. "I will listen to no more of this. . . ."

He strode around the table and held her arm tightly. "Answer me, Nan! You will not because the awful truth of what I say stares you in the face! Richard would like Edward of Lancaster for Anne, make no mistake! 'Twill be a bitter pill for Clarence to swallow when the time comes, for I doubt not that that young man sees the crown swerving ever closer. He hopes that the King's unpopular marriage and the sudden prevalence of Woodvilles in every corner will eventually cause Edward's downfall, leaving the path clear."

"Let me go!" Nan's thoughts reeled and she struggled feebly. His words had an ominous ring of truth about them, she knew Richard only too well after all this time.

John forced home his advantage. "Admit, Nan, that Richard paves his way to greatness cleverly. With his two daughters he will have two opportunities of putting his blood upon the throne of England."

She looked up into his face. "I do not know you, John Neville, you are a stranger to me."

Still he held her. "Nan, contemplate what I say. This very day our Neville kinsman Sir John Conyers rode into Middleham with a mighty following of horsemen. Conyers is as sly a dog as ever breathed, his reputation is less than savoury, and yet he comes here at Richard's invitation and is now closeted with Richard in his private rooms. All this afternoon they have been together, with strict orders that they are not to be disturbed, and I am expressly forbidden entry. There is some devilment afoot and Richard chooses Conyers as his tool."

His fingers were hurting her and she twisted her wrist, trying to strike free of him. Abruptly he released her. "I meant only to put the truth before you, I did not mean to hurt you. Believe me." He touched her cold cheek with his hand.

Her back was straight and her chin raised. "John, if you seek to turn me from Richard by all this then you are doomed to fail. I know what Richard is, what he was always. What I did not know was that through all I loved him and only him. I accept him as he is, John, no matter what he might do."

He turned and extinguished the slow candleflame and the heavy odour of wax filled the still air. The darkness was absolute. His voice came out of the blackness. "Even if he gives your daughter to Somerset's bastard?"

Her hand was on the door as Anne's tear-stained face flashed before her eyes. "I do not believe all that you say, John."

"Your new-found love has clouded your eyes, Nan."

She pulled the door open and the storm rushed eagerly in, whisking away the stillness which had become almost cloying. Raindrops brushed her face as she stepped out, her skirts dragging wetly through the puddles which lay deep across her path.

TWENTY-NINE

BY the following year the summer months were marked by the chasm which yawned between King and Kingmaker, and Richard sealed the separation with an act of treason. To his haven of Calais he went, taking with him his wife and daughters, his brother George Neville . . . and the King of England's brother, the Duke of Clarence. There in the month of July 1469, Isabel Neville became the eighteen year old bride of Clarence. George Neville performed the ceremony with a dispensation received from the Pope; but it was treason as Edward Plantagenet had not consented to the contract.

While the Earl of Warwick was in Calais, the north of England was suddenly astir with rumour and upset as a great army flurried about under the banners of one Robin of Redesdale. Here at last was Sir John Conyers, acting under Richard's commands, and taking the false name of Redesdale. His sole purpose was to lure Edward away from the safety of London and into Neville country. How very nearly the plan faltered when John Neville swooped upon Redesdale's army and almost routed them; this was John's first open rebellion against his brother and how potent it was. Only Redesdale's immense strength and numbers saved Warwick's plan; they lost John's pursuing force and gathered together again, surging south towards London.

Edward was forced at last into action, and at the head of a royal army he left London and rode northwards to meet with the rebels. During the ensuing struggle the King's force was overcome, and Edward was taken prisoner.

Warwick returned to Middleham and was there when his royal prisoner was brought north.

Nan watched from her window as Edward was led into the courtyard, his horse's bridle held by one of his own brother's retainers. The Black Bull of Clarence fluttered proudly above Edward's golden head, and Nan could see the triumphant smile on her new son-in-law's handsome face as he looked at his vanquished King. Clarence saw the crown only just beyond his outstretched fingertips now, soon . . . soon. . . .

The first party were followed into Middleham by Conyers and some of his men, and Nan saw Richard personally welcome his kinsman. The King dismounted, smiling amiably at all he met, and nothing in his bearing as he sauntered into the castle could denote the fact that he was a prisoner.

Alana touched her mistress' shoulder. "My Lady, there is one of Sir John Conyers' men outside. He wishes to speak personally with you."

Nan raised her eyebrow. Speak with her? "What does he want?"

"I know not, but there is something familiar about him, my

158

Lady, I feel that I should know him and yet cannot put a name to the face."

"Bring him before me then."

A thin man of dirty, unkempt appearance shuffled into the room, and Nan swiftly raised her spice-filled pomander to her nose. He smelled most foul. "You wished to speak with me, Sirrah?"

"My Lady, my face has changed pitiably, but I am known to you. I was in the past the one who brought letters to you from the Lady Eleanor Butler."

"Of course, now I know you. What is it you wish to tell me, have you a message from my niece?"

He licked his lips, his eyes not meeting hers. "My Lady, the Lady Eleanor has been dead for over a year now."

She gasped, her hand flying to her throat, then anger took her. "And you wait until now to inform me?"

He licked his lips again, and his hands began to twitch with fear. "I set out immediately to tell you, but my horse threw me and severely injured my back." For the first time Nan noticed the unusual stance he affected; crooked where once he had been straight. He stepped nearer, his hand outstretched, for he was sore afraid that she would have him punished for not acquainting her with the news. "My gracious Lady, the message I had could not be entrusted to another, as God is my Witness this is true, and so I had to wait until I could tell you myself. I have had no opportunity as you have only recently returned to England from Calais."

She surveyed him, grateful to the perfumed spices of the pomander. Jesu, but he stank! "Very well, tell me what my niece wished me to know."

"She was taken ill and died within two weeks of first falling low with a wasting sickness. She sent for me when she knew that she could not live and bade me come to you and remind you most earnestly of your vow. She was very ill, but even so she clutched my arm with the strength of a man, and she lifted herself from the bed where she lay and forced me to promise that I would tell you and you alone of what she asked. You must never tell the secret which was hers, my Lady, for the sake of her son's life."

Weakly Nan waved her hand at him. "Alana, reward him for his troubles." She turned away unhappily as Alana took

159

her purse and gave it into the grubby hands. The shuffling footsteps were heard again and then the door closed upon him.

Nan leaned her hot forehead against the cold stone wall, her fingers touching the rich colours of a tapestry which hung close to her. The mustiness of the hanging came to her nostrils. Eleanor, her sweetest Eleanor, dead. . . . Edward's sauntering walk and smiling face crossed her mind. Eleanor dead, unhappy, unacknowledged, alone and the man who caused her such pain was here, under the same roof! Suddenly she turned to the door and hurried out, her angry steps taking her swiftly in the direction of Edward's apartments.

The guards at the entrance, some of Clarence, some of Warwick, stood aside for her to pass, and a page hastily announced her to Edward who lay idly upon a couch. He leaned gracefully on one elbow, surveying her, and waving all his attendants away. Prisoner he was, but Richard had no wish to overstep any mark as yet with this ingrate named King. Edward's voice was lazy, a drawl. "Well, my Lady of Warwick, you wish to speak with me? Perhaps you come to welcome me to your hospitality?"

Her fingers clenched as she stared down at him, at the long muscular body and broad shoulders. In his fine clothes and with every movement he was royal. "I have some news which might be of interest to you, Your Grace."

"Indeed? Pray unburden yourself then, for you look as if you would joyfully thrust a dagger between my ribs."

"Aye, joyfully indeed, and my emotion has no bearing whatsoever on the quarrels between yourself and my husband."

His eyes narrowed and at last he stood. Now he towered over her. He put his hands on his slender hips. "What then?"

How she wished to strike that smile from his curving lips. "Lady Eleanor Butler is dead."

He started, his eyes widening briefly and then resuming their former mocking. "You have my sympathies upon the sad passing of your niece."

"I had thought your wife to be worthy of greater sorrow than that, Your Grace!" She almost spat the last two words.

"And what is that meant to communicate to me?" His voice was dangerously quiet.

"Exactly that which is obvious. I know that your present marriage is invalid because you were pre-contracted to my niece." She paid no heed to the danger which now raised its head around her, she thought only of forcing this uncaring man to acknowledge to her that Eleanor had been his true wife.

"And who, pray, furnished you with such a wondrous tale?" He turned slowly and picked up a grape from the table.

"I have not lent my ear to mere gossip and scandal-mongering. Your Grace, the tale I have from the lips of Eleanor herself."

The juice of the grape oozed between his firm lips and he put his kerchief to his mouth elegantly. "If you believe the story why have you not informed the world before . . . or more to the point why have you not informed Warwick, for I know *he* is not aware of such a rumour else he would have made good use of it."

"I have said nothing because I vowed upon the Bible that I would not. It is a vow which Eleanor reminded me of upon her deathbed."

"Ah! A vow!" He grinned, his relief apparent.

Her anger was revitalized. "Aye, a vow which saves you considerable embarrassment. Think what a tool this could be in the hands of your enemies . . . in the hands of your brother Clarence who would have your throne for himself! Oh dearly would he like to have such a mighty weapon with which to strike you down."

He whipped around. "I gave you no leave to slander my brother's name!"

"He slanders it himself! He gladly flew his banners above your captive head did he not? Such is not the action of a loving, faithful sibling!" Her fingernails bit into the palms of her hands, drawing tiny specks of blood.

He allowed the moment to cool before speaking again. "My Lady, there was no marriage contract . . . oh Eleanor thought the ceremony to be valid, but it was no true priest who said the words but my friend Hastings. . . ."

"Hastings indeed! That was not the name Eleanor put to me. Stillington, she said, *Stillington*!"

Now he pursed his lips and gazed steadfastly at his red-shoed feet. He took a deep breath. "I say again that it was no true ceremony, I was free to contract myself to my present Queen." His blue eyes were fixed on her again.

"And I say you lie . . . Your Grace!"

His breath hissed fiercely as he sought to control his own mounting anger. "Then, my Lady of Warwick, we must agree to differ!"

Nan threw caution to the winds, she sprang ardently to Eleanor's defence. "You have a son, his name is Edward of Wigmore, he is legitimate. The woman you call your Queen is now pregnant with your third bastard! Acknowledge the truth!"

He whitened a little. "You step beyond the limit which I am prepared to allow, Madam. I pray you cease now before matters pass further. Queen Elizabeth expects another child, it is true, but she bears me no bastard!"

He was very regal, very awesome, and she quelled a little. "Maybe not, if you have re-married Elizabeth during the past year." His tongue passed very slowly over his lips, and Nan knew that he had not legalized his alliance with the Woodville Queen. Elizabeth had no idea that her marriage was hollow, and Edward did not dare tell her, he was afraid to! A smile almost forced itself to Nan's curling lips as she looked up at the pride of the Plantagenets.

She turned to go, but he called her suddenly. "My Lady, do you intend to continue honouring your vow to your niece?" There was a concealed anxiousness about him.

"I will honour the vow." She was proud then, her Beauchamp breeding evident in every fibre.

"You speak as though you honoured every vow you made, my proud Lady!" He was smiling, gone was the anxiousness of a moment before.

She turned, uncertain of him now. "What do you mean?"

"I mean that you have not honoured one vow in particular —your marriage vow!" Once again his beringed fingers plucked a grape from the bunch which lay on the table.

The blood pounded in her ears as she stared at him. "I do not know. . . ."

"Oh come now, surely you do not forget your lengthy dalliance with Northumberland.

Her fingers gripped at a chair, tearing the fine stitching which adorned it. "How did you come by this knowledge?"

His fingers caressed a round, blue grape which nestled in the palm of his hand, and then he tossed it into the air and deftly caught it in his mouth. "Like yourself I do not lend my ear to mere gossip and scandal-mongering, and like yourself I came by the tale from the lips of the one most concerned in it."

She gasped aloud. "From John?" She could not believe it, John would not be so foolish.

"Aye, although I have every reason to believe that he is completely unaware of his confession. I am, as you will know, renowned for my idle ways, my boon companions, my mistresses, and so on. Well, Northumberland is a close friend of mine, but not one who follows my lower pleasures. He is a somewhat staid mortal, and my surprise was great when one day last autumn he elected to join me in a veritable orgy of drinking and wenching. His capacity for ale astounded me, but it loosened his normally guarded tongue. I found myself listening to the tale of his love for you, the Countess of Warwick, his beloved Nan . . . his brother's adulterous wife!" She closed her eyes faintly, but then felt his fingers gripping her chin firmly. She blinked and looked up at him. "Madam," he whispered, "we are both concerned now with a deep secret of the other. For no other reason than that I like Northumberland and enjoy his considerable support against Warwick, I will remain silent upon your indiscretions. If at any time John Neville should waver from my side and go back to your husband, then beware, for your secret is no longer safe. I will drive a wedge between the Nevilles, a wedge which nothing could overcome. Warwick would never forgive such a mighty blow to his all-consuming pride."

She grabbed at his hand, pushing it away and standing. "Then you shall know a like uncertainty, Your Grace. I will cast aside my vow if you betray me."

He nodded. "I have no doubt of that, Madam, no doubt at all. I see that we understand one another to perfection! We live upon a sword edge, do we not." He straightened and walked to the window, leaning forward on his elbow to peer out.

"Ah, the Black Bull of Clarence! See how my brother struts across the courtyard like a peacock! His hopes are vain, for Warwick will not put him upon the throne! The country will not put me aside for my brother. Mark my words, Nan Beauchamp, your mighty husband will not be able to carry this rebellion through." His teeth gleamed as he turned to look back into the room.

He laughed aloud as he saw the train of her brown velvet skirts disappearing through the doorway.

THIRTY

THE watch called the hour of midnight, and outside the guards changed, their voices clear in the autumn air. Nan turned in the warm bed, her hand stretching out to touch Richard . . . but he was not there.

She sat up, pushing her tousled hair back from her eyes. The curtains around the bed were drawn tight to exclude the draughts, but on Richard's side they were pulled back. She climbed over the bed and peeped out, shivering as the cooler air touched her.

Richard was slumped in an upright chair by the dying embers of the fire, in his hand a goblet of wine. He twisted the goblet by its thick stem, his eyes watching the swirling liquid. He sighed, leaning back, his hair aglow with the firelight, and the grey was merged into the rich chestnut of his youth.

It was over a month now since the King had fallen into his hands, a month during which the Warwick star should have been ascendant, but somehow . . . somehow. . . . He turned his head as Nan slipped from the bed, her white night robe shining in the dim light. She knelt at his feet, leaning her head against his knee and she felt his hand on the nape of her neck stroking her hair.

"Something is wrong?" She looked up at his tired face.

He drank from the goblet. "Aye, but I know not what! There is the rub! I have Edward in my hands, I have routed the accursed Woodvilles, and Edward smilingly does my bidding. Everything should be complete, and yet there is nothing to grasp in my hand. The country lies dormant, waiting, not rising for me or against me! The power is mine again, I have the King putting his seal to every proclamation I place before

164

him, but. . . ." He grimaced and jerked the empty goblet towards the embers. Droplets of wine splattered on the red hot logs, hissing and spitting.

She ran her fingers along his thigh. "That is what you wished, is it not. You have made it clear to Edward that he cannot cast you aside, that he is powerless without you. What else can there be for you?"

He smiled, the lines creasing on his face. "Sweet Nan. If this exercise has proved one thing to me, it is that where Edward is powerless without me, *I* am also powerless without him! That is the unpalatable pill! Edward obliges my every order, but some time I must release him, and he knows it. When that time comes he is not about to be so amenable! That much I know of Edward Plantagenet! If only the country had risen to support me, then I would have him where I wanted him! But this accursed lethargy which clutches England cannot be coped with. Edward knows my power is hollow, he knows that his supporters merely await his word . . . and there is nothing I can do to prevent my bloodless defeat."

Nan thought then of Edward's smiling demeanour. Of course he had realized very soon that this was to be Richard's fate.

Richard stretched over to a small table and poured another cup of wine. Slowly he drank, his shrewd eyes fixed upon the lazy blue flame above a large, half-burned log. "If I cannot rule England through Edward, then I must rule through another . . . or go under the waves of my own defeat and humiliation."

She sat up, turning her head to look at him. "You would murder Edward?"

He breathed in deeply, holding his breath then for a long while. Suddenly he stood, exhaling loudly. The movement of his loose robe caused a draught and the fire crackled and flared, smoking, eddying. "I do not wish to commit such a. . . . Nan!" He turned back to her, his shadow looming giant-like on the panelling behind him. "Do you think the realm would accept Clarence?"

She shook her head. "No, I do not. Such a course would need your every energy, your every waking moment to push it forward. Clarence is no King!"

He nodded, continuing his pacing. "Well, Edward had some irritating news today from London; his Queen is delivered of yet another daughter! Three pregnancies, three daughters! This means that Clarence is still heir to the throne. It *could* be done Nan, after all were Edward to fall and break his neck tomorrow then Clarence must legally have the throne."

She stood, holding her suddenly cold hands towards the warmth of the fire. "Do not entertain such ideas, Richard, for it would be a merciless and bloody murder, one which would sin against God!" She reached out for his hand as he paced, catching it and holding it to her cheek. "Richard, my dearest love, my Lord, put aside such a plan."

He came close, slipping his arms around her and holding her against his body. "I love you, Nan, and I fear that you have never truly realized how much I do so, but in this I cannot take your counsel. Edward takes England along the wrong path, I *know* it! We should draw close to France, not Burgundy! For England's sake as much as my own I must try to depose Edward and put Clarence in his stead. Clarence is malleable, my son-in-law, my ardent follower in all things. He would make a King whom I could bend, coax towards the right goals. . . ."

She buried her face in the soft hairs of his bare chest. He pushed her back against the oak panels which cloaked the wall, leaning heavily against her as he put his lips to her throat. As the shivers of delight moved over her, Nan thought fleetingly that he had not mentioned any leanings towards Lancaster, but then such thoughts vanished in the pleasure of his love.

"I tell you, my cousin of Warwick, were I to ride for London now there is little you could do to prevent me!" The King's white teeth flashed as he grinned at Richard's dark face.

Nan stared at the winding road before her, holding herself apart from the polite but deadly banter of Edward as he baited his captor. It was only a few weeks since Richard had told her of his plan to put Clarence on the throne, but already Edward's position had strengthened. Richard was now moving from Middleham to Pontefract, a move which had been planned for some weeks.

She smiled at Isabel who rode at her side. Isabel was without her husband who now sought to keep well away from his captive brother, but Isabel's beautiful face was bright and happy. She was with child, and she prayed fervently that she would present George with a son. The news of her pregnancy had not brought a smile to the face of Edward.

The autumn leaves swung down through the air, floating daintily to the thick carpet of bronze, gold and scarlet which lay along their path. Crisp and curling, they muffled the passing of the King's cavalcade. Harness jingled gaily, and the smell of warm horseflesh pricked their nostrils, and all the while there was Edward's light humming.

Nan watched the King's face carefully, for she felt sure there was something afoot, something which did not bode well for the Earl of Warwick. Sure enough, Edward's eyes flickered continually towards the approaching hills rising above the thickness of the forest. Her discomfort and apprehension rose in ever increasing waves. She turned to look at Richard, but his eyes too were upon the distant hills. There was no fear on his face, just an awareness that somehow he was riding towards danger; it was a measure of him that he did not turn back for Middleham.

The trees were scattered now, the leaves only in patches along the roadway. Suddenly the hilltop before them was alive with horsemen, bright and glittering in their armour, colourful with their banners alight in the sunshine. Silently they waited there, motionless. Nan's heart pounded and a scream of fear rose in her dry throat, but no sound would come from her stiff lips. Her eyes scanned the banners; all were those of the King's supporters. From Edward's low laugh of triumph she knew that this was a pre-arranged tryst between him and his adherents.

Another laugh rang out, but this time it was Richard's. "Your Grace, you have bettered me perhaps, but you have tasted the power of my name in the realm!"

Edward's face was for once serious. "Aye, and you have tasted the hollowness of that power!" His tone was hard.

The horses had not faltered in their cantering pace and now they rode into the heart of the great silent horde which straddled the hilltop. Then Edward reined in, smiling at two faces he loved dearly; Dickon of Gloucester . . . and John of Northumberland. John had once again put himself firmly upon Edward's side, and now Richard looked coldly at his brother.

"I greet you, brother John!" The words were spoken quietly, slowly, and he looked steadily at the white, tense face.

167

Not once did John speak, he looked unhappily at his brother, but he did not answer him. Richard laughed as if the moment were vastly amusing, and he flicked a fly from his horse's neck with the reins. "Fear not, sweet brother, I do not reproach you fully . . . a little, aye maybe, but fully, no!"

Now John flushed, pricked into reaction by this humiliation before a such an audience. "Your reproach, whether full or no, would not lie so heavily upon me, Richard, for it is you who err and not I!"

Richard raised his eyebrows and shrugged a little, as if John's words meant little or nothing to him. Only Nan knew how much they were hurting one another with their harsh words.

Edward manœuvred his mount between the two, speaking to John, but smiling coolly at Richard. "Well, Northumberland, your faithfulness to me has not gone unrewarded. The matter we spoke of some months ago shall be attended to forthwith. My daughter Elizabeth shall be the bride of your son, and your son shall have the Dukedom of Bedford to mark the occasion!"

Nan dared not look at Richard to see how he took this. She heard the squeak and crunch of leather as he moved in the saddle, then he spoke. "What is your will with me now? You have me vastly at a disadvantage!" How defenceless he looked when she opened her eyes. All around the men bristled with armour and weapons, but Richard was unarmed and splendid in his scarlet coat and black velvet cap. His golden collar shone, flashing as his mount shifted and stirred beneath him.

A great hush fell upon the gathering and her fingers tightened around the reins, her knuckles white and taut. She leaned forward, willing John to look at her. Do not kill him, do not kill him, she pleaded silently. The brown eyes swung at last to face her, and she saw briefly a sad yearning in them; he smiled faintly, shaking his head. She relaxed, knowing that Richard was not to die. Her hands were shaking, the reins damp and sliding stickily against her palms.

"The disadvantage is of your own making!" Edward snapped, his blue eyes hard.

Richard smiled, removing his cap and running his fingers through his thick hair. The wind caught at the hair, twisting and blowing. "True, I can make no excuses. I believe that I was right, and still am right."

168

The smile seemed to touch upon something dormant in Edward's heart. "You are free to go, Cousin!" he said curtly, turning away from the charm of that smile.

Richard inclined his head just once and then replaced the cap and pulled his horse's head round. Nan looked once more at the sea of cold, unfriendly faces and heard the murmurs of anger which rose from some hearts. Warwick should not go free, he should be disposed of now, *now, now*. . . . She did not know how long she surveyed them, but at last some of those stern faces turned away from her gaze, unable to meet her.

Dickon dismounted and caught at her bridle before she turned to go. "Think of me kindly, fair Countess, and speak of me warmly to the Lady Anne."

She hesitated and then smiled, leaning down that no-one could hear her reply. "Such sentiments would be better spoken in person to her, Dickon, she grieves much for your company."

The grey eyes were sad. "I cannot speak my love in person, you know I cannot! There is too much discord between . . . well, you understand well enough, I think."

"I will tell her." Nan kicked at her mount and it lunged forward, hastening down the hillside to where Richard's party waited impatiently for her. They vanished at last into the blessed cover of the forest, hidden from the unwavering stare of those hostile eyes behind. As she rode, Nan's teeth chattered uncontrollably and the nausea of great fear rose hot in her mouth. So very nearly Richard had lost his proud and unrepentant life. The red and gold of autumn swam sickeningly before her, merging together mistily. She heard Richard's cry as she slid from the saddle.

THIRTY-ONE

"MY Lady, my Lady. . . ." Alana's voice was urgent and broke slowly into Nan's slumbering. Again she shook the sleeping figure.

Nan sat up then, the sleep fleeing to the shadows as she blinked in the candlelight. "Whatever is it? Isabel?" Her thoughts winged to her daughter who was well gone in her pregnancy.

"Nay, the Lady Isabel sleeps on, as does the Lady Anne. Warwick Castle has a visitor." Alana looked a little uncomfortable.

"Who is it?"

"It is the Earl of Northumberland, he is alone and wishes to speak with you."

Nan struggled into a robe. "Something must be very wrong for him to come here thus. Jesu, if ought has happened to my Lord. . . ." She paused as another thought struck her; what if John had come over to Richard's side, what if Edward should carry out his threat then to make known her secret. . . .

Alana's hand was reassuring. "He bade me tell you that the Earl is well enough."

"Where is Northumberland waiting?"

"I took him to the small room at the far end of the great hall, there is a fire there still. . . ."

But Nan was already gone, her bare feet flying along the passageways and down the twisting steps. Her heart pounded with fear and she prayed silently that John had not changed his colours. Richard must never know, never!

For six months she had been at Warwick, coming there immediately after Edward's escape from Richard's custody. She, Isabel and Anne had seen little of him or Clarence and rumours were widespread of the troubles they caused around the kingdom; but no-one really knew the truth of what was happening outside the castle walls.

The hall was still heavy with the scents of the last meal of the evening, and her nose was assailed by memories of chicken, roast meats, baked fish, spices, and sundry other foods. Beneath a trestle a hound chewed still on a large bone, and the grinding of its huge teeth sounded unnaturally loud in the vast, silent room. She paused, glancing around. The servants slept on the floor, their huddled shapes lit by the fire which roared brightly in the huge fireplace.

She heard the sound of boots against the floor, and walked towards that sound. She pushed open a small door and entered the chamber. John wore a very heavy cloak, its hood was

170

pushed back from his dark hair, and now he poked at the rushes with his boots, his fingers drumming on the table.

"My Lord of Northumberland, you wish to speak with me?" Her voice was uneasy.

He started as she spoke, turning sharply to look at her. His eyes moved over her, warm, remembering. "So formal, Nan?"

She was disconcerted, but her fear of his intentions was still uppermost. "There is too much to separate us now, John."

He bowed his head, nodding. "Very well, I will say what I came for and then leave you. I warn you that in a day or so you must expect the return of your husband and Clarence. England grows too hot for Richard now and I think he will be in some haste to leave."

"That is all? You merely come to warn me?" She held her breath.

He raised his head in surprise. "Yes, that is all, it is sufficient surely? Richard has been continuing his plottings and disturbances. Conyers has been fanning the flames of rebellion in the north and now yet another of our kinsmen has joined the fray. Lord Welles, our second cousin, has been rousing Lincolnshire to fever pitch, calling men to arms in the names of Warwick and Clarence. The object is plain enough, Richard is attempting to put Clarence on the throne, but unfortunately for my brother everything has gone wrong. Welles was overthrown, captured and beheaded, confessing before he died that his instructions came from Warwick and that Clarence was to have the crown. Richard and Clarence managed to escape capture, and their whereabouts are not known and Edward has attempted three times to contact them, commanding them to explain their treasonous conduct. They have ignored these commands, and now he seeks them out and his temper is not a little frayed. He intends to pursue them until capture now. My other brother George he has detained as being implicated in Richard's activities, and the King's fury has been whipped up further by the knowledge that there have been continued contacts with France. Richard will have no option but to flee the country, for if Edward has him in his grasp. . . . There is no hope of Richard gaining control of Calais, Edward has seen to that. Burgundy will not harbour the man who has for so long worked against their alliance with

171

England. That leaves only France, Richard's jewel, he will have to throw himself on Louis' goodwill."

Wearily Nan sat in a chair, burying her face in her hands. Why, oh why could not Richard have been less proud, less ambitious; why could he not have left his politics by the wayside, just this once. . . . Was there no point at which he surrendered?

John watched her, longing to go to her, but he knew at last that there was nothing left of what once had been between them. She was cold now. "Nan, I come to ask you not to go with Richard."

She stared at him. "I thought perhaps you came to join him!" She smiled.

"No, I am as far from his schemings as ever I was. I am Edward's man, as Richard once said. Do not go with Richard, for Edward will never forgive or forget, and his anger is such that your womanhood will not protect you from his revenge!"

"I will not desert Richard. I love him, and obey him."

"If Richard finally, and openly, takes the field against Edward, then he is doomed. He will be forced to raise the colours of Lancaster, for he must surely admit now that no-one is going to lay down their lives for the weak, spineless Clarence! Fighting for Lancaster is the only way he will be able to raise numbers enough to even consider taking the field in earnest. To Richard the French alliance means everything, and he will take any path which might lead him to that end, even if that path should mean the restoration of the House of Lancaster! You *know* I speak the truth!" He strode over to her and gripped her shoulders, shaking her violently. "God's Blood, Nan, if he turns his colours yet again what then will be the value of Warwick's precious name and reputation! He is mad with the lust for achieving *his* aims, *his* ambitions, and now he will take down with him all who cling still to the Warwick that was!"

She struggled free, raising her hand and striking his face sharply. "Should I then accept your word, my Lord, the word of a brother who once confided in me his great misgivings in Richard's ability to put *York* on the throne? Richard prevailed then, did he not? And he will again!" Oh how she defended Richard now.

172

He dropped his hands from her as if she had spat upon him, and suddenly her anger was gone. In its place was a feeling of guilt, and of self-dislike at the way in which she spoke to him. "John, forgive me, it seems that each time we meet now we quarrel and speak abusively to one another. I thank you, most gratefully, for coming here and attempting to save me, but please know that I cannot leave Richard. Please understand." Should she tell him of Edward's knowledge and threat? Should she, or would such information be better left untold. . . .

His hand touched her cheek. "I understand only that I love you still."

Footsteps sounded loudly outside the door, and Alana's voice echoed around the slumbering hall. The servants awoke abruptly, rubbing their eyes and looking with fearful eyes at one another. "My Lady Anne, I beg of you. . . ." Alana called again.

The door opened and a small figure in a long night robe came in. Anne's flushed face was eager as she look around for John. "I heard you arrive uncle, but when no-one came to awaken me I came alone to greet you." She hurried to him, holding out her hands.

He grasped the small hands warmly. "It seems my niece remembers me with kindness." Then he raised his eyebrows. "Or have you perhaps some ulterior motive in seeking me out, minx."

She blushed and bit her lip. "Have you seen the Duke of Gloucester?"

"Ah, now it becomes clear! So much for wishing to greet your poor uncle! Yes, I have recently seen him, and he is well. You may rest easy, Anne, for he has no love other than yourself, I vow he leads the life of a monk!"

Anne's eyes were suddenly brimming with tears. "Will he still want me, uncle, when all this is done?"

John glanced quickly at Nan. "Why should he not?"

"Because I am the Earl of Warwick's daughter and the King will not want his only remaining brother to wed a Neville. Dickon ever was Edward's true brother, I am so afraid that he will do his brother's bidding in this and forsake me."

He sighed, not wanting to cast her down and yet unhappy to build her hopes. "While matters stand thus between your

173

father and the King, I fear that Gloucester will never ask for you. He will wait, such is his way."

"Are you going back to London now? Is he there?"

"I may answer yes to both questions."

Anne walked to the fireplace and then glanced at the open door where the servants' curious eyes peered in. She hurried over and slammed the door to, leaning back on it and staring at John. "Take me with you, take me to London that I may go myself to Dickon."

"Anne!" Nan was horrified.

John whistled softly, shaking his head. "My little niece, I cannot and will not do such a thing! I will not come between your father and you, our differences may be many but I will not add that to my list of sins."

"Please!" she dragged her hand over her tears. "Please take me."

"Once again I say no, Anne."

Nan went to her. "You had best go to your room, Anne, and I will forget this night's work! Your words are not those of a gentlewoman!"

Anne flung away from her, her voice breaking with emotion. "I have tonight a chance to go to Dickon, whom I love and who loves me, and yet you both deny me that chance."

Biting her lip unhappily, Nan put her hand on the bowed golden head. "Anne, you cannot take such a course. What if Dickon has no wish to receive you under such conditions. You will embarrass him considerably by fleeing to his protection in this way. Think child, think!"

The weeping subsided a little, but Anne was obviously unconvinced. Her jaw was set stubbornly and she glared fiercely at the uncomfortable John. He picked up his gloves and raised his hood over his head again.

"I think my presence becomes a little unwanted, I will go. God keep you, Nan!" He kissed her cheek gently and then was gone. The servants stood aside as he passed.

As his footsteps died away she realized that she had said nothing to him about Edward's threat.

THIRTY-TWO

Two days later Richard returned. He and Clarence rode swiftly into Warwick, closely followed by their retainers, and before Richard had even dismounted he was shouting orders for new horses to be prepared and waiting within the hour.

Nan, Isabel and Anne awaited him in the solar, and Isabel's pretty face was pale and wan. She sat uncomfortably upon a chair, her hand pressed against her swollen stomach, but her eyes brightened as she saw Clarence.

He ran the last few yards across the hall to her, taking her hands and pressing them to his lips. Nan warmed a little towards him for this, but in all other respects she could not like her son-in-law any more now than she had done when he first came to Richard's household as a small boy. Anne watched her sister's reunion with her husband, and an unhappy veil descended over her eyes. She look away, biting her lip.

Then Richard was there. He was pale and tired and obviously had not slept for some time. His face was unshaven and his hair untidy and windswept, but Nan did not care for that as he embraced her. She could smell damp leather and perspiration, and she could feel the stiff hair against her cheek. His skin was cold and moist from the raw weather outside. He held her hands then, drawing back from her and looking closely into her face.

"Nan, matters have gone amiss with me and I fear we must flee the country."

"I know. Your brother was here to tell me."

Surprise crossed his face, and then hope. "John? Is he. . . ."

She shook her head. "He has not changed allegiance, Richard, he came only to warn me as a friend that I would soon be receiving a visit from you. There was nothing more." She looked away uneasily.

She felt the slackening of his grip upon her fingers, saw the disappointment in his eyes. How he needed John at his side. After a moment he drew himself together again, releasing her hands and going to a trestle where some food had been hastily laid. He picked up a small chicken and greedily broke off a piece. Clarence joined him. Their appetites were enormous. Richard wiped his lips with a napkin held out by a small page. "We make for Calais, *my* Calais!" He smiled.

175

Nan's heart fell. "You cannot, Richard, for the King has commanded Calais to close its gates against you!"

For the first time she saw Clarence react. His already pale face was suddenly bereft of all colour, and his hands commenced a shaking which even Isabel could see.

"What is the matter?" Isabel was anxious.

He ignored her, his eyes fixed firmly on Richard. "If not Calais then where?"

Nan could guess the reason for his fear. If Calais would receive them then his chances of gaining the throne were still alive. Already his self-confidence had received a severe jolt when he realized that England was not about to rise as one for the banners of the Black Bull, even if supported by the legendary Ragged Staff! He had hopes still of Richard's magic weaving a spell for him if Richard could gain the mastery of Calais and therefore of the seas, but now. . . .

Richard bit again into the chicken, his eyes thoughtful. At last he spoke. "We go for France then, there is no other course!"

"Never!" Clarence's fear and apprehension mounted. "We *must* try Calais, it may be that they will ignore my brother's commands."

Richard shifted uncomfortably, tossing the half eaten chicken back on to the platter. "I think we must face the fact, however unwelcome it may be, that our hopes of taking the crown and placing it on your head are severely dashed! Without Calais I am virtually powerless, Edward can raise a greater number of men to his banners than you and I put together."

Nan knew then that Clarence was aware of Richard having been in contact with Margaret of Anjou. The words of John Neville sprang into her mind. Words fought for place upon Clarence's frightened lips. In France there lay Lancaster, and he was a scion of the House of York. In France there lay another answer to Warwick's problems, another possible King who would be willing to receive Warwick's aid.

Anne suddenly stepped forward, touching her father's arm. "Father, may I remain here in England?"

Richard stared at her, frowning. "No, I take my family with me, no-one shall I leave to fall into Edward's hands."

She would not release him. "Please, I will come to no harm. I will go to the Duke of Gloucester."

Nan held her breath. Oh Anne, you have chosen your moment unwisely. "Put aside your hopes of Gloucester, my daughter, he is not for you!"

Anne's mouth opened, and she swayed in misery. This was the first time Richard had put any obstacle before her match with Dickon. There was another in that room who looked dismayed. The Duke of Clarence's pale blue eyes looked apprehensively at Richard . . . and then at the beautiful, fair-haired Anne.

Isabel struggled to her feet, holding on to the back of the chair to support herself. Clarence looked at her and his face was suddenly hard. He no longer saw in her the pathway to the crown through the support of her father. "You had better prepare yourself for the coming journey, Isabel!"

Nan rounded on him in horror. "Isabel cannot undertake such a journey. She is eight months with child, would you have her lose the babe?"

Sharply he rounded on his mother-in-law. "Madam, Isabel is now the Duchess of Clarence, and as such she is *my* responsibility! She journeys with us, that is my command!"

Isabel looked reproachfully at her husband, but he would not relent. Silently she left the solar, taking the rebellious-faced Anne with her.

A short while later they all rode out from Warwick, knowing that the King's men were not far behind them. Southwards they rode, southwards for the sea and escape. As they left the castle confines, Nan heard Clarence once more beg Richard to make for Calais, and this time Richard agreed to attempt such a course.

Sickeningly the small ship lurched again, the howling gale driving the creaming waves over the lower decks. The spray whipped through the angry air, striking Nan's face like so many tiny needles as she struggled to where Richard stood with Clarence at his side. It seemed that the captain's voice came from a long way off as he shouted commands to his weary men.

Her veil and skirt tugged fiercely in the turmoil. She clung to the handrail, her fingers slipping on the damp, slimy wood. How far away now the joys and comforts of Warwick. Her eyes turned to the nearby coastline, the well-remembered outline of Calais; so near and yet so very, very far away. She looked then at Clarence, her dislike evident upon her cold face as she silently condemned him for their present plight. If it were not for him they would be ashore now, ashore in France where Isabel could receive attention. . . .

Richard's arm was around her waist, tight and strong. "Nan, you should remain below, Isabel has need of you!" He shouted the words close to her ear, but even so the greedy gale whisked them away, carrying his voice into the shrieking vortex of sea and air which gained momentum it seemed with each passing second.

Her eyes implored him. "Can you not gain entry yet? Has no word been sent to the garrison of Isabel's condition?"

He shook his head, his damp hair clinging to his face. "You saw what happened. When we tried to make for the harbour they fired cannon across our bows, and the sight of the Ragged Staff drew still more shots. A longboat has braved the elements once to bring word that the King has commanded them to keep us out. At this moment Edward's word counts for vastly more than does mine! I sent a message back with the longboat that Isabel's babe came before its time, entreating them to either let us land or to send wine and herbs to ease her travail. As yet we have seen and heard nothing else." Seeing Nan's distress he pulled her a little closer, straddling his legs to gain more balance. The wind dropped a little, the howl fading minutely, and now she heard his voice clearly, felt his lips against her ear. "How is she? How much longer will her labour continue?"

A gigantic wave broke over the heaving ship and she buried her face in his chest as the water gushed fast, feeling the icy coldness as the retreating deluge sucked at her legs and skirts. Slowly the ship righted itself, preparing to meet the next onslaught.

"She is bad, Richard, very bad. More than a day now she has been in labour and I have known few babes survive such an ordeal." Her anger and resentment, and her fear for her daughter rose sourly within her and she turned savagely on the pale Clarence. "You, Sirrah, are responsible for her misery now! You should have allowed her to remain in England, you are no worthy knight! May God curse you!"

Clarence's eyes widened with horror as she cursed him, his

178

hand crossing his chest as if to fend off her venom. Richard's arm tightened around her. "Nan, that is enough, the matter is no business of yours now!"

"No business? She is my daughter . . . your daughter!" Tears sprang to her eyes and still she stared at Clarence, her gaze full of enormous hatred.

The ship yawed alarmingly, and Clarence's already uneasy stomach at last gripped him. His cheeks were drained of any colour and a greenish hue stained the rest of his face. He hung helplessly over the rails, vomiting again and again, and Richard called for some help to take the young Duke down to his cabin. Clarence was almost unconscious with the violence of the nausea as they half-carried him away.

Nan felt Richard's body stiffen and she thought at first that another wave was poised above the tiny ship, but now dimly she heard the lookout's voice calling through the whine and whistle of the wind. Richard was turning to stare at the shore. Slowly the ship rose on a great swell and as it did so they saw for a fleeting moment a tiny black shape leaving the safe haven of Calais. Oh so very slowly the little craft came nearer, and with each dip of the oars Nan's hopes rose; Jesu grant they came to take Isabel ashore, that maybe they would take them all ashore.

The boat was almost alongside at last, the oarsmen's eyes wide with fear as they saw the violent sway of the ship; now it towered above them, now dipping lower until they could see right over her decks. Time and again they sought to throw a line on board, time and again it fell useless into the seething waters.

The line was aboard! She leaned over to look, her finger-nails scraping the green slime of the rail as the ship moved again. The boat was drawn away by the rising waters, but not before the men had hastily tossed a tightly bound wicker basket into the sea. It hit the curdled waters, causing the white spray to fly, but all sound was lost in the screech of nature's fury. Now the oars dipped again, turning the light craft back to the beckoning shores. The undulating seas soon hid them from view, leaving only a glimpse now and again as the waters parted momentarily. Nan's heart fell. There was no hope then for Isabel. . . .

The basket was hauled on to the decks and as the ship

straightened Nan made her way as quickly as she could towards the dark little doorway which led down to the equally dark cabin where Isabel lay. Richard dragged the basket behind him, and they stepped thankfully into the cabin, the door slamming of its own accord behind them.

While Richard bent to slice the ropes which bound the basket with his dagger, Nan hurried to where Isabel still tossed on the narrow, damp board. Ankarette hovered anxiously above her beloved mistress, now and then pressing a towel to the wet forehead.

Isabel's hollow, pain-filled eyes looked hopefully at her mother. "Can we go ashore?"

Richard drew forth wine bottles from the basket. With his dagger he forced one open and handed it to Nan. Ankarette raised Isabel's head slightly and they pressed the bottle to her lips. Suddenly she pulled her head away from it and the wine poured down her neck and on to her shoulders. Nan threw the bottle away in horror as Isabel screamed her pain to the heavens. Terrified of her sister's agony, Anne hid her face in her hands, sinking to her knees at the side of the narrow bed. Richard crouched where he was, his face white and frightened.

Alana's voice remained calm as she drew Ankarette's fleeing courage back in to the cabin. Together mother and daughter worked over Isabel's writhing body while Nan held the twisting, scratching hands.

Then it was over. Isabel lay still, her eyes closed, her face almost yellow with exhaustion. Nan turned to Alana, her glance dropping to the tiny, lifeless form held in the woman's arms. A boy, a little boy! Alana picked up a large cloth and wrapped the tiny body in it, hiding the little face which had so briefly seen light but never life.

Nan's hands began to shake as she pulled the sheets closer around her daughter. Isabel turned her face away, tears creeping from beneath her closed lids and sliding down the begrimed cheeks. Anne looked now, but could not bear the grief. She rose and ran blindly towards the door, and as she opened it the storm howled in at them, the damp wail of the wind a fitting background to the stunned, unhappy scene within.

Richard stood slowly and approached the bed. In his hand he held a bunch of herbs which had lain at the bottom of the basket, herbs which if sent a little sooner would have spared a little of Isabel's agony. He dropped the green bundle on the sheet as he bent over his daughter, putting his hand to her cheek and kissing her gently. She reacted by turning her face away immediately, saying nothing.

Nan put her hand on his arm. He took a deep breath before speaking and then she strained to hear him. "I will send her puking husband from his sick-bed, he will needs must find his sea-legs now! She has need of him, no-one else, may God help her! He must bow to the inevitable, we sail for France!" His voice caught and she saw that the wetness which lay on his cheeks was not of the storm's doing. He drew her close as if he feared to lose her, then he was gone to command the captain to set sail for France.

THIRTY-THREE

THE French voices floating on the summer breeze lay musically upon Nan's ears. She looked out of the arched window at the people who strolled lazily in the sunshine, their lilting words carrying freshly to the room where the English ladies sat.

It was June, and for some months now they had been living under the spreading, benevolent wing of Louis, King of France, Richard was treated like a visiting monarch, fêted, idolized, cultivated. The regard which Warwick had for the French King was in every way reciprocated. Where Richard needed Louis' protection and his offices to effect a reconciliation with Margaret of Anjou, the French needed Richard in the same way. The English King had turned his face from France, and Louis badly wanted a friendship with England . . . therefore Edward of York must go, and Lancaster must return. It was all so simple, so logical.

Nan put down the book she was endeavouring to read, and listened instead to Isabel's clear, distinct voice as she read in French to her sister. Isabel was fully recovered from the loss of her baby, and now her health had returned. She blossomed in the warm French atmosphere. The only mar on her horizon was the coldness of Clarence. Since he suspected Richard was going to turn to Lancaster, he had grown increasingly unpleasant and harsh towards his bewildered wife. Isabel could do no right, and when she tried to placate him, he grew haughty and withdrawn. Nan's dislike of him deepened and he sensed her hostility.

Anne sat quietly listening to Isabel, but she was obviously deep in thoughts other than the heroic exploits of French legendary heroes. In her hands she held the playing cards she had been using before Isabel had picked up the book, and her fingers moved on them now and again. Nan's soft heart yearned for her younger daughter. Poor Anne, the Duke of Gloucester might just as well not have existed as far as Richard was now concerned. Nan had said nothing to Anne of her fears concerning Richard's as yet uncertain flirtation with the House of Lancaster. True, Richard had said nothing openly about his plans, but there was John's warning to ponder on, and such a thing was not beyond Richard's vast ambition. It could well be that he wanted Anne to wed the heir of Henry VI . . . if the mighty, vitriolic Margaret could be persuaded that her future lay in an alliance with Warwick.

Nan's fingers crept to her throat, trembling as she looked at Anne's bowed head. If all this came to pass, what lay ahead of her poor child? That she would be unwelcome in Margaret's household was inevitable, and Anne would have to bear all Margaret's past hatreds and frustrations. Through Anne Margaret would avenge herself on Warwick himself. Aaaah, Gloucester, Gloucester, you should have taken your choice of bride when the chance was offered, your delay has cost you dear. . . .

A burst of laughter from the garden drew Nan's attention away. Outside Clarence walked with a young French nobleman. The laughter was hollow, and the smiling Frenchman was obviously ill-at-ease with the English Duke. Clarence was elegant in his wine-red coat and oatmeal hose, and the white plumes in his fashionable hat bobbed defiantly in the breeze. Defiantly, aye, for Clarence was as unpopular as the Devil himself in Louis' France. Had he gained the English throne and shown himself to be of a mind to obey Warwick, then the French would have loved him; as it was Clarence had been

182

unsuccessful and was nothing more than the hated English King's brother and heir.

For the first time Nan found herself feeling a little sorry for this shallow princeling. If he did not already know what was afoot with Richard at the French court, then he must surely soon be apprised of it. What would his attitude then be? His suspicions were nothing more than that, the proving of those suspicions would be a bitter blow. And what of Richard himself? If he came to an agreement with Margaret then his Yorkist son-in-law would prove something of an embarrassment would he not? Clarence would be placed firmly on the outside of both parties in England, essential to neither Edward nor Warwick. But which one would be more likely to receive Clarence back into the fold? Edward! There was no joy in a separation within the royal family, and Clarence at his side was infinitely preferable to Clarence with Warwick. Yes, Clarence would throw himself on Edward's mercy, he had no other choice. But all this was only if. . . .

Trumpets sounded across the undulating French countryside, and Nan's lips parted in a smile. She recognized that sound of old. Richard was returned from Louis. Eagerly she waited, and soon enough the door opened and he was announced.

He filled the room with his presence, his eyes alight with triumph. She knew from his demeanour that everything was going according to his minutest hope. The Warwick legend was reborn, twicefold! He swept her into his arms, and she could feel the excitement, the trembling anticipation quivering inside him. He was longing to return to England and continue the fight against his former protegé. There was a brightness in his eyes as he looked at her. "Ah, Nan, it is good to be with you once more!"

The door opened and Clarence came in, his face taut with anxiety. He walked to Richard, endeavouring to appear casual and unconcerned. "Your visit to court was fruitful then?"

Richard's smile faded a little. He took a deep breath and glanced at Nan. "Aye, my visit was as fruitful as I could have wished. There are many things I wish to speak of with you."

Clarence smiled and the smile was not warm. "That I can

imagine. I know well enough that *my* future has been taken care off!"

Richard's face tensed a little, but he was amiable still. "My son, what has been put aside for you is handsome indeed."

"Aha, then you have put aside the throne of England for me? I vow that that is the only prize which I would term handsome." The sarcasm was heavy.

"Do you choose to listen, or have you decided already that I have sold you for less than your considerable worth?" Richard put his hand up to loosen the high, stiff collar of his pleated doublet. "I have met again with Louis, and this time Margaret of Anjou was present also. . . ."

"Ah, so it is Lancaster!" George's face was red with anger and fear.

"Do not interrupt me, Sirrah, for Prince you may be but I will brook no such ignorant behaviour!" Richard's mercurial temper rose swiftly, dangerous in its control. "You must know that there is no hope of putting you in Edward's place. The only hope of disturbing Edward's tranquility lies in resurrecting Lancaster. Louis is prepared to aid and abet such an invasion as he knows Margaret of Anjou would be friendly towards him."

"And how is this alliance to be sealed?" Clarence's eyes narrowed as he looked not at Richard but at Anne. She returned the look blankly, not understanding.

"How is an alliance normally secured? How was the Burgundian alliance secured? By marriage of course!"

Now Anne understood at last, the truth slowly sinking into her lethargic senses. "No . . . no. . . ."

"Anne!" Richard took her hands, drawing her towards him. "Anne, I have arranged a grand match for you, none other than the heir to the House of Lancaster, Prince Edward himself."

The blue eyes were wide with horror and disbelief. "Never, please say that you jest for I would not marry Edward of Lancaster!"

He held her still, ignoring the tugging of her hands as she sought to break free. Nan's heart ached for her daughter, but she could do nothing. Richard looked at Clarence. "The contract has already been drawn up and the betrothal will take place next month at Angers Cathedral. I have undertaken to return Henry VI to the English throne. For you, George, I have secured the entire wealth of the Duchy of York, and in the event of the marriage of Edward and Anne proving barren, then you have the throne. You will be heir, George!"

"I am that now." Clarence spoke unemotionally.

Anne struggled again and this time pulled free of her father. "How I despise you, my father, how I hate and despise you! You give me to the House of Lancaster when I would wed the House of York!"

Richard stiffened, hurt at her outburst. In his eyes the marriage was grand, offering her the chance of becoming England's Queen, and he could not understand that she would not welcome such a dazzling future. "You have no will in this matter, Anne, I bid you be silent!"

Anne stared coldly at him, then she turned and walked from the room. Isabel soon followed, looking savagely at her father. Clarence hesitated only a moment before joining them.

Richard looked at Nan, raising his hands helplessly. "You would desert me also?"

"Well, you must understand Clarence's attitude if you cannot understand Anne's."

"Aye, well it would not surprise me if he returned to England. I confess to being surprised that he came to France at all, he would have stood a better chance throwing himself at Edward's feet. He knew in his heart that there was no hope after Welles' rebellion fell by the wayside. He would not face up to the fact though."

Nan waited a moment. "Anne loves Gloucester, you choose to forget that?"

"Love? What is love when crowns are at stake? She will one day be Queen of England, and hopefully the mother of future kings."

"She will be marrying Somerset's bastard!" Nan reminded him gently.

"She will be marrying the future King of England!" His sharp words closed the conversation firmly.

185

"WHAT manner of man is Edward of Lancaster?" Nan sipped her wine and watched Richard's face as he poked idly at a scurrying spider. The spider froze, curling up.

"Hmm?"

"I said, what manner of man is Edward of Lancaster?" The spider uncurled and made haste for the shadows.

"Forgive me, Nan, I was thinking of my brother John."

Her fingers shook a little on the stem of her glass. "It is a pity he veers so strongly towards Edward," she murmured faintly.

"That is just it, my love, I have reason to believe that his allegiance has been severely shaken by recent events in England! It seems that Edward has made great efforts to secure the dubious support of Henry Percy, that same Percy who lost to John the Earldom of Northumberland. Now, of all things, Edward has taken the Earldom from the faithful John and given it back to Percy! True, he gives John the mighty title of Marquis Montagu, but it is a title, no more. . . . What manner of exchange is that for my brother after the princely revenues of Northumberland? I know my brother, and he will be stricken by this treatment after the efforts he has made on Edward's behalf. Already I have written to him begging him to join me."

Nan's trembling hand threatened to shatter the delicate goblet and so she very carefully put it down upon the table. Her dismay was great. John must not, could not, join Richard now . . . Edward would. . . . But she must say something, Richard was looking at her. "Is not the king's daughter still betrothed to John's son?"

"Betrothals can be broken easily enough, John knows that. Ah, but it would be good to know that John was at my right hand again." He smiled as he turned to look fully at her, hope shining in his eyes.

She returned the smile, but her lips were strangely awkward. "He is a fine soldier."

"Fine? There is none to compare with him the length and breadth of England!" He stepped over to her, a laugh rising in his throat as he drew her to her feet. "Nan, the pendulum

186

swings yet again, I know it, and my blood surges to the knowledge!"

Anxiety still gripped her. "Why are you so certain that John will turn his colours?"

He smiled. " 'Tis, I think, no vain hope. I know my brother." He went to pour more wine. "Nan, the moment fast approaches for an invasion of England, and with Anne wedded to Margaret's son the alliance will be complete. . . ."

She forgot John and her worries, thinking instead of the unhappy Anne. "What is he like, this scion of the House of Lancaster?"

He shrugged. "He has been brought up to believe himself the true heir to the throne of England, to believe that his father King Henry has been odiously treated by the usurping House of York. He looks across the Channel and sees Edward sitting comfortably upon the throne while his father languishes in the Tower. What can be expected other than that he is a bitter soul?"

Richard was refusing to meet her eyes and she knew that he was not altogether happy with his daughter's bridegroom. "He is only seventeen is he not, an impressionable age."

"Aye, and the impressions he has absorbed are not conducive to a happy future with the House of Neville. My name and everything connected with me he hates, as his mother has so avidly taught him."

Nan could have wept for Anne. "Richard, what torment do you give our daughter into?"

Pain showed in the hazel eyes for a moment, pain which he hastily smothered behind a mask. He had to maintain his stand, his personal feelings must not enter into this important matter. "Madam, a contract has been drawn up. My word is my bond. I need Margaret's support to take up arms against Edward, and so I will abide by the terms agreed." Again she briefly saw the anguish he disguised so well. He loved Anne dearly, but the sacrifice of her happiness was as nothing compared with the realization of his dreams of a French treaty.

The door opened and Isabel peeped in "Forgive my interruption, but I think it would be better if you came to talk with my sister, mother. She is weeping again and nothing I say will help her."

Richard turned away angrily. "Foolish wench! Can she not

187

see what a magnificent prize is about to come into her hands?"
This is Richard, thought Nan, he really cannot understand how
Anne can reject what he offers.

"I think I had best go to her." Nan was almost apologetic.

"Go then, and imbue her with a little common sense!" The
goblet tinkled as he put it on the table and began to replenish
his wine.

Nan followed Isabel, seeing her elder daughter's sour face.
"What is it Isabel?"

"Very well you know what is the matter!" Isabel halted,
her skirts rustling crossly. "My father tosses my husband
aside so easily in favour of Margaret of Anjou's son."

Nan was wary. "You father has done what he deems to be
best for England."

"England! He has no thought for England, he thinks only
of Warwick!"

Anger rose in Nan's breast. "The same words could so
easily be applied to your husband, Isabel, and so I bid you
mind your tongue in future when speaking of such things!"

There was a silence after this outburst and they walked
slowly on towards Anne's rooms. "You have always preferred
Anne to me, have you not?" Isabel spoke quietly, her eyes
glistening with unshed tears.

"Isabel, what a terrible thing you say of me! I am concerned for your sister now because of the unhappiness which
stretches before her. You have married the man you love,
and you loved him well before there was any talk of crowns
and kings. His present predicament matters not at all, you love
him and you have him. Think then of Anne. She has always
loved your husband's brother, and knows that he loves her in
return, and yet she is forced into marriage with a man she
knows not at all and who she must suspect of hating her and
her family. When you view matters from my eyes, Isabel, it is
Anne who needs my love and comfort now, not you."

Isabel bowed her head. "Forgive me," she whispered.

Nan embraced her, realizing as she did so that already they
had reached Anne's door. "Perhaps Isabel I had better talk to
her alone."

"Yes, I understand. Mother . . . I must tell you that I think
my husband is considering returning to England. I do not
know, it is merely a suspicion. He . . . he does not confide in

188

me now, he does not join me unless he has to for appearance's sake. I fear that his wrath against my father is directed at me as he dares not direct it at father openly."

"You are right, I think, Isabel. He is hurt, but he will rise above his troubles." Nan hoped in her heart that her words of comfort would bear the truth, but she had grave doubts about George of Clarence.

Isabel walked slowly away and Nan knocked quietly upon the door. She heard Anne's low voice calling her and went in. Her daughter's face was red and puffy with all the tears shed.

"Oh mother, I cannot bear it, I cannot bear it. . . ." Anne's tears rose anew at the sight of her mother's anxious, kindly face.

"Anne, it is the fate of all women that they are the property of their menfolk, to be given and bartered for at will. My own life was such. I could not like your father even slightly when first I knew him, indeed I actively hated him . . . but time changed, healed, soothed. I love him now."

"Perhaps if I had not loved so desperately elsewhere. . . ."

"Anne, within a week you are to wed Edward of Lancaster. You must face that fact!"

"Perhaps if Dickon knew. . . ."

"He would do nothing! There is nothing he can do, he cannot spirit you from here! You must cast aside all thoughts of him now, you must concentrate on what is going to be. Believe me, it can be done!" Oh, how true those words. She knew the pain of wanting one man when her future lay with another.

Anne sat quietly now, her hands twisting and untwisting, pulling and knotting her kerchief. "You will help me? If I know that you think of me I can be stronger.

"Anne, my dearest Anne, I will do all I can to help you. Be sure of my comfort at all times."

They sat in amicable silence for a long while, absorbing the strange sounds of the French castle, the foreign scents, and unaccustomed style of the furniture.

"Mother, you know how matters have deteriorated between Isabel and Clarence?" Anne looked at Nan.

"One would have to be blind, deaf and dumb not to realize that he now treats her abominably! I have no liking for him!"

"Nor I. In fact the dislike which rests between my brother-in-law and myself virtually amounts to hatred. It ever has been so. The thought that the English throne will now probably come to me and not to him drives him to deeper malignancy. He was pleased when he knew that I could not marry his brother, but his pleasure so quickly was dispelled when he realized the man I was really to marry.

Nan was surprised. "I had not realized that it was so between you and he."

"Oh yes. He bears me great emnity." Anne picked up the tarot cards which lay at her side and began to set them out upon a gaming stool.

THIRTY-FIVE

ANNE'S slight figure shimmered in the smoky light. The torches flickered in the rising wind which drew through the French castle. It was July, a day which had been hot and humid but which now brought promise of rain. Again the torches brightened in a swirl of warm air, and outside the evening light faded perceptibly as the storm clouds loomed nearer. Anne bowed her head, staring at the golden platter which lay before her, its contents untouched. It was her wedding feast and yet she had not eaten, and she had not spoken all day except for taking her vows in the cathedral. More torches were brought as the storm overhung the castle, and with them the scene leapt into clearer perspective.

The bride was dressed in a gown so fine, so brilliant, that many had gasped at its extravagance. Richard had spared no expense when he gave his daughter away in marriage; she looked every diminutive inch a future Queen. Her pale face somehow enhanced the peacock blue silk with the golden panels of pearls and silver stitching. Around her throat were twisted row upon row of large, perfect pearls. Upon her head she wore a steeple headdress after the exaggerated French fashion, and the finest of golden lace was drapped over it, trailing down and looped eventually over her arm. In the eyes of many she was now the Princess of Wales, future Queen of England.

Edward of Lancaster was at her side. He was seventeen, a little more than two years Anne's senior, but he was almost the same height as his new bride. His figure was sturdy, muscular . . . and the expression in his eyes was awesome. His life had been a succession of bloody years, his only knowledge that of hatred and revenge. His few years had left their indelible mark upon Margaret of Anjou's only child. Now he drank deeply of his wine, wiping his thin lips with his embroidered sleeve. As became a royal bridegroom he wore a coat of purple velvet, but already the beauty of the garment was marred by the dark stain of wine where he had carelessly spilled his goblet. Purposely he avoided speaking with Anne, always taking care that his head was turned away from her.

From her position further along the dais, Nan watched the wedding guests, but her heart reached out to the sad, pathetic figure of the bride in her magnificent silks and jewels. But if Anne's gown was magnificent, the crimson and gold of Anne's new mother-in-law was in truth the most impressively regal garment in the room. Henry VI's Queen had entered the hall alone, and the train of her gown had required the services of four pages to carry its heavy length. Margaret was now forty-one, and the face once renowed for its dark beauty was sour and lined.

Margaret's son did not draw his looks from his dam. Not for him the black hair and eyes, the dark skin and small figure; from the face of Edward of Lancaster there stared the tawny ghost of Edmund Beaufort. Somerset had been elegant, handsome, every fibre a man of noble and exalted lineage . . . but his illegitimate son by the Queen of England was uncouth. He looked so very like the long dead Duke, but somehow everything was slightly wrong, slightly out-of-place. Nan thought of him as being like the Duke when seen in a nightmare, and dimly remembered with the coming of dawn.

Richard raised his glass to Margaret, and after an obvious hesitation she returned the gesture, but she almost curled her lip with hatred as she looked at him. This then was the joining of Neville and Lancaster, the alliance which stunned England and dealt a cold fear into the heart of King Edward IV.

Soon Richard would be returning to Edward's realm, at his

side a great army of vengeful Lancastrians, and not a few dissatisfied Yorkists. Nan sighed and pressed her lips together; poor muddle-headed Henry VI would be brought forth from the Tower and placed yet again upon a throne he could hardly remember . . . *if* the invasion were successful.

Strangely enough there was one face at this gathering which Richard had certainly not expected to find still at his side. George, Duke of Clarence, was still in France, still very much in evidence at Richard's side. Now he sat opposite Nan, his golden Plantagenet hair proclaiming his birth for all to see. He had hardly taken his eyes away from Edward of Lancaster from the moment of first seeing him. Even now his dark glance fell upon the bridegroom who replenished his goblet yet again. Nan saw in Clarence's blue eyes the fire of jealousy and spite; but for this Lancastrian upstart, the great army would surely be riding for Clarence. The skin drew white over his knuckles. Nan looked away.

The feast was almost done and already the servants were hurrying to remove the trestles and strew fresh rushes upon the food-stained floor as the guests prepared to dance away the remaining hours. Jugglers performed before the dais, tossing balls and streamers into the air, making wonderful patterns, but their deftness and brilliance did little to awaken Anne's interest. Her hands she cupped together in her lap, and her eyes were downcast.

Prince Edward glanced at her, and seeing her continued doleful expression, he sighed loudly and banged his goblet down upon the small table now placed at the side of his chair. He slumped inelegantly, twisting his lips as he leaned his elbow against the arm of the chair. To Nan's perverse amusement she saw Margaret's lowering gaze fall upon her surly son and she leaned forward, poking him sharply in the back. He started, turning to see who touched him. Margaret's lips moved angrily, her voice a low whisper of fury. As he began to reply the minstrels finished playing and a heavy silence fell upon the gathering—a silence broken only by the bridegroom's loud retort: " 'Tis not drunkenness, mother, merely utter and exquisite boredom!"

A gasp went around the room and all eyes swung to where Richard stood. Nan looked at him too, but he made no movement to signify that he had heard. She could only see by the whitening of his mouth that he had not only heard but that his every instinct bade him take a rough hand to the insolent princeling he could now term son.

A page bowed low before Nan, bidding her to speak with the Queen. Margaret's chill gaze was upon the Countess of Warwick as she made her way towards the dais. When at last Nan knelt before her, Margaret carefully and deliberately kept Warwick's wife in such a position of servility. "Madam, we have not spoken together for many years. I would tell you how I welcome your return to my household."

Nan raised her face, disguising her feelings, but her thoughts ran slyly behind her open countenance. Indeed you must welcome me, how it must salve your bruised pride to have Warwick's Countess at your beck and call . . . it must be nearly as sweet as having the Neville Earl himself on his knees before you! "As I also welcome returning to you." How Nan's Beauchamp blood curdled to be speaking so sweetly to this woman, how had she found it to maintain the innocuous smile and bowed knee.

Margaret pursed her lips, her dark eyes narrowing cunningly. "Edward of York was indeed a foolish ingrate was he not, to spurn his mentor, the man who 'made' him."

Nan's green eyes flashed, but she chose her answer carefully. "Perhaps, Your Grace, the matter may be looked at in a different light. Were it not for Edward of York's behaviour, my Lord may never have perceived the error of his ways, may never have . . . returned to the House which should rightfully be upon the throne. Your husband, our sovereign King Henry, was wrongfully deprived of the crown." May God forgive me, she thought.

Margaret watched her in silence, then she raised her jewelled hand and at last allowed Nan to stand. "Hmm, you please me, my Lady, your presence will be soothing I think."

"Soothing?" The word escaped Nan's surprised lips.

"Indeed so, is it not soothing to know that you and your daughters are at my side when Warwick rides out to raise *my* banners in battle?" The meaning was plain enough; Margaret did not trust Warwick, and she regarded Nan as a hostage, a reminder to Richard that he must uphold his side of the bargain. Nan smiled suddenly. Henry's Queen had not changed, the years had not diluted the strength of her hatreds and mistrusts. Margaret accepted the smile at its face value and inclined her head graciously as she waved Nan away.

Richard claimed his wife then, drawing her to one side. He did not speak for they had both stopped to watch the bride and bridegroom walk out on to the floor to lead the first dance. The cheers which echoed around the room were hollow and Nan saw that Margaret did not even clap her hands as the bridal pair began the measure.

Again the wind howled about the castle, drawing eerily through the rooms and passages. The torches flared, spluttering and pouring forth black smoke. The wind seemed to find an endless number of cracks and crevices through which to suck and blow. The rushes moved noisily on the floor. The eddies of wind were warm, lifting Anne's golden veil in a cloud about her head as she moved. Her beauty was ethereal as she danced, and instinctively Nan knew that Anne had blotted out the unsavoury figure of her new husband and replaced it with the slight, dark memory of Dickon.

A low rumble of thunder coursed across the dark skies, and a ripple of uneasy whispering ran through the wedding guests.

Nan turned to Richard. "The elements disapprove of this day's work."

He frowned. "Do not talk of such things! July is a month frequently endowed with thunderstorms, or am I mistaken?"

She soothed him. "I merely jest."

"Jest? Then it is surely a bad quirk which bids you jest on such things!"

"Oh come now, forget that I spoke. Tell me, is there further news from England?"

His ill humour faded and he smiled. "I have received a letter from John! Oh, it contains nothing to raise my hopes, he is still most careful to remain impartial. But since we parted he has never answered any of my communications, and so I deduce a hopeful light from his having written at all. He wavers I think, and that is sufficient for the moment."

That awful apprehension she knew so well gripped Nan again, and her fingers stole over Richard's arm. She could not bear for Richard's faith in her to be shattered by such a discovery as would come his way if John truly did join him. He touched her fingers gently. She sighed. "John has my sympathy in his dilemma."

"Why so? His problem is caused by the same weakness which strikes at every man. He seeks to guess which side will bring him the greatest reward . . . it is folly to choose the wrong banner."

"I do not think he can be judged so lightly. I think that maybe his conscience is *truly* torn."

Richard ignored the words. "I mark how closely Clarence sits upon my tail. At first I was surprised, but now I think I have solved his reasons. He will wait until the very last moment before finally deserting me, because until then there will still be a slight chance of the throne coming his way. Once he seeks to return to Edward his hopes of seizing the throne become minute."

"Richard! It could be that Clarence will remain with you anyway! Has your lust for power and your infernal pride completely annihilated all human kindness from your heart?" Nan was irritated with him.

He smiled unexpectedly. "My sweetest Nan, how else can I be now? I know deep within me that Clarence *will* desert me, I have not misjudged his shallowness. As to John, well perhaps I was unnecessarily harsh, but you did seem somewhat quick to defend him."

A blush stole over Nan's face. "I . . . have always been fond of him."

"I know. I love him dearly myself, and perhaps that is why I feel his loss so keenly. Never has any one man been able to strike so deep into my heart with his defection." He leaned back against the wall, his hair stirring in the wind which leaked in through the ill-fitting window next to him. She looked at his face, seeing the tiredness there, the lines, the deep care in his eyes. "I look around me Nan, and I see no-one upon whom I may lay my complete and utter trust, except perhaps my brother George. The grand son-in-law I have acquired this day will not be true, and why should he be? I seek to replace his father upon the throne for my own ends, not from any grand conscience . . . no matter how I may protest to the contrary in public."

"But what of the French alliance? Is that not what truly governs your actions?"

He looked at her. "I pray so, Nan, I pray so. I hope that my rebellion is not solely motivated by my urge to teach

195

Edward a lesson for turning from me!" He looked away as some raucous laughter broke out amongst the guests.

Nan saw that the ladies were leading the white-faced Anne away. The ancient ceremony, much loved by everyone except the bride and groom, was about to begin; the bedding of the newly-wed pair. Nan excused herself from Richard and made to follow, but she was delayed by one of the French noblemen who insisted upon talking to her. As a result some ten minutes had passed before she at last could leave the hall and make her way to Anne's apartments. Already the ladies had spirited the bride to the inner rooms, for Nan could not hear their laughter as she hurried along the passageway. Outside Anne's apartments she hesitated, for she could hear voices from inside the first room, and one was a male voice. What was a man doing in there now?

Queen Margaret's voice crept unasked through the door. "Remember my son, this night you may sleep with your bride, but beware my anger should you seek to consummate this marriage!"

Nan stiffened. Edward sighed, his shoes scraping against the floor as he shuffled his feet. "Mother, she is now my wife . . . and a very pretty one for all her Neville blood!"

"Exactly, she is a Neville. Her only political attraction lies in her parentage! Should this campaign go against Warwick, then a Neville wife will be an encumbrance and not an asset. Remember, you do not accompany the invading army, but remain here in France to await the outcome. An unconsummated marriage may be annulled without undue fuss, and a more suitable bride found for you."

Again his shoes scraped on the floor and Nan heard him sigh. Then he exclaimed in a burst of irritation. "Must you always harbour that accursed piece of metal? Whenever you are worried about something, you bring it out of your purse. . . . 'Tis a habit which grates upon me vastly!"

Margaret's voice was unexpectedly hurt. "It is a memento of someone once dear to me."

Nan heard the gentlemen approaching for the bedding ceremony. She could no longer hesitate at the doorway without being seen. She must go in . . . as she pushed upon the door she heard a tinkling sound.

The door swung open at her touch and a small, tarnished

metal object rolled at her feet. She stared at it and then at Margaret, who avoided her gaze uncomfortably. Slowly Nan bent to pick it up. There was no mistaking what it was, the years rolled away and for the second time that evening Nan thought of Edmund Beaufort, Duke of Somerset. In her hand rested a folly bell.

THIRTY-SIX

THIS was her last night with Richard for a long time to come. On the morrow he would leave France on the long-awaited invasion of England.

The bedchamber was warm, lit by the firelight. Outside the air was chill in the September night, but inside. . . .

Alana drew the brush through her mistress' long, silky hair, while Richard lounged upon the bed watching. There was something sensuous, almost catlike, about the dragging of that brush. Soon Nan dismissed Alana, and turned to look at Richard.

"I do not look forward to the morning."

"Well, the sooner it is begun then the sooner we are re-united, sweetheart. But even the leaving of port will be difficult, there is a Burgundian fleet blockading the Channel at Edward's instructions." He was smiling. He had no fear of the coming bloodshed and danger.

How much longer could his life be charmed, for how much longer could he evade even being wounded? "I pray that you live and return safe to me."

"I will." There was such a supreme lack of concern that she was almost convinced of his apparent invincibility.

"And what of the other lords who accompany you. Good Lancastrians most of them, names like Oxford and Pembroke! Once your avowed enemies, but now your comrades? Is there really and truly a trust, a bond between you all?"

"Of course. There can be no other course for me now. I have tossed my dice and my score is shown. I cannot now withdraw and go on bended knee to Edward. They know it and so they trust me, just as I trust them."

She fingered the brush, tracing the outline of its handle in the dusty surface of the table. "You do not know really what awaits you in England. Your faithful northerners have raised some sort of insurrection which is again aimed at drawing Edward out of London. Pembroke is certain to raise Wales to your banners. But what else is there? There is much of England which is cloaked with an impenetrable mist now, maybe it will rise for you, maybe for Edward! There is too much left to the dubious services of luck. Edward has not been idle during these past months, he has gathered together a huge army, and all he needs must do is wait."

He smiled again, holding out his hand to her and drawing her near. "True enough, but the dice of which I spoke is heavily weighted on the side of those who invade. Edward cannot know how we intend to conduct our campaign, he must wait for us to move first. It is also true that Edward has amassed a formidable army, but there is another in England whose army eclipses that of the King!" His hand caressed her arm, slipping beneath her robe and touching her warm skin. She slipped on to the bed beside him, her senses tingling at the closeness.

"Who? There can surely be no-one. . . ." She stopped, her lips parting. "John! Is it John?"

He lay back, laughing now, and drawing her down beside him. "Correct! The Marquis Montagu has a mighty force!"

He rolled over until he was leaning heavily upon her, and then he pressed his lips against her throat.

She closed her eyes, but somehow she could not give herself fully to the embrace. That fear rose unasked, unwanted. "You have heard from your brother?" Please God, no, no. . . .

He raised his head, forcing himself back from the delights of the embrace. "Not from John, no, but from brother George. It seems that John took himself along to visit George in his prison and was closeted for a long time with him . . . unburdening his soul!" Nan's heart almost stopped within her at these words. She knew from Richard's attitude that he still had no notion of her past, but what if John's infernal conscience had bade him tell everything to the quiet, sanguine George? Richard put his hand against her breast. "George tells me that he is certain that when the time comes I will find the Marquis Montagu at my right hand. George is seldom wrong in these matters, and I have never known him be wrong about John." His lips were on her breast now, and he would brook no further talk. She drew him close, holding him tightly, lovingly, but she could not enjoy his love because of the terrible alarm which seeped through her entire being. If he discovered the truth then never again would she feel his body close to hers, feel his lips kissing hers, murmuring endearments!

Tears were near and she bit her lip to hold them back. He lay beside her, his fingers twining gently in a lock of hair and she took his hand and laid it against her cheek. If Edward chose to inform him, Richard would be in England and she in France with no opportunity of explaining, of trying to. . . . "Richard, take me with you tomorrow."

"I cannot, Even had I so wished, I have now given my word to Margaret that you will remain with her, as do Isabel and Anne."

He reached over and extinguished the candle which stood close to the bed, and the darkness of the room swept over them. After a moment her eyes became accustomed to the moving firelight and she turned her head to look at Richard. His eyes were closed now, his hand still curled about her long hair. She pressed her knuckles to her mouth, tasting the tears which lay wetly on her cheeks now. What should she do?

She thought desperately of Edward. His Queen was with child again, surely this time it must be the hoped for son. Edward; cunning, clever, as politically brilliant in his own way as Richard. Would he ever consider keeping such a secret? She knew the hope was useless. Edward had too many grievances against Richard to seek to protect her good name. She must tell, now, she must do it. . . . She touched Richard's shoulder, shaking him slightly. He stirred, but his sleep was deep.

At first she was relieved that he did not wake, but then she knew that she must try again. Her hand reached out—and then stopped. If she told him then she would definitely estrange him, he would never be able to forgive her such a sin. But if she remained silent? What then? Well, if John joined him, Edward would surely acquaint the Neville Lords with his knowledge, slowly dropping his poison into Richard's ears. She stared at the fire, trying to imagine the time when Richard was informed. Perhaps it would be just before battle, in order to most shatter his nerve, his concentration. Maybe he and John would even be together at the time, conferring. It would shake Richard, yes, but would he believe it? There was a chance that he would think it to be a trick of Edward's to drive a wedge between his powerful foes. John would surely deny such a tale, he would never be foolish enough to admit outright to Richard that he had slept with his wife. Her hand dropped away from Richard. Was she not a little like Clarence? He delayed and delayed because there was a slight hope of his achieving his dream . . . she would also delay, because of that slight hope. Any possibility, no matter how slight, how vague, was to be seized at. She looked at Richard, drinking in every loved curve of his face and body; never, never could she bear to lose him. She must smother her conscience, conceal and dissemble, he would not learn the truth from her lips.

She lay back, wriggling into a more comfortable position. She listened to his regular, easy breathing. Her love for him surged strongly and she put her arms around him, feeling his heartbeats strongly against her breasts.

When dawn broke she was still wide-eyed, sleepless. But when Richard arose a little later she slept at last. He smiled down at her and kissed her cheek, but she felt nothing. He slipped from the bed and drew on a robe, knocking on Alana's door and whispering to her that Nan was to remain undisturbed.

His party was long gone when eventually she stirred. From her window she saw the flotilla of his ships sail on the morning tide.

THIRTY-SEVEN

"YOUR Grace, it is now February—five months since my Lord returned to take England triumphantly in your cause.

Your husband is again on the throne of England and Edward has fled the country. Why cannot we go to London now, to allow all to see once and for all that the House of Lancaster is supreme?" Nan's anxious tone caused Margaret to raise an imperious eyebrow.

"My Lady of Warwick, it is true that your worthy Lord has overwhelmed the Yorkists, however I have received word that Edward is only awaiting favourable winds to return him to England to take back the throne. I cannot and will not risk my son's life until every last stirring of Yorkist sympathy has been subdued. Remember, with my son ends the House of Lancaster. No, we remain in France a while yet."

Nan took a deep breath to calm her anger. Richard's continuous requests for Margaret to go to England loomed large in her thoughts as she turned once again to the Queen. "Madam, can you not see that the victory lacks conviction if you and your son remain safely cocooned across the Channel? The people accept King Henry, but you and I both know that he is a mere figurehead to them . . . it is yourself and above all *your son* to whom they now turn!" She held her breath as she awaited the outcome of her last attempt at making Margaret seen reason.

The Queen raised her head from her book again. "I remain unconvinced that the time has come for such an undertaking, my Lady. In the past my impulsive actions have cost me dear, this time I cannot afford to make a wrong decision *or* act hastily."

"Hastily!" Nan could not withhold the exclamation. "You delayed once before, after the second Battle of St. Albans. That delay cost you the campaign, for the Yorkists stole London from under your nose!"

Margaret whitened with anger, and Anne who sat nearby looked apprehensively at her fearsome mother-in-law. "My Lady of Warwick, I am your Queen and I forbid you to speak in such a grossly offensive manner to me! In token of my esteem for your husband I will say no more, but right now I would read a little more comfortably if I was without your presence in this room!"

Nan flushed and her embarrassed gaze met the equally uncomfortable glance of her elder daughter. Isabel looked quickly away, continuing to sort threads with Anne, who this time did not even lift her head from the colourful pile of embroidery twines which lay in a basket on her lap. Without further argument Nan curtseyed swiftly and hurried from Margaret's presence.

Once outside she took a deep breath of relief, glad to be away from the Queen's oppressive presence. Margaret over-shadowed everyone and everything, dark and brooding; her son was a mirror of herself. Anne walked in fear of him, and Nan suspected that he had made various threats to his wife, perhaps even carrying out some of them.

She wandered to a window and cleared a space on the frozen pane to look out at the wintery scene which surrounded the castle. Snow, snow and yet more snow. Everywhere glistened and shone with the beautiful white coat which hid beneath its silky softness all scars, all blemishes. All was fresh, crisp, almost newborn. Fingers of frost patterned delicately across the cleared patch of window and she breathed upon it and peeped out again. Somewhere out there, across the Channel, Richard awaited her.

His fleet had evaded the Burgundian blockade, aided it must be admitted by a fortuitous gale which scattered the enemy, breaking its ranks and rendering it useless against the sixty or so ships which Richard led successfully across the Channel to the English shore. Edward had been enticed from the south by the insurrections in Yorkshire and had been caught un-awares by news of Warwick's invasion. The country had risen in parts to Richard's banners, and Pembroke had succeeded in rousing the Welsh; as always the men of Kent were as one in the shouts for the great Earl they loved. In the north close to the King's army lay the mighty numbers of John Neville's followers; John Neville with his ailing allegiance, nursing his considerable complaint against Edward. As Richard had hoped, and Nan dreaded, John had turned his colours and all his immense force had elected to remain with him. Edward had little choice but to flee, he knew he could not withstand such numbers. Taking his brother Dickon with him, he took the coast road and soon left the shores of England behind him . . . but for how long, that was the question! Queen Elizabeth had fled into sanctuary with her three daughters, and shortly afterwards had given birth to a son. A son. England had a Yorkist heir now, and Edward would surely come back to fight for such a future.

In London Richard had had a tense reunion with John. That the meeting had been uneasy Nan knew from Richard's letters. Gone was the camaraderie of the past, Richard had found that he was not entirely happy with his brother. This was now John's lot, he was not trusted implicitly by either Lancaster or York.

How miserably Nan had passed these months. Every day she awaited the messengers from England, fearfully opening Richard's letters, her eyes searching for the dreaded news. Edward was bound to strike out at the Nevilles from his haven in Europe, he was bound to enlighten the Earl of Warwick as to his wife's infidelity with his brother. Daily she prayed, her fingers passing over her beads time and time again, her knees aching from the long hours she spent in prayer. The news had not arrived. Nothing happened. There was no mention, no hint, in Richard's letters that he was aware of anything. Were her prayers answered? She could not believe that Edward had maintained a silence.

Several large snowflakes wandered through the still, iced air, soon joined by more. In a short while, less than a minute it seemed, the air was filled with ever-increasing numbers, and the silent blanket thickened upon the ground. A horseman went by, the hoofbeats muffled, and she watched the deep, clear-cut impressions of the hooves. The greedy snow filled the cavities quickly, blurring the outlines, soon leaving a mere procession of dimples . . . eventually leaving nothing to signify that horse and rider had passed that way at all.

Her fists clenched. Holy Mother, how she longed to be with Richard again. Her body yearned for him. How cold was her bed in the mornings when she awoke, her arm stretched across an empty mattress, an unruffled coverlet. She whirled around guiltily for the door had opened. Margaret stood there.

"I have reconsidered, my Lady. Perhaps you are right, delay at this time could possibly cost us dear. We shall leave for England shortly, I will write this day and inform the Earl of my decision."

Nan smiled, a great weight lifting from her heart. "Your Grace, your decision must surely be the right one."

Margaret bowed her head. "I sincerely hope so, my Lady, I sincerely hope so. What other chance will there be such as this? Edward is out of the country, and King Louis fully occupies the Burgundian allies of York with a war upon their own doorstep." Her black eyes clouded as she look across the room at Nan's dark figure framed in the doorway. "I pray God that I have not left it too late."

Nan looked at the window. The hardening frost allowed a brief glimpse of the countryside where now the snow billowed thickly. The trees beyond the walls were invisible through the seething white mist.

THIRTY-EIGHT

THE men's voices sounded eerily through the dense fog which had held the ship captive for so long. Nan pulled her winter cloak more tightly about her, but the fur had now absorbed the beads of moisture from the still air and felt clammy against her skin. She shivered. It was Easter, the month of April, and such was the weather sent to greet their home-coming. Above her head a large warning torch burned loudly, showering sparks over her, sparks which died upon the damp decks beneath. Her face was lighted by this single great flame, lighted as she strained to see through the grey curtain which stretched endlessly on all sides.

They had long since lost contact with Margaret's ship, being unable to remain even within hailing distance, and now the sailors relied solely upon their instinct to guide them to the shore which they knew to be close by. She swallowed, frightened by the uncertainty of the moments which passed so slowly. But soon she would be with Richard, soon she would embrace him again. . . .

Shouting broke out amongst the men and sailors ran past her along the slippery deck. They pointed, talking excitedly, and she followed the direction of their fingers. Her heart leapt; was that the dim outline of land she was so briefly shown? Again the fog swirled thickly, eddying, alive . . . then it parted momentarily and allowed the anxious eyes of those on board to glimpse that beloved sight, the coastline of Hampshire, England, home!

Alana hurried to her. "See Alana, God has answered our prayer, we are safely brought to England."

"Aye Madam, I heard the men's voices. God be praised, I had not thought to see England again when that accursed fog descended upon us."

Nan's smile faded. "I hope that the Queen's ship has been as fortunate." She glanced again at the fog which hovered a little way off, threatening to close in on them at any moment. Margaret had with her both Isabel and Anne. Only the lack of comfortable accommodation had prevailed upon the haughty, suspicious Queen to allow Nan to travel separately. She still wished to have the persons of all those dear to Warwick under her watchful eye.

Now guiding torches were alight upon the shore, and the welcome sight of Portsmouth drew near. The sails hung limply against the air, useless. The men hurried to the oars yet again and soon the sky was filled with their chanting and the creak of the oars. People lined the small harbour as the craft approached, and Nan saw how they huddled together, whispering as they tried to make out the banners which clung to the mast, invisible, unintelligible. She smiled to herself. You shall soon see who comes, you shall soon know that great Warwick's banners mount this ship! She held her head proudly.

The anchor was dropped noisily into the still waters, and soon a rowing boat was lowered. Alana tugged her arm. "My Lady, see there, the Queen's ship has already put in and would seem to have been here a fair while. They were maybe more lucky than ourselves."

Nan smiled with relief. They were safe then, her daughters were safe. There was a stir amongst the crowd, a muttering. The rowing boat rocked violently after the slow, easy rolling of the larger craft, but soon enough they reached the wharf.

She looked up as she stood, reaching for the slimy rungs which were her route up to the cobbled street above. Three figures she saw clearly, Margaret, Isabel and Anne . . . and now they were joined by the wary shape of Prince Edward. Her call of greeting died upon her lips as she saw their white faces, anxious and unsettled. Something had happened!

Gathering her cumbersome skirts together as best she could,

205

she started up the rungs. It seemed an age before at last she stood before them, smoothing down the crumpled velvet. "What has gone wrong?" Her frightened eyes fled from one face to the next, searching, pleading. Richard's name came into her mind. Richard.

Anne's face crumpled. "Oh mother. . . ."

Isabel could not meet her mother's eyes and she stared with great concentration at the mast of the ship. Alana climbed the rungs and now stood with Nan, her hand steadying Nan's shaking arm.

It was left to Margaret herself to speak. "My Lady, I have grievous news for you, indeed for all of us, but more especially for yourself. There has already been a great battle, a great confrontation, between our forces and those of Edward of York. I fear that York was triumphant."

"And Richard?"

"Prepare yourself my Lady, for Warwick is dead."

Nan stared, not comprehending and not wanting to comprehend. "There is some mistake, some terrible error has been made. Richard is not dead, he cannot be! Who brought such news, I will have his miserable head for spreading such infamy abroad!" Her voice was rising with each word, perspiration gleaming wetly against her forehead. Alana held her firmly, anxiously.

Margaret showed a kindness towards the stricken woman. She took the shaking hands. "My informant is none other than the Earl of Devon. He is here now with the Duke of Somerset, they pledge their support to our cause and even now I am preparing to leave with them for Exeter to raise another army. Pembroke is still in Wales with his loyal Welshmen, together we will still be able to crush York, and avenge Warwick's death." Margaret gestured behind her and for the first time Nan saw the great mass of soldiers and horsemen who filled the narrow streets. Above them hung the Dolphin banners of Devon and the Portcullis of Somerset, grandson of the long-dead Edmund Beaufort.

The fog was lifting, allowing the pale April sunshine to filter through on to the chilled land. Nan wished now for the swift return of the all-concealing mist. Richard. She could not, would not believe it! She smiled weakly. "I know he is not dead, it was an error, an error."

Anne hurried forward and put her arms around her mother. "Listen to us, mother, there is no doubt about the news. The Earl of Devon *saw* father die, he *saw* them plunge a dagger into his throat!"

Nan's eyes closed faintly. Richard's face swam bloodily across her imagination, his eyes open but not seeing, his lips parted but not speaking. "No." She whimpered a little, her knees lacking the strength suddenly to hold her. She sank to the rough cobbles. Anne released her, looking down at the bowed, weeping figure.

She turned to her mother-in-law. "Your Grace, she cannot travel with us in such a state. Should I remain here with her?"

"No, you travel with your husband, my Lady, your allegiance whether you wish it or no, is now entirely with us."

"Anne, go with your husband, do as you are bid." Nan's quiet voice interrupted them.

Alana hurried over to Isabel, and took her aside. Soon they were deep in conversation. Nan stood. "Your Grace, I will not go with you to Exeter. There can be no place for me now, I have no further will to fight."

Prince Edward raised his eyebrow. "No will, Madam? Have you no thought of revenge for your husband's death?"

Her hand moved slightly. "Will revenge breathe life into his corpse?"

"That it will not do, but surely it will atone a little for his loss."

"Nothing upon this earth can atone for such a loss . . . nothing . . ." Edward shivered at the lifelessness of her voice, it was as if death had crept into her. Nan wished only to hide her face from the world, to sink into obscurity with her grief. "I will seek sanctuary at Beaulieu, the White Monks will receive me."

"You will immure yourself forever? Come Madam, such is not the answer!" Margaret frowned at Nan's seeming capitulation, her voice harsh.

Nan looked coldly at her. "That is my wish, and you are powerless to gainsay it."

The Queen turned away. "Very well, if that is your wish then so be it. We leave directly." She began to walk away, stopping as she found that Isabel and Alana were in her path.

They stopped their hurried whispering and stood aside, and Nan noticed how cool, how full of hatred was Margaret's face as she looked at Isabel. She leaned closer to the shrinking girl, closer until her face was only a few small inches away. "I have no wish to see your face near me, my Lady, get you away from here!" Her voice was a hiss, and indeed Margaret resembled a viper in that moment.

Isabel's blue eyes were round with fear and she scuttled away, running to her mother. Nan put her arms around her, thinking now only of Isabel's plight and nothing of her own. Her mind was somehow numbed to the shock of Richard's death. She had pushed away into her subconscious self the fact that she was alone now, that no more would she hear his voice, touch him, kiss him, love him.

"Why is the Queen so spiteful towards you?" She shook Isabel a little.

Anne hesitated close by, only to be taken roughly by the arm and pulled away by her surly husband. Her head turned unhappily to look back. She was lifted onto a waiting horse and soon the air was filled with clattering hoofbeats as the great cavalcade moved away, turning westwards for Devon and a new beginning.

Nan waited patiently for Isabel to reply. "Mother, I . . . I fear that my husband deserted father and went into battle for his brother Edward. He is now in London awaiting my coming. That is why Margaret hates me so, because my Lord was in part responsible for what happened at Barnet."

"Barnet?"

"That was the place where the battle took place, where. . . ."

"Do not say more, I do not want to hear, I do not want to hear!" The hysteria returned a little as Nan put her hands to her ears as if to fight off the words which Isabel sought to use. Not yet, oh please God, not yet. . . .

"Mother, come with me to London. I am sure that the King will receive you kindly." Isabel's voice was gentle as she perceived the depth of her mother's grieving.

Ankarette hovered nearby, holding the reins of two palfreys. Behind her were a small number of men, maybe six in all, which was all Margaret would allow for the traitorous Clarence's wife.

"Edward will not receive me kindly, my daughter. I am the wife of a traitor, and not only that, I was party to my husband's activities. I raised no voice of dissension, I am, in Edward's eyes, as guilty as Richard. My only course must be to seek sanctuary. For me it matters not which House rises to power; for you I could wish York . . . for Anne I could wish Lancaster. Go now to London, be reunited with your husband. I will pray for you that he loves you sufficiently to overcome the undoubted disadvantage of having a Neville wife."

Isabel looked unhappily at her. Could she be sure of George? She turned away and walked to Ankarette. She did not look back as her small party left the cobbled square.

Nan remembered little of that journey by fishing boat across the bright April waters of the Solent to Beaulieu. She was hardly aware of the magnificence of the scenery of the estuary as they negotiated the River Beaulieu to where the Cistercian Abbey nestled at the lower neck of the New Forest. It was well named "beautiful place" but Nan's dull eyes took in nothing. She had no remembrance of the welcoming faces of the White Monks as they greeted her and offered her shelter and sanctuary.

Later she stood numbly in the small, dark room which they gave her. Alana disrobed her, taking away the stained cloak and unfastening the rich gown beneath. "I shall wear bright clothes no more, Alana, for now I must wear widow's black." The silence lay heavily upon them and Alana commenced to brush the dull hair.

Nan could not bear the silence any longer. They must talk of something. "What did you speak of with Isabel?"

Alana's hand hesitated in its brushing. "I asked her to tell me of Barnet, my Lady."

"And did she?"

Alana put down the brush. "Do you wish me to tell you now?"

Sighing, Nan sat down on the hard board which was to be her bed. "I must know, must I not? I cannot forever seek to ignore what has happened."

"Before the battle, when Edward came back to England, he came ashore in the north and marched southwards through England. Between Edward and the Earl lay the army of your

209

brother-in-law, Marquis Montagu." Alana looked cautiously at Nan, remembering what had once passed between John Neville and her mistress, but Nan did not move. "No-one knows for certain what happened, but somehow the King managed to slip past the Marquis' army unharmed and un-hindered. It is now thought, in view of what has since hap-pened, that the Marquis deliberately withheld his hand from attacking Edward." Nan smiled to herself; that could easily be true, for John had come with an unwilling heart to his brother's camp. "The Duke of Clarence slipped away with his forces and made his peace with his newly-returned brother. News of all this apparently reached George Neville, and he thought the battle lost before it was fought and threw himself upon Edward's mercy." Poor Richard, thought Nan, surrounded by desertion from the outset. "The great armies eventually converged upon Barnet, with the Marquis having apparently recovered from his earlier unsureness and once more putting himself with the Earl. The battle commenced and all was well with the Earl, until a terrible case of mis-taken identity turned the tide. That same fog which so recently enveloped us stretched across the whole of England that day, and was so dense that the opposing armies had difficulty in identifying one another's banners. In the mist the Marquis' men saw coming up on their flank an army which they thought to be flying the King's banners of the Sun in Splendour. They turned to attack this army, only to find out too late that it was not the King but the Earl of Oxford, their ally, with his banner of the Star with Streams. Oxford's men broke line with cries of 'Treason', thinking that the Marquis had changed his allegiance yet again. Morale was crushed with this and soon the Marquis' lines failed. The Earl saw the Marquis fall . . ." Nan gasped, her face paling. John dead too, not John too. . . . ". . . and he tried to make his escape to which his horse was tethered. He was hampered by the weight of his armour and the pursuing men soon caught him and . . . well, I will not explain what happened next." Alana's voice died away, soaked up by the mellow stone walls of the silent Abbey.

Nan sat quietly, her hands folded in her lap, staring at the floor. "John fell with Richard after all then."

Alana shifted uneasily. "It is said that he died at his own

hand, my Lady, although I know not if that be true for such is mortal sin." She crossed herself devoutly.

"Poor John, my poor John. He could not surrender to the King, and neither could he escape. His heart was not in the fight, Alana, he came to Richard's side but his loyalty was really to Edward. I can well believe that he took his own life rather than continue." She raised her eyes to the narrow window, at the tiny portion of England which was visible to her. She felt a great sadness for John, a sadness which did not lack love. He had meant much to her, had given her fulfilment at a time when her life lacked warmth and kindness, and when her passionate nature demanded more than Richard gave of himself. Richard. His name filled her. Outside the birds whistled and sang; Warwick, Warwick, Warwick. The abbey bell boomed out suddenly, the sound reverberating throughout the building; dead, dead, dead.

With a loud cry Nan stood, pressing her hands frantically to her ears. She swayed across the room, leaning her face against the cool stone wall. Tears poured down her cheeks, hot and salt. Slowly she sank to her knees, the stone tearing at her face, her fingers scraping uselessly, clawing as if to sink into the wall itself. She huddled there against the wall, hiding her face from the world, weeping endlessly for her dead love. Over and over again Alana could hear one word clearly, one word which seemed to hold the orb of Nan's existence in its rich, beloved sound. *Richard*.

THIRTY-NINE

ALANA watched as her mistress walked across the short grass which covered the courtyard inside the sheltering walls of Beaulieu. The June sunshine dappled the white wimple and long black robes she wore, somehow diluting their severity. Alana watched sadly, for in the two months since Barnet, her mistress had grown thin, not seeming able to rise above her loss. Shelter they had within these dreaming walls,

211

but always there were to be seen King Edward's men outside. So far they had not come in.

At first the women had been afraid, thinking that Edward would violate sanctuary in order to secure the person of the Countess of Warwick, but now it seemed that he merely sought to keep her under strict surveillance. Her movements within the Abbey were suddenly restricted, and it soon became obvious that the monks themselves had been warned not to allow her to communicate with anyone outside. From the first appearance of the King's men the friendly smiles had faded from the faces of the monks, now they looked at Warwick's widow with fear in their eyes. They did not dislike her, indeed they had a quiet respect for the gentle manner of the highborn lady who lived amongst them now; but they greatly feared Edward's wrath.

Not long after her first arrival at the Abbey, the Abbot himself had brought news to Nan. There had been yet another great battle between York and Lancaster, and now the hopes of Lancaster were forever dashed. Edward of Lancaster was killed at the Battle of Tewkesbury, and his mother and wife taken prisoner. Anne was a widow then, and in Edward's hands. The Abbot had made it known then to Nan that the real reason for his fear of her remaining within the Abbey, was that after the battle many Lancastrians had taken sanctuary in Tewkesbury Abbey, but that the Yorkists had broken down the doors and shed blood within the holy walls. She had smiled at him, and said: "That will not happen here, for if such be the threat then I will gladly give myself into the King's hands rather than have any such desecration in your Abbey."

In the clear evening sky the seagulls called as they returned from the land. Their white wings flashed in the warm light, beating rhythmically as they sought their night-time resting places. Nan stopped her walk and put her hand to her eyes as she looked up at them. Distantly a trumpet sounded, but she did not notice as she resumed her walk, her soft slippers picking daintily between the white and yellow heads of the daisies which littered the grass. She looked forward to these hours when she could walk in the fresh air. Again the trumpet sounded and now she heard it. She stopped and looked nervously back to where Alana stood.

212

Alana hurried away to a position where she could see who approached along the road. She strained her eyes, crossing her breast fearfully as she saw that a great company of men approached, with long banners streaming above them. She tried to make out the cognizance. At last she could see . . . a White Boar . . . the Duke of Gloucester! "Holy Mother!" she gasped, gathering up her skirts and running back to Nan.

"It is the King's brother, Gloucester!"

"Well, if Edward has sent his beloved young brother to winkle me out, then no doubt I shall go! Who am I to resist such a grand and exalted messenger?" Nan's voice was resigned, flat.

Alana was horrified at the spiritless tone. "Who are you? You are a Beauchamp, the heiress of the greatest inheritance England has ever known . . . and most of all you are the widow of Richard Neville!"

Now the hoofbeats could be heard, and the trumpet sounded close by. They heard Gloucester's name called out at the Abbey gates, heard the request that the doors be opened to receive him. There was an ensuing conversation with the monks but Nan could not hear it well enough to understand.

Her heart leapt with fear as she saw a monk hurrying across the grass towards her. He clasped his hands before him, bowing his head beneath its concealing cowl. "My Lady, the Duke of Gloucester would speak with you. He bids me tell you he will come to your presence completely alone."

"Alone?" Nan's green eyes widened, her thoughts flying back to the Dickon she had known. Would he stoop to murdering her within the sacred walls of Beaulieu? She recalled his long grey eyes and solemn, wise expression, a wisdom which went beyond his years. No, Dickon would not harm her, of that she was sure. "I will speak with him. Alana, when he comes I would have you withdraw to a suitable distance that he might speak freely with me.'

"Madam, I. . . ."

"Do as I say, Alana. It may be that he has some offer to make to me from the King."

The monk hurried away again and they watched a small arched doorway swallow his white-robed figure. Nan's eyes remained fixed upon that doorway, waiting, watching. Her hopes began to rise a little. At last the door opened again and another figure appeared, a figure vastly different from the sombre monk. Dickon, the most important man in the kingdom next to the King himself.

His slight figure was splendid in a doublet of russet velvet and wine red hose. His short travelling cloak was flung back from one shoulder, held back by an enormous jewelled pin formed in the shape of the White Rose. There was a Yorkist livery collar across his shoulders and from it hung a pendant of the White Boar of Gloucester. He had discarded his hat and his dark brown, unruly hair swung free in the evening air. His grey eyes were kind as he bent over her hand.

"You would have words with me, Your Grace?"

He smiled. "Indeed, and I would assure you that it is only words I face you with. Do not fear the great company of men to ride with me, the King's brother needs must ride in such splendour." He smiled again, almost shyly.

"Speak then. What message do you have for me?"

"Message? I do not understand."

"I presume that you have come to me on behalf of your brother the King."

"Indeed I have not, he has no knowledge that I come to you. I would imagine his anger would be great if he did know!"

She was taken aback. "What then?"

He turned and began to walk slowly along the grass, his pointed shoes making no sound. She walked with him, not taking her eyes from his bowed head. He glanced up. "You will know of course that the Lancastrians were defeated at Tewkesbury?" She nodded. "There can be no more unrest from the House of Lancaster now that . . . Prince Edward is dead. Margaret of Anjou will agitate no more, there can be no reason for her to do so as she is widowed now." His grey eyes looked calmly at her.

"Widowed? What happened to King Henry then?" Nan stopped.

"He . . . er, died! Nay, ask me no more, sweet lady. Mine was not the hand which extinguished him, indeed I can only suspect that he was thus despatched. His continued existence was a great and very real threat to my brother's throne; were I in Edward's place no doubt I would have thought and acted upon the same impulse."

214

Henry dead. Nan closed her eyes, remembering her youth at Warwick Castle. "Poor Margaret, how she must hate the name of England. From the moment of her coming to this wretched land she has known nothing but strife and unhappiness. I can in some manner sympathize with her, she was placed from the outset in an untenable position."

He grunted. "Do not utter such treasonous words in Edward's hearing, my Lady!"

"I am hardly likely to be afforded an opportunity."

He pursed his lips. "It cannot be that Edward intends to keep you in here for the rest of your days. His anger is great at the moment, but it will pass as he feels more and more secure upon the throne. I will say though that his harshness towards you is causing comment, he is not usually so hard with women."

She stopped as they reached the wall and turned to retrace their steps. "I had hoped that you brought me some word from the King. Until I receive some indication from him then I dare not venture forth for I am a traitor against him. What dreadful death would await me? I must remain here for I am a coward, Your Grace, and have no strength to face a bloody execution." She licked her lips, hesitating to ask him a question which burned within her. "Dickon, tell me . . . where have they buried my Lord? They have given him a burial within the Holy Church?" Her eyes pleaded for a reassuring answer.

"Both he and his brother, the Marquis Montagu, lie at the family burial place at Bisham Abbey. They were buried according to the rites of the Holy Church. Was no word sent to you?"

"No, I did not know. The only news from outside which I have heard of is the battle at Tewkesbury."

He took her hand. "You should have been told, my Lady, and I apologize . . . both for that and for other things which are about to happen to you at the hands of my House. You are to lose your vast fortune, my Lady, every last vestige of it."

She snatched her hand away. "Richard's inheritance yes, that is to be expected. The King will confiscate that as his right."

215

"Not only the Neville estates, Madam, but all your own Beauchamp and Despenser fortune. Everything."

She clenched her fists, fear creeping through her. Without her fortune she was helpless. "By what authority?"

He took a deep breath, choosing his words with care. "You are to be treated as if you were dead, as if you too had died upon the field of Barnet. Your fortune is to be divided equally between your daughters."

Her head reeled. What hope had she? Thoughts of George of Clarence crossed her mind and her lip curled unpleasantly. "No doubt Clarence rubs his hands together eagerly. Poor Isabel, she has a purpose again, if only to bring such a fortune into her weakling husband's paws!"

Gloucester became agitated, and his fingers twisted at the dagger at his waist. "It is partly on account of Clarence that I seek your company now, my Lady. I am certain, although I have no proof, that it has been at his instigation that all this has come about. He is certainly most anxious that you remain walled up within this Abbey. After Tewkesbury, your daughter Anne was sent into the household of her sister Isabel. Many a time have I sought to speak with her, but always I have been turned away at the door."

"By Anne?" Nan was amazed.

"I do not know if she even realizes I have been seeking her out. My brother is trying to keep her away from the world, hoping no doubt to somehow annexe the entire Warwick inheritance for himself."

Nan was silent, watching the thin-faced Duke as he paced up and down before her. Her expression was thoughtful. "Tell me, Dickon, is your interest in my poor Anne on your own account or on account of her value as an heiress?"

He paled and then grew angry. "Madam, you ask me that?"

"I do Sirrah. It was because of your hesitation that Anne was forced into marriage with Edward of Lancaster. Such hesitation was not really necessary had you loved her sufficiently. Edward's anger would have been a momentary thing, even he could not survive the loss of both his brothers' loyalty."

He nodded unhappily. "I know, I know. At the time, however, I thought my course to be the best. I wished to have

216

Anne with Edward's blessing. Such is my way. But now I am in a quandary, you see I do not know if Anne loves me still. It could be that she willingly conceals herself from me."

"What if she does? What if she now despises you?"

"Then were she the greatest heiress of England and France combined, I would not pursue her. I love Anne and would wed her, but only if she so desires. She was the wife of Edward of Lancaster, mayhap she knew him long enough to love him. She would indeed resent me if such were the case, for I was of the army which slew him."

Nan smiled at his. "Anne knew her husband long enough to walk in fear of him, that much I do know. Also that the marriage was never consummated because Margaret of Anjou wished matters to be kept in such a state in case they wished the contract annulled. If it is my opinion you have come here to seek, then it is this. I believe Anne still loves you and is being hidden against her will. She would certainly not go willingly to Clarence's custody, for they hate one another very much."

As she spoke a great sadness lifted miraculously from Dickon. His grey eyes were alight now, his lips parted in a smile. "My sweet lady, this day you have given me new hope. I will return to London and leave no stone unturned until I find her. Already George and I quarrel openly over his behaviour and Edward grows irritable, but from now on I will gladly risk the King's disfavour in order to gain Anne." He kissed her cheek.

"God be with you, Dickon, and may you find my daughter."

He grew more serious then. "You must not sit back and await Edward's first move, my Lady. Put pen to paper, write letters to everyone you can think of who may be able to help your cause. Even to the Queen herself, for she can have no reason now to hate you. I will help in every way I can, but I may not openly give aid to one named as traitor to my brother's safety. You do understand? I will contrive by some means or other to send assistance to you, you shall not lack for anything if it is in my power to prevent it. I have a well-trusted servant, his name is James Tyrell; you may know that when he comes here then he comes direct from me."

He left her alone in the lengthening shadows.

217

FORTY

OH my love, for a whole year I have been without you. Nan looked out through the narrow window at the small portion of the world she could see. The April daffodils were creamy against the young green grass, and the birds filled the air with their song. Twelve months Richard had lain cold in his grave. She closed her eyes, blotting out the living beauty of springtime. Would she ever love this season again?

Her fingers ached and she glanced down at them, seeing the ink stains which no amount of scrubbing could remove. The letters she had penned knew no number, she had beseeched the aid of everyone she could think of who might conceivably use his or her influence to help the unfortunate Countess of Warwick. But nothing . . . all these months and not one of those she approached had even replied to her. Here she must remain, it seemed, alone, forgotten, damned. How far away now the joys and memories of Middleham and the wild moors of Yorkshire. Ah, the springtime in Yorkshire. . . .

"We have a visitor, my Lady!" Alana's eyes were bright with happiness as she stood in the doorway.

Nan turned, her black skirts rustling. "Who is it?"

Alana stood aside and in came her daughter, Ankarette. "Ankarette! How pleasant it is to see you again!" Nan held her hands out to the girl who immediately came to her, kneeling and pressing Nan's hands to her lips. "What brings you to Beaulieu?"

Ankarette stood, pulling a face of displeasure. "My impending marriage is what allows me a chance of visiting you here. I may not remain for long as I have come well out of my way, I am supposed to be journeying to Cayford in Somerset."

Alana's smile was gone now, and concern crossed her wrinkled face. "Who do you marry? Is he of your own choice, my child?"

"No, Master Roger Twynho would never be anyone's choice, I fear! The marriage has been arranged for me, with no thought of my feelings whatsoever."

Alana went to her daughter. "You have met this Roger Twynho?"

The girl shuddered. "I have indeed, and he is not of comely appearance! He is old enough to be my grandsire, and he dribbles excessively! He looks for someone to cook his meals and mend his clothing, tend to his animals, and so on . . . no doubt I shall fulfil the requirements admirably!"

Nan could sympathize with this rosy girl's acid tone, for what happiness could there lie ahead for her with an aged husband such as she described. Alana, however, knew her daughter too well. "Daughter, you are concealing something from me! I know you, my girl, you have a lover!"

The girl's face stained red with embarrassment and she glared repoachfully at her mother and then with a little fear at Nan. Such revelations before the Countess of Warwick!

"Tell me, Ankarette, who arranged this match for you?" Nan smiled kindly at the nervous girl.

"My lady, it was entirely arranged by the Duke of Clarence!"

Alana grunted disparagingly. "I could have thought as much! One would not expect better from such as he! I beg your clemency, my Lady, I should not speak thus of your daughter's husband, but I do not find him to my liking."

"No I, Alana, nor I." Nan's words were spoken quietly.

"And now, my dear daughter, I shall have the name of your lover!" Alana returned like a loosed arrow to the subject her daughter dearly wished forgotten.

Ankarette untied her travelling cloak, tossing it away. Her crisp brown skirts trailed across the floor as she walked to the window, committing a great crime in her mother's eyes by turning her back on Nan. A pause hung on the air as they awaited her answer.

"His name is John Thuresby and he, like myself, is in the Duchess of Clarence's service. He is in no position, however, to offer for my hand, and anyway what could he say when the Duke himself commands I shall marry elsewhere." Her voice was sad now, she made no attempt to conceal her unhappiness.

Nan went closer to her, standing a little to one side and looking closely at her. "Ankarette, why is Clarence so interested in your marriage?"

The lashes were lowered, the flush a little deeper. Ankarette turned her face away hurriedly. "I cannot say, my Lady."

219

"Come now, George Plantagenet is not one to bring himself down to matters concerning his wife's servants! What happened?"

Alana was staring at Nan now, then her eyes moved to the trembling figure of her daughter. "You have not been dallying with the Duke himself, girl, if so I. . . ."

Ankarette laughed and the sound was little short of hysteria. "Jesu no, little could be further from the truth!" She bit her lip, then took a deep breath and turned to face the other two women. "The Duke of Clarence wishes to be rid of me, and also of John Thuresby. The reason is that we have discovered certain things concerning the Duke's private affairs, things which he would rather were not made public."

Nan raised her eyebrows. "If this be the case why does he not send his henchmen to dispose of you permanently?"

"Because the Duchess Isabel is also aware of what we have discovered, and she has threatened to reveal her knowledge if the Duke touches a hair of our heads."

"Isabel threatens Clarence?" Nan could scarce believe it of the timid daughter she knew.

"Aye my Lady, her life is not happy with the Duke. He makes it well known that he regrets having married her, saying that he was coerced by the Earl of Warwick."

"Coerced! The young puppy was eager enough to rush into the marriage at the time, of that you may be sure. But enough of that . . . what is this secret knowledge you have?"

The Abbey bell boomed out and Ankarette started. She paced across the room nervously, debating whether to impart her discovery to still more eager ears. She bit her lip, and as the sound of the bell died away, she decided to tell them everything. "Well, John Thuresby came to the Duchess' household originally from the service of Robert Stillington, the Bishop of Bath and Wells and also the Chancellor of England. The Bishop has become more and more friendly with the Duke of Clarence, seeing that they possess adjacent lands in the west country and therefore have much to do with one another. The Duke is more than passing fond of wine, and often in the past John had served wine to him when he dined with the Bishop. When John left the Bishop to join the Duchess of Clarence's service, the Duke would often send for him to serve wine when the Bishop came to the Duke's table. Thus

220

John was often alone with them when they drank, and ashamed to say the Bishop also drinks a deep cup."

All this while Nan's pulse had been quickening. At the mention of Stillington the earth had seemed to spin before her, surely after all this time there could be no possibility of the secret pre-contract of the King and Eleanor coming into the greedy hands of Clarence?

Ankarette was continuing: "It seemed, so John said, that the Duke was still of the opinion that he was the rightful King of England. He used to say that under an Act of Parliament passed by the Lancastrian Government before the Battle of Barnet, he was the heir to Prince Edward of Lancaster who died without children. He thought that as this Act had never been revoked it was therefore still law and the crown should be his. He often said all this and John thought that the Bishop was pondering upon telling the Duke something which weighed heavily upon his mind. One day when they had been drinking a long time, they discovered that more wine was needed and sent John to bring some. As he was leaving them he saw that a large jug, still full, lay upon the hearth close to the fire, and he bent to retrieve it. They thought themselves alone and continued their talk, with the Bishop at last saying that which had been hovering upon his ancient lips for so long. He told the Duke that he too thought Clarence should be King, but that he had other reasons for believing Edward to be an unsuitable King. The King's marriage to Queen Elizabeth, he said, was not true because many years ago he had betrothed the King to Lady Eleanor Butler. Your niece, my Lady!" Ankarette looked earnestly at Nan.

Nan nodded. "I am aware that Eleanor was my niece, Ankarette!" The girl's disappointment showed in her face, she would dearly have liked to know the entire truth and she guessed now that Nan knew more than she was prepared to tell. As for Nan, she would also have liked to unburden herself of the dark secret she had kept all these many years, but even now she honoured her vow to her dead niece.

Ankarette turned away and glanced at her mother. "The Duke, John said, seized eagerly at what the Bishop told him. He thought it was a mighty weapon to use against the King, knowing as he did how desperately hated the Queen's Woodville family were throughout the land. He could imagine the

221

great nobles coming to his banners in order to wipe out the Woodvilles and place him upon the throne in the stead of his brother. He already thought of himself as King George!" She almost spat the last two words, so great was the hatred she felt for Clarence.

Nan was a little confused. "But how did Clarence discover John's knowledge? Surely your lover was not fool enough to tell him!"

"Oh no, John was in a difficult position. He did not know what to do because he knew that they would be angry if they discovered him still to be there. He thought for a while and then decided that the only thing he could do was pretend to fall asleep. He had at his side a full jug and he guessed that if they discovered him they would think he had returned unnoticed by them and had fallen asleep as he waited to serve. This is exactly what happened. He was punished for his idleness, but no more. Nothing more would have come of it had he not told me, and I been foolish enough to tell the Lady Isabel. I have been with her all my life it seems and we have always told each other everything, and now I carried on with this childish trait and told her this. She is with child again and is very prone to sickness each morning, and apart from this her health is very poor now. The Duke cannot bear to be with her when she is thus and talks loudly of his discomfort in her presence. She was eventually provoked by his behaviour, and being with child and therefore given to weeping and depression, she turned upon him. During the argument which followed she faced him with what she knew through me, and it was my misfortune to be the only other person present as they argued. The Duke is sharp-witted enough and it did not take him long to see how the tale had come to his wife. He knew that John and I were lovers and he guessed that John had not been asleep when they thought him to be. That is why John has been sent away with all manner of threats ringing in his ears and why I have been betrothed to the odious Master Twynho, who is apparently a faithful servant of Stillington's and will watch me closely. We owe our lives to the poor Duchess who threatened to tell the King what she knew if her husband harmed us."

Nan swallowed sadly. "My poor Isabel, is her life really

222

so terrible? And you say her health is very poor . . . in what way?"

Ankarette stared uncomfortably at Nan. "Well, I did promise the Lady Isabel that I would not tell you of this when I saw you . . . she knew I was coming here you see . . . but I think you should know, you are her mother. The Duchess has begun occasionally to cough blood, and is frequently overtaken with dizziness and fainting spells which have nothing to do with the child she carries within her. Her skin is like wax, so pale that blue veins may be seen through it."

Nan's hand flew to her mouth. Oh no, not that, not that. . . . Isabel, my child.

Alana frowned darkly at her daughter. "The Lady Isabel was right, Ankarette, in wishing such tidings to be kept from her mother. You had no right to disclose it."

Ankarette was almost in tears. "I thought she should know, mother, I only did what I thought was right."

Nan sighed, putting up her hand to halt the flow of words. "And you were right, Ankarette, I *should* know of my daughter's ill health. Can you tell me anything of my other daughter, the Lady Anne? I have had no news of her this long time now."

"There were great troubles between the Duke of Clarence and his brother Gloucester over the Lady Anne. For a long time after the Battle of Tewkesbury she was with us in the Duchess Isabel's household, but then suddenly the Duke took her away, poor little thing, and we saw her no more. It seemed that he hid her somewhere when the King finally decided that the Duke of Gloucester's suit would be accepted, that Gloucester could marry the Lady Anne *and* have half of the Warwick inheritance." She paused then and looked with embarrassment at Nan, for she knew that it was really Nan's inheritance which was now given between others. "The Duke of Gloucester came almost every day demanding to see the Lady Anne, but he was turned away, and before Clarence finally hid her completely she wept every time she knew he had come because she loved him. Then the Duke of Gloucester found her, we do not know how or where, but he took her to St. Martin le Grand's and placed her in sanctuary until such time as the marriage contracts could be finalized and he could marry her. Now they are married and are living in the

223

north, Gloucester was given the castles of Middleham and Sheriff Hutton as part of his share of the Lady's fortune."

"Ah, so there is some sweet news in this unhappy realm!" Nan was glad. She could have wished for no finer future for Anne than a life with Dickon. He had kept his promise and left no stone unturned until he found the girl he loved. "Oh, how I would wish to join them there, at Middleham, and end my days in that place."

Ankarette took up her cloak. "I fear I must go, Master Twynho will be awaiting my arrival and the escort I bribed to bring me by way of Beaulieu will brook no lengthy dallying." She stepped lightly over to her mother and embraced her. "Fear not on my behalf, mother, for I am well able to take care of myself. John has gone to a place not far from Cayford and I shall see him again, that is all that matters to me.

"Be on your guard, my foolish maid, for you will be playing with fire if you risk meeting your lover again."

Ankarette smiled brightly and hugged her again. Then she was gone.

The room settled back to its former silence and Nan resumed her position by the narrow window. The daffodils swayed in the light breeze and a sparrow hopped amongst them, pecking busily at the ground. Suddenly a large black cat pounced upon the sparrow, crushing the daffodils and trapping the tiny bird with its cruel claws. Nan turned away, shivering; even the pleasantness of the spring day was spoiled.

FORTY-ONE

WEARILY Nan raised herself from her cold, aching knees, drawing her cloak tightly about her thin shoulders as she went to sit on a hard seat in the chapel. The winter wind gusted fiercely through the arches and columns of Beaulieu and Nan could no longer withstand the rigours of its icy strength. She was fifty-one years old, but seemed older. Gone now was the delicate beauty which had once been her glory. Her hair was dull, greying, and only retained its golden brilliance at the tips. She listened to the tolling of a bell and to the last dry leaves of the dying trees as they scuttered loudly over the stone flags. In another month or so she would have been incarcerated at the Abbey for six long years. Six years. Why was it that the King steadfastly refused to allow her her freedom? She still wrote countless letters, but all were always ignored. The quarrels between the Dukes of Clarence and Gloucester were surely over now. Between them they had secured her entire fortune, Clarence by far gaining the greater division, and she was helpless, alone. Edward was being unusually severe upon her.

The candles upon the altar moved and fluttered, playing with her dancing shadow upon the cold grey walls. The flames winked in the gloom, sending their wandering glow over the golden vessels which stood against the rich wine-red velvet. Moonlight shone strongly through the stained glass of the window, casting rainbow hues across the floor. The patch-work pattern sprang over her dark cloak as she sat, huddled, trying to summon enough will to resume her prayers. She must pray, pray and pray again for salvation. . . .

Gloucester had done what he could for her. She knew that he had pleaded many a time with the King, asking that she should come into his custody, saying that he would be completely responsible for her . . . but always Edward refused. Dickon's servant James Tyrell came twice a year to visit her, and it was through him that she learned of family matters of interest to her. She knew that Isabel was now the mother of two healthy children, a girl named Margaret and a son named Edward. She knew also that Anne was unhappy because her marriage was barren as yet, but very happy in her love for Gloucester. John Neville's widow, the plump, empty-headed Joan, had married again less than a year after John's death at Barnet, and her new husband was Sir William Norreys. The son of John Neville, once so proudly created Duke of Bedford and betrothed to the King's eldest daughter, was now plain Sir George Neville, stripped of his fine Dukedom and without his royal bride. He lived in the household of Dickon of Gloucester. It seemed that Gloucester was trying to shelter all the unhappy souls cast out at the death of great Warwick.

A door banged loudly, banging again as the wind rose sharply outside. What kind of weather was this for April, thought Nan, shaking her head. April, the most hated month in her year, the anniversary of. . . . A hand knocked upon the nearby door and she saw the door slowly begin to swing open. The moonlight flooded in, lying with a silver sheen upon the floor. A tall, slender figure stepped into that blaze of sudden light, his dark brown hair as clearly visible as if in daylight, but his face obscured by the black, opaque shadow. Her eyes widened, her fingers trembling as she made the sign of the Cross before her. It was John Neville! John! She cowered back fearfully in the seat, her eyes large as she looked at the ghostly figure before her. She could not drag her gaze from that slim figure as he walked towards her. He was speaking but she heard nothing but the pounding of the blood in her ears. Her senses screamed before her lips parted, and the perspiration leapt to her cold skin. Peal after peal of her shrieks rent the darkness before she lost consciousness.

The cup of wine was warm and sweet against her lips as her eyelids opened. She was no longer in the chapel but in her own meagre room. Alana was chafing her mistress' thin, lifeless hands. Nan heard the crunching sound of a man's boots upon the fresh rushes and turned to see who was there. The candles blazed behind him, but she saw his face at last as he leaned towards the fire. She relaxed, seeing that dark brown hair again and knowing that it was not the shade of John Neville who had returned to her but James Tyrell, from the Duke of Gloucester.

"You are recovered, my Lady?" Alana's worried face loomed over her.

"Yes, yes, I am well. Forgive me for frightening you, but I thought, I thought. . . ." Her voice trailed off as she gazed once more upon Tyrell. The candlelight was behind him again and she was struck anew with his strange resemblance to John. Why was it that she had not noticed before? Her brow cleared; of course, he had never before called at night. In daylight he bore no likeness whatsoever to the dead Neville.

He spoke and his harsh northern accent drove away all lingering memories. "I must have frightened you sorely, my Lady, I crave your forgiveness."

She waved her hand to dismiss his apologies. "You did nothing, Sir the blame lies with myself for allowing memories

226

from the past to override the present. I imagined you to be someone else, it was but a trick of the moonlight."

Alana was more fierce. "Aye, that *and* your enforced stay in this damp place! A pox on Edward of England for treating a lady thus cruelly. If matters progress much further he will have your death laid at his feet!"

Nan silenced her with a frown. "It is the King of whom you speak, Alana, and I doubt not that it is treasonous to utter such words of him. Master Tyrell, what is it you would speak of with me?"

"I am sorry that my visit must be in the hours of darkness, my Lady, but my master bade me on no account to come when I might be seen. It appears that the Duke of Clarence has become suspicious that his brother is sending succour to you and has been sending his spies to watch all messengers of the Duke of Gloucester who travel in this direction. I had a merry time riding in circles through the New Forest, but I know that I lost them."

Nan pulled herself up and Alana propped her up with cushions. "Am I to understand then that the Lords of Gloucester and Clarence are still quarrelling with one another? I thought that when my daughter Anne was finally wed with Gloucester and the apportionment of *my* fortune agreed, that all would be peaceful in the House of York."

"Outwardly it may be so, my Lady, but there is little love lost between the King's brothers. It is the Duke of Clarence who perpetuates the trouble; there is not only the dispute over the estate, but also the place in the King's heart held by the Duke of Gloucester. The King leaves little room for doubt as to which of his brothers he loves and trusts the more, and it is certainly not Clarence. Even so, Clarence is very powerful in England, and it is because of his insistence that you are still kept here. The King fears to offend his surly brother too much, and the fickle George has made it plain that he considers your freedom would cause a vast rift! Clarence does not want it remembered that he quarrels and argues over your inheritance when you are still actually alive. The treatment meted out to you would not be liked throughout the land if the people truly realized what was happening. They still remember your dead Lord with love, and they certainly recall your father."

227

Wearily Nan stood, smoothing down her black skirts. "I must wait then for some disaster to befall my odious son-in-law Clarence before I may breathe freely again." Her glance fell upon a leather purse which lay on the table. Smiling she took it up, hearing the welcome chink of coins. "My thanks, my heartfelt thanks, go to my other son. His kindness to me is not unappreciated." Her heart warmed to the unseen Gloucester. "Have you any word of my daughter Isabel? I worry at her health."

Tyrell's kind face saddened. "Her health declines, I fear. She is with child again and her physicians fear that she will not survive another confinement."

Nan bowed her head. Daily she expected now to hear of Isabel's death. She knew in her heart that her elder daughter was dying, but somehow the tears would not come. Nan could weep no more. "At least then she will be spared the approaches of Clarence, for I know that he cannot bear her to be unwell, it disgusts him."

Tyrell pursed his lips. "It is a wonder that she is with child, for Clarence has been enamoured of another woman for many months now. He has fallen deeply in love with the Duke of Burgundy's daughter, Mary. She is the child of the first marriage, before Burgundy wed the King's sister. Clarence drinks too much and becomes violent, even striking the Lady Isabel sometimes. His drinking has become a byword in the land and he talks wildly when in his cups, so wildly that one cannot distinguish the truth from fantasy. He speaks treason when drunk, and the King grows weary of him. Once, I am told, the Duke said that the King's marriage to Queen Elizabeth was bigamous! I wonder at the King's patience with such a man!" Tyrell shook his head in wonderment.

Nan suddenly wanted to laugh, laugh at Edward's uneasy soul. Two people he thought to be in possession of his secret; herself and Stillington. Now he was beset by his own jealous, drunken brother with his twisted threats. And what of the Queen? Nan remembered the ice-cold beauty of Elizabeth Grey and her avaricious grasping of power and wealth; if she should become aware of her true situation, what then? Her smile faded. "I have much to despise the Duke of Clarence for. I spit on him, Master Tyrell, I spit on George Plantagenet as the lowest vermin which breathes and crawls upon its fat belly on God's earth! May he rot in hell for his crimes, may he rot in hell!" She was breathing heavily, her anger and unhappiness sapping her energy. Her breath caught in a dry sob. She walked from the room, her head held high, leaving her curse lying tangibly upon the cold air.

Tyrell crossed himself before such immense, deep hatred. He gathered up his cloak and hat, then he seemed to remember something important. He touched Alana's arm. "Mistress Burden, there is some happy news which I was to tell your mistress. The Lady Anne bade me tell her mother that she is at long last with child! She feared that she was not to be blessed with a child, but now . . . well. . . . You will tell her?"

"Of course I will, rest assured, Master Tyrell."

A short while later he was riding away through the Forest, back to the Yorkshire Moors which Nan so longed for, back to the castle where Anne waited.

FORTY-TWO

It was the New Year, cold and drab. The Year of Grace 1478 entered stealthily, dragging its damp feet with painful slowness, and it brought with it news of death.

Nan was in the courtyard, it was only early morning but the monks did not make any attempt to restrain her from leaving her rooms. Her heart was heavy, heavier than it had been since Barnet, for Isabel was dead. A mere day or so before Christmas Nan's elder daughter had died after giving birth to another son, a sickly infant who had shortly followed his mother to the grave.

Hoofbeats clattered dully through the outer gateway, rattling along the narrow roadway towards the inner gate. Nan watched the messenger as he rode across the open space of the courtyard. She did not know him and he certainly did not look like the retainer of some great lord . . . she walked on, immersed in her own misfortunes and losses.

The minutes passed, how many she did not know, but suddenly her eye was caught by the plain white robes of a monk hurrying across the grass. He waved his arms excitedly, calling to her. She stopped.

His face was red with the effort of running, for he was a portly man. "My Lady, come quickly, it is Mistress Burden. . . ."

"Alana? What is wrong?" Nan's fingers stole to the golden crucifix which hung against her breast.

"She has received a letter, and when she read it she cried out, clutched at her breast as if in great pain and then fell to the ground. We cannot rouse her from the faint."

Nan's slippers pattered over the moist grass, echoing as they entered the Abbey buildings. In her room Alana lay motionless upon the hard bed. The monks crowded over her, their faces worried, their heads shaking unhappily as they murmured together.

"Stand away from her! Would you have her die from lack of air!" Nan pushed them away roughly, her fear and anxiety making her forget her manners. She looked at the wrinkled, white face against the pillow, taking the cold hands and squeezing them. Alana's breathing was faint, but steady, and Nan sighed with relief. There was hope then. "Bring more blankets, as many as you can, and build up the fire. She must be kept warm."

Obediently the monks went upon their tasks, and Nan cast around the room for the letter which had caused the trouble.

A crumpled parchment peeped out from beneath the bed and she bent to retrieve it. She placed the parchment in the purse at her waist and administered to Alana's needs. Soon the blankets were piled high upon the prone figure, tucked tightly under the thin mattress. Fresh logs were tossed upon the dying fire and before long it roared and crackled with renewed vigour. The monks bowed to her and hurried away, only one remaining.

He seated himself close to the fire, folding his hands before him, his face concealed by the large cowl of his habit. Nan hesitated to read Alana's letter before him, but she soon realized that he dozed, for his head nodded slowly forward until his chin rested on his chest. His loud rasping breaths filled the air.

Nan drew a small stool to the side of the bed and sat down, feeling in her purse for the letter. The writing was soiled but quite legible although of a large, round style which Nan did not recognize. She turned it over briefly to see who had sent it and saw the name John Thuresby. Her brow creased . . . the name was familiar. Of course, this John Thuresby was Ankarette's lover. Nan pressed her fingers to her tired eyes, rubbing them to concentrate upon the letter. Her sight was no longer so sharp. . . .

"Mistress Burden. I did not know to whom I should write this, my last letter, but someone must know the truth of the great injustice which has been done to your daughter and myself by the noble Duke of Clarence. I could think only of you because I know that Ankarette told you the circumstances of our dismissal from the Duchess Isabel's household. At the end of last year the gentle Duchess at last passed away, leaving this world of pain and grief which she had endured for so long with such fortitude. She died after childbirth, although she had looked nigh unto death for many a month before. The baby died not long after, being a mirror of his mother's ill health. The death of the Lady Isabel left myself and Ankarette in a difficult position, because it was only through her that we still lived. The Duke seized upon his opportunity, because of the knowledge we secured long ago of his plotting with Bishop Stillington, and accused Ankarette of poisoning the Duchess. He accused me of doing away with the baby. With the death of the Duchess died our safeguard, and he knew that no-one would believe our protestations. He wished us silenced forever. He did not stop at mere accusations against us, though; he took the moment to implicate the Queen and her family. Clarence stated that Ankarette and myself were in the employ of the Woodvilles and that the deaths of the Duchess and her child were made in order to strike at the unpopular Duke. He has been quarrelling openly with the Queen these many months now. I fear that the jealousy which has ruled George Plantagenet for so long has finally unhinged his mind, so bent is he upon following his insane plans. Ankarette and I were both seized in the night and spirited away to Warwick, where in the morning we were brought before a court manned entirely by the Duke's men. The verdict was inevitable, we were both found

231

guilty of these so-called murders. My beloved Ankarette, your daughter, was taken immediately to the gallows and she gave no murmur as they led her away. She walked proudly to her death, Mistress Burden, stopping only once before Clarence and he waxed so white with fear that he hurried away. I am to follow her tomorrow morning, but have persuaded my guard to allow me to write this letter, and as you now read I shall already be dead. Forgive me for unburdening my heart to you thus, know only that we have died unjustly for a crime we did not commit . . . which no-one commited save in the mad eyes of the Duke of Clarence."

Nan crumpled the paper in her hands, closing her eyes with the horror of what she had read. Holy Mother, that Alana should have received this! She looked at the motionless face and put her hand briefly to the sallow cheek. Isabel's death had been sad, but Ankarette's was indescribable in its injustice. Oh George Plantagenet, there is surely a place in Hell for you. . . .

Clarence! Nan stared at the curling, licking flames of the fire. What would Edward do now? Not only had his wayward brother attempted to implicate the Queen in his plottings, but he had taken the King's law into his own hands by trying and condemning two people without the King's permission. Could Edward afford to keep such a brother at his side? It was surely as John Thuresby had said, Clarence was no longer sane. Thoughtfully she continued to stare at the fire, and then suddenly a new idea came to her.

On impulse she stood and went to the sleeping monk, shaking his arm violently. He was so startled that he almost overbalanced and fell into the fire.

Nan's voice was urgent. "Has there been news from London recently, news concerning perhaps the Duke of Clarence?" She held her breath as she waited for his reply.

He pulled his habit back into shape after his startled awaking, licking his lips and mumbling. Then he sighed, scratching his head. "It is strange that you should ask, for this very day a pedlar called who had come direct from London. He said that the city is humming with interest because the Duke of Clarence has been arrested by the King. There is to be a trial, it seems, and the charges are to be brought by the King himself. I know not what will befall our land, my Lady, when the King of England strikes down his own brother!" He shook his head, mumbling again.

Nan stood up straight, her green eyes alight with hope. At last, at last . . . Clarence had overstepped every limit which Edward was prepared to allow him. If the Duke was imprisoned, possibly coming to trial, then surely his hold over Nan was gone.

Trembling she moved back to the bed, tucking in the blankets more firmly. "Ankarette will be avenged, dear Alana, she will be avenged. The King will punish Clarence this time." Her whisper shook with hope.

Seven years she had been forced to remain in this Abbey seven years alone and ignored by all except the Duke of Gloucester. She was a grandmother, and yet had never seen her grandchildren . . . three she had, for Anne was now the mother of a son. Would there be a chance now that she could go to Anne, leave this place?

She must write again, write and write and write. She went to her own room, sitting at the table and taking a fresh sheet of parchment. She picked up the quill and dipped it in the ink. Slowly, laboriously, for her fingers were stiff, she wrote to the King.

As she finished and applied her seal to the parchment, the monk came from Alana's room. "Mistress Burden is conscious now, my Lady. She will live."

FORTY-THREE

WITH infinite patience Nan arranged the intricate folds of her black gown. There were no great preparations to be made with her appearance now, no elaborate headdress or tightly-fitting gown, no jewels or necklaces. . . .

"What think you, Alana, will the King of England approve of my appearance?" She smiled at the woman who lay back on the hard bed. It was some weeks since the letter had arrived telling of Ankarette's death, and Alana was still weak, but daily she grew stronger.

Alana lifted her chin proudly. "He cannot fail but be impressed with your dignity, my Lady."

"Let us hope that he has come in answer to my last letter." Nan bit her lip, fearing almost to think about Edward's reasons.

"One thing is certain, he will not have come all this way to Beaulieu in order to merely pass the time of day."

Gathering the dull skirts in her hands, Nan left the room and made her way through the Abbey to where Edward awaited her. She soon knew that he was near for the corners bristled with his men.

She was shown into a room and at last she saw him. He was holding a carved Madonna and Child in his beringed fingers, but he put the precious thing down when he saw her. His eyes swept over her, and he no longer saw the beautiful woman who had once been loved by two of the greatest magnates in the land. He saw a thin woman of fifty-two, old before her time, with a tired face and sad eyes.

She in turned surveyed him. The handsome youth was gone, leaving instead a slightly corpulent giant of thirty-four. The years of easy living, of drinking and eating and licentiousness had left their mark upon the golden Yorkist King. His voice, however, had not changed. "My Lady of Warwick, I trust that you are well."

She curtseyed. "As well as seven years here can allow."

"I will not be reproached, Madam, for you supported Warwick in his rebellion, you raised no objection when he allied your House with Lancaster! In my eyes you are as guilty as he of treason!"

Nan's eyes were steady as she looked at him. "I do not reproach you, and all you say of me is true. But remember this, it was Richard Neville the man whom I supported so earnestly, not Richard Neville the politician. I would have been well content had he lived amicably at your side. My only hope now is that you show me mercy and allow me to leave here to end my days a free woman."

He drummed his fingers upon the table. "Let us not prevaricate, my Lady, the reason for my visit must be obvious to you. Before anything further, however, let me tell you that my brother Clarence is dead, and Stillington imprisoned in the

234

Tower. They are the only two others to be in possession of a secret which I wish covered up. What can you tell me which will make me lenient towards you, which will make me consider you trustworthy?"

Nan's head was reeling. Clarence dead! "Dead you say?"

"His activities could be borne no more. He chose to boast to my Queen that he knew of my pre-contract, and no amount of warning would make him hold his drunken tongue. I could not afford to allow him to live, I had my children to consider, my son Edward who will succeed to the throne after me. George was tried on a charge of treason, and it was not difficult to amass a great wealth of evidence against him . . . he had been most active over the years, as you will know! He was sentenced to death, but I could not allow my own brother to be publicly executed, and so he was executed privately in the Tower." He closed his eyes and she could see how terribly these events had affected him. Fratricide is a heinous crime.

"Your Grace, what can I say to persuade you that my lips are sealed? Only that should I so have wished I could many a time these past years have shouted your secret to the world and remained safe within these walls in sanctuary. I made a vow, a vow which I have honoured. There is another reason too. At the time when John Neville left you and rejoined my husband, you did not divulge my adulterous association with my brother-in-law. I thank you for that."

He sucked the air in through his lips, exhaling in almost a whistle. His drumming fingers increased their noise and he looked agitated. "Oh but you see, Madam, I did *not* keep your secret, I *did* divulge all to Warwick."

Her lips parted in horror. Oh no, surely not, surely Richard had not died knowing of her unfaithfulness. Oh please no!

He smiled sadly. "I told him, and sent a trusted servant to deliver the message in person. The servant returned and told me that Warwick had laughed at such a tale. He laughed that I could imagine him foolish enough to believe such infamies of his beloved Nan. So you see, my Lady, you were safe all along, Richard Neville could not and would not believe in your infidelity. He did not even think the matter worthy of telling John Neville. Such was his faith in you."

Nan could have wept for her dead Lord. "My poor Richard, how I betrayed you, my love, my love. . . ."

235

"Spare your sorrows, Madam, I could have wished him less ardent in his love for you. The battle I won, but it would have been a sweeter victory had I split the Nevilles asunder!"

Nan's sorrow fled. "Had you treated John Neville with the trust and courtesy his undoubted love for you warranted, then the Nevilles would never have reunited! But once again we digress. Your Grace, my health does not improve, nor my age diminish. I have no wish to remain here until my life ends."

He smiled faintly. "Do I detect a veiled threat in your words?"

She was so tired, so very tired. . . . "There is no threat, Your Grace. Read into my words only one meaning. I wish to be free of this place and it is in your power to grant me that freedom."

For a long, long while he looked at her. She knew that he was thinking deeply on the strength of her wish for freedom. Would she break her vow if he ignored this latest request? Clarence was dead, he no longer stood between this woman and her liberty.

Steadily she met his gaze. Seven years out of a life is a long time. She did not think she was prepared to continue.

Suddenly he nodded. "Very well, Madam, you shall have your freedom. My brother Gloucester has made repeated applications to have you live with him and so he shall be granted his wish."

She was almost weeping with relief. This above all things was what she had wanted, to go to Anne at Middleham. "I thank you. I thank you."

His next words were totally unexpected. "Eleanor's ghost haunts me at nights, I see always her dark eyes, so beautiful, so very gentle. I have tried to trace my son by her, but have been unsuccessful."

"I had always thought you cared nothing for her. You cast her aside with little or no thought for your son then."

"The strength of my desire for the woman who is now my Queen went beyond the desire I felt for Eleanor. I realize now what I lost, for Elizabeth is unbelievably cold. She willingly allows me my mistresses, almost stooping to procuring more for me! No man likes his wife to be so accommodating, so lacking in care. Such coldness frightens me. Only in one thing does she show any human feeling, and that is in the furtherance

236

of her family's fortunes. For them she will fight like a she-wolf. For me as a man she cares nothing, for me as a King she cares a lot! And there you have my marriage. Even the wisest of Kings can be the greatest of fools. Never was I more foolish than when I tried to dilute the power of the Nevilles by bringing the Woodvilles to the fore. I wanted Elizabeth and the fact that she had such an immense family merely added to her attraction for I wished to teach Warwick a lesson." He smiled a little sadly. "You will no doubt say that I deserved all I received."

"Maybe, but who am I to pass judgement upon you. As to Eleanor's son, I am afraid that I cannot help you discover him. She hid him well before she died."

He took up his cloak and swung it around his shoulders. "Mayhap Eleanor was right. I think maybe that I would merely seek to salve my conscience by finding him now. Well, my Lady of Warwick, the secrets of the past begin and end within these four walls. You shall have your freedom and I shall trust to your good faith. I shall send word to my brother Gloucester of my decision."

The daffodils raised their creamy heads to the pale April sunshine as the new day awoke. The crisp moorland air was heady as the small party rode through the fast dispersing morning mist. James Tyrell paused as they forded a rushing stream, the waters of which were swollen still from the snow which clung to the higher peaks. The horses picked their way carefully through the icy waters, dipping their muzzles gently to drink briefly before moving on towards the north.

Gradually Nan's eager eyes recognized the rise and fall of the hills, the well-remembered moors of the past. She urged her mount faster, delighting in the drumming of its hooves upon the hard roadway. It seemed that another, more spectral horse galloped at her side, a huge charger caparisoned in red, bearing the Ragged Staff emblem on its flank. Richard. Richard. Tears coursed down her cheeks as her lips moved to his name.

The mist still swathed the valley and suddenly the road dipped before her, vanishing into the white stillness. Beyond, rising majestically, full of martial splendour, stood the towers and battlements of Middleham. Breathless she reined in. She was alone, having left the others behind. The horse stamped and snorted in the silence.

"How often have I dreamed of this?" she murmured. Then she urged her mount down into the shadowy valley. The ghostly hoofbeats of that other horse joined their sound to the ringing air.

Nan, Countess of Warwick, had come home.